The Pedlar's Omen

Raz Scully

The Pedlar's Omen

Published 2020 by Highland Creations
Cover and Layout copyright © 2020 by Highland Creations
Cover design by Highland Creations
Cover Art copyright © by Lukaschaloupka/Dreamstime
ISBN-13: 978-1-952299-16-2 (eBook)
ISBN-13: 978-1-952299-17-9 (Paperback)

www.razscully.com

3FCC1C007F0168FF6362DDAD2B424E17F92D2DEFEFB25A48F2608A0A8952E914

To my wife who has been patient, loyal, and long suffering with me all these years. God knew I would need fun in my life and He wasn't sparing in the least when He brought you along. My life is forever better because you have been in it!

To Him, when my world seems to fall to the darkest of places, You are there. You reach out, not in anger at my failures, but to lift me back up... because You actually like me.

Delivery

Roger's eyes snapped open with the sound of a muted explosion, the slight shaking of his bed, and the subtle jerking feeling of the artificial gravity lagging behind with the rapid shift of directions.

"A little help would be appreciated!!!" a female voice yelled over the intercom. "I'm a mist pilot, not a fighter pilot!"

Roger threw the blanket aside and hit the floor running. The Pedlar's Omen was a small ship, so getting to the small bridge was accomplished in seconds. He strapped himself into the seat at the navigation and gunnery controls.

"Shutting down nonessentials for extra power," Roger said as his hands rapidly flipped switches and accessed terminal commands. The sound of motors and pistons could just be heard coming from the rear of the ship as the defense turret extended from its resting place to the top surface of the ship.

Sonja continued to jerk at the controls, evading bright red bolts of destructive energy. A bolt hit the starboard side, sending a wave of light blue energy scattering just above the surface of the ship. The comms switch was flashing and pinging.

Roger pulled up the controls to override the automatic targeting of the turret. The automatic targeting system was a budget item that the ship dealer had thrown in. Roger rolled his eyes when he thought about how much the added cost was verses its effectiveness. Still, it was cheaper than hiring a dedicated ship gunner, on datapad anyway.

Five targets, fighters in size, lit up his screen. There was a larger ship closing off in the distance, just out of range. He didn't waste time. The small cannon cut loose a hand full of shots on the closest ship. The fighter silently burst into flame and debris until its oxygen supply ran out. The remaining four fighters quickly spread out. "Guess they weren't expecting any fight."

"Not real worried about the fighters. I'm more concerned with the big boy behind them. Shields down to 42%."

"I saw that. You get an ID on the larger ship?"

Roger was having a harder time killing off the remaining ships now that they were being evasive. On the flip side, the Pedlar's Omen was getting shot at a lot less. It gave the shield generator a chance to catchup. He caught sight of Sonja reaching for the comms switch, then thinking better of it. He knew it was starting to piss her off.

"Carrakus Invader."

"So much for out running them or escaping them planet side."

Two more ripples of blue energy scattered over the ship's form. The brief increase of laser fire exchange cost the other side another fighter.

Sonja couldn't handle it anymore. She flipped on the comms switch.

"... down your weapons and prepare to be boarded. If you will just cooperate, we will release you planet side unharmed."

"Yeah, like a raider's word is worth anything!" she hit a button to reply. "We don't have any children on this ship for you to molest, so blow off chomo!"

The voice on the other side went into a cussing rage that Roger cut short with a comms override. "Sometimes I regret telling you stories about my past life as an officer."

The fighters got more aggressive and the larger ship off in the distance picked up speed to overtake them.

"Your prison stories have made these hell hole trips more fun. I never would have known how to get under their skin if you hadn't told me about how lowlifes are and what really pisses them off."

Roger stayed focused and downed the remaining fighters

before the shields could completely collapse under the barrage of energy. The Invader that was rushing on them would be a real problem soon.

Sonja put the pedal to the metal towards the planet that had to be at least a half hour away yet. "You realize we are going to have to fight that thing, right?"

Roger didn't answer. He pulled up information on what was known about the Carrakus corporations Invader ship design. It was based on a military style cargo ship. Heavily armored and had just a few defenses. The few defenses maxed out as much teeth as the law allowed for civilian ships. Roger could only guess what modifications the raiders may have done with it. It was at least five times the size of the Pedlar's Omen. Secretly, he wished he could get his hands on that ship. It would make his life so much easier.

"Don't even think about it!"

"Think about what?"

Sonja stared at him with her dark brown eyes. "I've seen that look before. We are not even going to attempt to take that ship. As much as I hate these hell hole jobs, I didn't sign up for suicide missions. There is no way the two of us could capture that ship."

Roger let out an exasperated exhale. "I'm not planning on taking it. Even though a larger ship would make our lives easier. A larger ship would mean being able to take jobs that are more respectable... not to mention safer than what we have been doing."

She turned back to her controls. "I understand. As much as I would like that too, you need to get your head out of the clouds and focus on what is going on and keep us alive. Now is not the time to dream about owning a bigger ship!"

Roger's focus remained on the ship's stats and layout.

Moments seemed like an eternity, with the Invader gaining on them to Sonja. "What's your plan, sir?"

Roger was quiet a moment longer, she seemed to pickup on his hesitancy to say what was on his mind.

"Captain Roger Vance..."

Roger closed his eyes. "Remember our little mishap maneuver with the Hijab Pirates?"

"Oh god! Surely you are not serious about repeating that!"

she started breathing heavier as she shook her head, "Maybe it was better for your head to be in the clouds after all."

"I take it you remember then. Good thing, because that's what it's going to take to deal with this Invader ship."

"Didn't I just mention that I didn't sign up for suicide missions?!"

"If you have a better plan, I'm all ears. Better make it fast though. Our window of opportunity is short."

She didn't have anything. Roger was the one who always came up with the plans. He always saved their lives in the end, even if just barely. Still, he had never abandoned her or left her behind on any mission despite his crazy ideas. Exasperated, she answered, "I don't have anything. Are you ready to execute?"

"Ready or not, we're out of time. Do it."

Sonja exhaled and pulled back hard and fast on the flight controls. The frame of the small cargo vessel groaned under the strain of the tight loop. The two passengers sank in their seat as the cockpit's gravitational system struggled to counter the shift in directions to keep the occupants from blacking out.

"Ship is not designed for this," she said through clenched teeth.

Within seconds the Invader was now running head to head with them. Its weapons had already been deployed. The distance between them got short really fast. The weapons systems of the Invader opened up, spraying red bolts of death at the Pedlar's Omen.

"Looks like they don't care about the cargo anymore..." Sonja said.

"Maybe if someone hadn't pissed them off beyond all reason, they might. They also might if they knew what we had." A thought came to Roger, "Assuming we haven't lost it all through a cargo hold breach. Maybe they know something we don't yet." The very thought of losing the cargo and not getting paid made his blood boil.

The Pedlar's Omen ducked, dived, and rolled as it charged at its target. Roger attempted to shoot the weapons out on the Invader. Sonja was too erratic though.

The shields of the small vessel began to fail. Explosions

against the hull of the Pedlar's Omen were getting more and more frequent. Interior lights occasionally flickered.

"Don't hit the pearl, don't hit the pearl, don't hit the pearl," Sonja whispered over and over to herself.

Roger was growling as lights lit up red all around him. He had only managed to stop one of the eight lasers that were trying to kill them.

"Hope your ready," Sonja yelled.

"Yes."

Sonja maneuvered as if to crash into the vessel. The Invader pulled away. "Oh no you don't!" She dived towards the ship at a steeper angle than she would have liked. The thrusters sputtered for a moment. Sonja's heart leaped up into her throat as panic gripped her. They kicked back on with a burst of speed. The Invader's shields rattled with the Pedlar's Omen's as the two energy barriers repelled each other. "NOW!"

Roger triggered an emergency reserve of extra power into the shield generator. There was a bright flash of light that engulfed both ships.

Sonja pulled up. Her dive was too steep, and she yelled out. The bottom of the Pedlar's Omen ground against the hull of the Invader. The shields of both ships had collapsed. "Going for the thrusters!"

Roger was racing to restore functions after the overload. Having done this before, he was hoping to have an edge over the crew of the Invader. "Weapon online again!"

"Their thrusters seem to be offline. Now or never."

Lights were flickering all over the surface of the Invader. Their thrusters were colorless, and the ship was adrift. Roger turned the small turret cannon on one of the thrusters and unloaded for all it was worth. The weapon didn't seem to do a lot of damage, despite how easy it was to hit.

The Invader's thrusters began to flicker back to life.

"I think we might be screwed!" Sonja said.

Roger kept firing into a particular spot on the side of the main thrusters. "Not yet," he said with a cool, steady tone.

One of the rear defense lasers began to pivot, looking for a target. Sonja tried to keep the ship steady, tracking the drifting ship's trajectory so Roger could finish pounding whatever it was he had found to take down the large ship. The small laser of the Invader picked away at what little shields Roger had managed to regenerate.

The thrusters of the enemy vessel came back online in full. Roger glanced at the depleting energy reserves available to the weapon. They were almost gone. The vessel started to spin on its attacker slowly but surely.

Sonja did as best she could to keep up. The Pedlar's Omen was still not fully functional either. The flight controls were sluggish.

The side of the main thruster exploded, sending debris out like shrapnel off a grenade. Roger kept up his fire in the same spot as his target slowly turned away. The small back laser stopped firing.

Sonja noticed escape pods jettisoning from all over the ship.

There was a secondary explosion. Oxygen and fuel mixed with explosive forces and fire. Together they ripped through the interior of the large cargo ship. Sonja pulled away as fast as the small cargo ship would manage. Integrity of the Invader weakened and pressurized gases exploded outward into the vacuum of space.

The Invader split into three chunks. Its lights went dark. Debris filled the area surrounding it.

"How are we looking for landing planet side?"

Sonja changed over her display to get diagnostics. "System is running really slow. Guessing, that means one of the computer banks got hit. Looks like we will be able to land after the power systems recharge over the next hour. However, three of the capacitors are offline. We have to have at least two of those back online and charged up to get into the mists."

"The pearl still intact?"

Sonja didn't really want to look. Her finger slid over the display to pull up the pearl and phantom drive system. She smiled slightly, filled with relief. "Everything shows good to go. Just need the power reserves for the phantom drive to get us into the mists."

"Guess we need to take a look at how bad the damage really is. How long before the wreck burns up in orbit?"

"Hoping to get a souvenir, are you?" She plotted the information into the computer to get an estimate.

"There are no starship facilities out here. This place is barely an outpost for the Corvus Commonwealth. Their unwilling to commit that kind of resources when there are too many raiders out here still."

"Oh god. You're telling me we may have to make our own parts and repairs?"

"If it's that bad, yes."

"The wreck will fall to orbit in 5 hrs. At which point whatever doesn't burn up will fall into one of the oceans."

"We need an eyes on damage assessment ASAP then."

Sonja unstrapped from her seat and got up. She looked at him seriously, "I really hope we are getting paid well for this hell hole job. Proper repair costs when we get back are going to be pretty steep if the damage is as bad as I suspect."

"You'll get your fee. This job is the highest paying job I've taken so far. Though now I'm not sure it's worth nearly dying for."

"I'm not worried about my fee. You know my past seriously limits my employment opportunities. So you might say I have a vested interest in you staying financially afloat."

Roger got up from his seat. "Just as any details of your past don't seem to be any of my concern every time I've asked, my financial situation is none of yours. You will get paid, I will have the ship repaired, and we will keep doing jobs. The day will come when we can upgrade from this little tub, and perhaps then you can run your own ship."

"It's not that easy."

Roger shook his head and stared at her a moment. "Clock is ticking. Let's see how bad this really is. Maybe we got lucky and the repairs will be quick and easy."

Sonja just looked at him with a concerned look on her face. "Fine," she said as she walked out of the cockpit.

Dropoff

Sonja lined up the cover panel and reattached it with the fasteners just as Roger walked by. He finished scrubbing the soot off his hand with a rag as he looked over at how Sonja was doing.

"You might just make a good grease monkey yet if you keep that kind of good work up," Roger smiled.

Sonja rolled her eyes. "I didn't sign on to be a ship engineer. I only do this because I want this ship to fly like I need it to." She stood up and faced him with a smile, "If you start making me do repairs as often as I have been doing, we'll need to talk about my contract again."

He looked down at the floor, "Yeah, you really do deserve a lot more than I pay you. I really hope to be able to pay you what you're really worth sometime soon. You end up saving my hind end too much."

She stepped closer to him and lightly tapped him on the chest with her tool. "Hey, I'm good with it," she said softly. "I'm just the pilot here. You are good about taking care of EVERYTHING else, which is normally an eight-man operation. I didn't mean to cause you to be hard on yourself."

He looked up. Their eyes locked with each other. "Besides, if your going to keep a tally of saving lives. I may bail you out once in a while, but you have saved me multiple times. Often from my own stupid rash decisions. If anyone has an unbalanced side of a budget, it's my side. I owe you. I'm sorry for being such a pain in the posterior."

"You don't owe me. You are very good at what you do. I'm grateful that you stick around and put up with me and the danger I put us in just to make a living." They just looked at each other silently for a moment. "Speaking of danger... I got my end of things patched up enough to get us planet side. How are you doing with yours?"

"Just finished as best I could. We still need to replace a computer bank and make some more parts for the number three thruster. It would be easier to do it planet side."

"Let's do it then."

Sonja didn't wait for him to get out of the way. Keeping her eyes on his, she just kept smiling and stepped forward out of the closet and brushed her body against his to get past him and down the maintenance passage and back to the bridge.

As she exited the maintenance passage out of sight, Roger realized he had been holding his breath once she pressed against him to get past. Work, focus on work, he thought to himself. He went to get his body armor on.

Several minutes later, he joined Sonja at the bridge. He took his normal seat at the navigation and weapons systems.

Roger pulled up the delivery information and began the contact process.

"This is Devin Outpost, hearing you loud and clear, sir. How can we help you?"

"This is Pedlar's Omen. We have a delivery for you guys. Package ID Delta Alpha nine nine six four Echo. Confirm."

"One moment please," the male voice said. "I'm not seeing... oh. OH... my god, you guys are four days early! This is an absolute godsend!"

"I don't like to be late. Which landing site would you like us to put down at?"

"We only control one landing site now. Raiders have been hitting us hard down here. We're in desperate shape. The supplies you are bringing us are going to save a number of lives and help us get things turned around. Go to landing site Bravo Four. I'll dispatch a team to meet you there to receive the supplies."

Roger looked at Sonja, "ETA?"

"Six hours for touchdown."

"Devin Outpost, ETA for Bravo Four is 6 hours."

"Copy six hours, Bravo Four. See you soon."

Sonja and Roger were both quiet for the rest of the flight.

"Roger, I'm seeing a lot of different movement on the ground."

"Noticed that too. When we get to the landing site and I offload the cargo, I want you to move the ship. Find a place to hideout until I have this delivered."

"Understood. You sure you don't want me to tag along?"

"You may have to save my skin if things go badly."

"You're probably right. For future I should hire you to teach me how to fight and how to use weapons."

"Really? Why would you want to do that?"

She didn't answer immediately. "I plan to hang around. It would be good for me to round out my skills a little more. Especially with the clientèle that we deal with. What would happen if a raider managed to get aboard the Pedaler's Omen? If they have any combat training at all, I'm screwed."

Roger thought about it. "I've had that thought before. You haven't ditched me and I wouldn't be able to live with myself if something happened to you. So consider it mandatory training as a condition of continued employment. I'll add it to your contract."

"I appreciate your thoughtfulness."

Roger felt the ship swing in an arc as Sonja slowed the ship and maneuvered to land. He felt the vibrations in the floor as the landing gear emerged from their resting cavities and locked into place. The ship did its slight bounce as the landing gear touched down and automatically adjusted for level.

"Down and locked. Keeping the engines hot for immediate departure."

Roger acknowledged and went to the cargo hold. Inside the tight space, he removed all the mechanisms that attached the cargo to the interior frame of the ship.

The cargo crates were loaded on a mini truck that Roger had stripped the cab off so all that remained was the driving controls and a seat sitting on the left side of the engine compartment. It was the only way to get the truck to fit into the Pedlar's Omen cargo hold.

Also crammed into the cargo hold were two trailers. Both

modified to get them stripped down enough to fit into the cargo hold with the mini truck. There was one trailer on either side of the truck. All three were loaded with as many crates as would fit on them.

Once he had everything detached, he went to the side door access that had a ramp for personal to enter and exit. He activated his helmet radio. "Radio check."

"Loud and clear."

"Copy," he access the control panel to open the door and drop the ramp. He pulled his sidearm and checked it before replacing it. "Exiting."

"Copy."

Roger came down the ramp checking all of his surroundings. It wasn't much of a landing site. It was a large circular piece of ground on the backside of a rocky hill. Only one little shack with some basic equipment for communications and solar power. The air was hot and arid. A carved path served as a road down off the hill and into a large valley filled with patches of trees in a sea of grasslands.

Roger guessed it might be late fall as the grasses looked to be dead and the leaves of the trees ranged from red to yellows. The sun was nearly at its peak and the temperature was already pretty hot. The view from the landing site over the valley was good.

"Looks like they are not here yet. See if you can get them on the comm. Go ahead and drop the cargo too."

The back bottom belly plates of the Pedlar's Omen shifted and opened up. Pistons activated and gradually lowered the floor of the cargo bay to the ground. After it came to a stop Roger hopped up into the driver's seat and started it up. He pulled it forward and backed it up to one of the trailers. He got off and attached the trailer, then repositioned the machine to attach the second trailer. He drove out from under the Pedlar's Omen.

"No contact. I think comms are being jammed."

"I've finished unloading. Button her up and do a flyby of Devin Outpost. Maybe they are just running late."

The cargo floor retracted to its home position and the protective plating resealed the belly. The ship lifted and the landing gear retracted as the Pedlar's Omen sped off. Roger walked to the slight cliff like edge to see the rest of the road down the hill. There was no one there. The dirt road made two switchbacks as it descended to ground level and merged onto another dirt road.

The main dirt road looked like it went east, which was where Devin Outpost should have been.

"Crap! Roger, you're going to have to help them. The outpost is under siege by raiders, maybe a dozen or so guys on the ground. I'm now being chased by the two fighters that were assisting!"

"Damn it," He ran to the mini truck. It was the fastest way to get to the outpost, but the last vehicle he would choose to jump into a fight with. "I'm on my way!"

He could see the Pedlar's Omen flying evasively in the distance. He drove the truck as fast as he dared and not loose control. Once he was clear of the switchbacks, he poured on the speed, as much as his mini truck would go. It was enough to kick up a good dust trail behind him. "How are you holding up Sonja?"

"I've taken a bit of a beating, but I'm holding out better than I thought I would. They don't seem to be very experienced pilots. Turret managed to get one of them. One left. We really need to upgrade that targeting system. I'd be willing to pitch in for that upgrade."

"The goal is to not have to do these kinds of jobs anymore."

"Yeah, yeah, yeah."

Roger heard an explosion in the distance and heard it over Sonja's radio. "What was that?"

"A major problem!"

Roger saw the Pedlar's Omen pull up from the tree line. Black smoke was pouring from one of the main engines.

"Someone down there has a surface-to-air missile system! I can't hang around here!"

"Get clear. I'm coming up on a roadblock not far from the outpost." Roger saw another projectile trailing white smoke chasing down the Pedlar's Omen. "SONJA! INCOMING!"

She banked hard left and up. The missile impacted on the top of the ship and sent debris flying. She rolled and pulled away in another direction. The targeting computer managed to get a fix on the pursuing fighter that was unleashing bolts of death. The turret shot nailed one of the two thrusters of the fighter.

The fighter started to spin out of control, and cork screwed in an arc towards the ground, exploding on impact.

"Halt you!" some guy in what could barely be called a uniform yelled out. He was joined by four others. All of them had light laser rifles leveled at him.

Roger slowed and brought his mini truck to a stop.

"Where do you think your going?"

Roger just pointed at the outpost.

"Dude, Franky," a skinny guy said. "I know that armor he's wear'n. He's a LEO. They wear those in prisons where I did time."

"Really!?" Franky said. "I don't like LEOs."

The skinny kid piped up again, "Little out of your jurisdiction, aren't you?"

"Yes, he is. This is Blood Fang territory," Franky said. "Say, what have you got in those boxes, LEO? A contribution for the cause?"

The four of them laughed. Two more raiders had come from the direction of the outpost. They had a bound blond hair woman as their prisoner.

"Ah, what luck. Bring her here."

The two men brought her to Franky. "You're mighty pretty." He smiled as he looked over at Roger. "Would be a shame if something were to happen to her. I suggest you get off that thing and keep your hands up were we can see them."

Roger shut off the mini truck and triggered a lockout command so they couldn't run off with it anytime soon. He got down and stood beside it with his hands just slightly to his sides with open palms.

"That's some nice armor you're wear'n. Take it off!"

"Not happening!" Roger said.

Franky went from smiling to mad in the space of a heartbeat. He slung his rifle over his back and pulled out a pistol. He grabbed the woman by the back of the neck and forced her in front of him. His left arm wrapped around her shoulders to hold her secure against his body. The top of her head was about his chin level. He put the pistol up to her temple.

The woman was starting to freak out and cry hysterically.

The large gag tied across her mouth prevented most of her sound.

"I SAID TAKE IT OFF!!!"

The woman blinked. Roger caught something. He confirmed what he saw, using commands in his helmet to replay and magnify. Roger didn't say a word, just moved his head as if to say, oh really.

Roger drew his sidearm and shot the woman and Franky through her. His left arm swung out and his forearm armor discharged a projectile at another man. Laser shots spewed out all around him. One shot caught him in the chest and another in the thigh. The armor absorbed most of the damage.

The man hit with the projectile went into convulsions as the extremely high voltage passed through his body. He collapsed to the ground.

Roger stepped back to get some cover from the truck from two of the men. He discharged his pistol at the two men he couldn't get cover from. Four men were down, three dead, one incapacitated, and the woman was dead. Two remained.

Roger discharged the hot and nearly spent energy clip and slapped in a fresh one. He heard movement behind him. Roger spun around and fired as he dropped to a knee. The man fell with two burned holes now in his chest. Roger moved around the back of the truck to find the sixth raider.

The raider was taking cover at the front of the vehicle, thinking Roger would come around the front. Roger took the shot of opportunity before the man could realize his mistake.

There was gunfire being exchanged at the outpost. Roger walked over to the man that had been tasered. The man was struggling to move. Roger kicked him over so he was flat on his back. He put a hole in the man's chest. Next he walked over to the man called Franky.

Franky was clinging to life. He was on his back, the dead woman on top of him. He still had his pistol and was trying to bring it up to shoot Roger. He was too weak to do so. Roger kicked the pistol out of his hand and then squatted down and looked at Franky.

"Why... did... you... kill... her?"

"Pretty simple. She's one of yours."

Franky coughed and laughed. "How... could... you... tell?"

"When she blinked. I saw the tattoo on her upper left eyelid. You guys and your stupid rites of passage. Raider tradition, females take a tat when they join. A star with a dot in the center on the top left eyelid. Not that you would have gotten my armor anyway without killing me first. But I'll sleep better knowing she was just another low life like yourself."

"Damn man," Franky coughed some more and tried to take some deep breaths. "Guess I'm going to prison for life... for this one."

"Nah. Prisoners are too expensive to keep alive out here, government budget cuts and all. I'm sure you know how it is." Roger stood up and shot him one last time.

He dragged the bodies off to the side of the road. The gunfire had stopped and he could hear outpost personal hollering at each other about checking the dead.

Roger got back in his truck and fired it up. He delivered the supplies of medical equipment and weapons to a very grateful community. They exchanged information. Roger told them about destroying the Invader ship, at which there was a lot of rejoicing. Once everything was unloaded and a message was transmitted that the delivery was received to Roger's contract holder, he left back to the landing site.

The engine was still smoking when she landed back at landing site Bravo Four. Roger loaded up the trailers and mini truck and secured them in the cargo bay. Sonja was patching up holes before they could head back into space. Roger joined her up on top of the ship. His heart sank when he saw the damage up top.

"I tried to avoid it, Roger. Honest."

"I know. You did good. I'm starting to think you might be a lier about being a fighter pilot though. You seem to be able to give them a run for their money every time."

"Not a fighter pilot. This is the truth."

They patched up as much as they could with what they had and made the Pedlar's Omen space worthy. The sun had set a couple of hours before.

"We need to get out of here. I don't want to be ambushed by more raiders tonight." Roger said as the two of them walked up the cargo area ramp.

"I just hope we don't come across anymore fighters or

other larger ships. We're out of patching material."

Meeting

A woman stood in the midst of a small bullet hole riddled warehouse. Vegetation was slowly reclaiming the place with vines growing through what once used to be windows and holes blasted into the walls. Thick layers of dust pooled by past winds had given birth to weeds in various places all over the warehouse. Crates and furniture were piled together near entrances and large windows to form some sort of barriers for cover of some long forgotten battle. Faith Jerin couldn't care less at the moment as she scrolled through reports on her datapad. The place was away from prying eyes and easy to secure for now.

She could hear movement of footsteps in the distance. "About bloody time," she muttered. She loosened the buckle to a pocket on her leather jacket and secured her datapad.

She pulled the sidearm that was holstered at her right hip. Quickly she inspected it for readiness before holstering the weapon again. It wasn't her typical weapon she was used to, but it would do. She kept her stance, feet shoulder width apart, one hand loosely holding the other at her belly. She waited patiently, being mindful of her surroundings, yet mentally preparing for the encounter ahead.

Two guards escorted a clean cut, and respectable looking man dressed in a business suit. They approached from what used to be the main entrance of the warehouse. Both guards wore a recon class body armor and had out light blaster rifles at the ready. Patches on the shoulders of Faith and the guards were the same government issue. No displays of rank or names could be seen on any of them.

As they came near, Faith addressed them. "I'm terribly sorry we have to meet in this manner, Mr. Robinson. The Corvus Commonwealth needs your help, and these are perilous times for all. I hope you understand."

"I have to admit, I was shocked at being rounded up like I was. I thought at first I had been kidnapped by some crime lord. I do agree, these are perilous times. You already seem to know who I am. You are?"

"Apologies again. My name is Faith Jerin, regional director of the Interior Intelligence Division. I'm on the move a lot these days with everything going on. Hence we are meeting here and not a formal government office. Again, I apologize."

"Ah, I understand. I had a sense that I would be subject to something that would be very difficult for me that I would have no control of. I just didn't know the details. Hence I still had the peace of I AM when I was escorted from the parking lot late last night."

The last statement caused Faith's eyebrows to raise. She turned her attention to the guards. "Leave us. Keep watch over the perimeter." The guards acknowledged the order and promptly left the building.

"We are free from prying eyes and ears. Many believe the religious sect of The Way are a relic of the past. Statistics show that believers in I AM are only 4-5% of Corvus population. Sometimes I find the truth is different than what is portrayed in documentation. So I'm curious, as one of the few recognized leaders of this religion, is your following still very strong? Do the numbers actually reflect the truth?"

A look of disappointment fell like a wet blanket on Grant Robinson's face. "Unfortunately, many have turned away from I AM to seek their own pursuits. I've watched over the centuries as followers get distracted by the things of this natural world and wander away. And as the people wander away, so have the laws of this nation eroded and gradually been replaced with lawlessness. It's a disheartening thing for me to witness. I never thought I would see the day."

Faith watched the religious man with a careful eye. She

chose her words carefully. "I have seen the corruption in our government first hand. It truly is appalling," Faith shrugged her shoulders, "However history shows that nations do rise and fall with time. Some believe the old values of the Corvus Commonwealth can be restored and with it the former glory. What are your thoughts about this?"

"I believe that I AM, the creator of all heaven and natural things, lifts governments and takes them down. It is our willingness to submit to the ways of I AM that determine the kind of government we are subjected to."

"Interesting opinion."

"A truth. One that is not always popular these days."

Faith switched from having her hands in front of her to having them behind her back. "Speaking of truth. What can you tell me about the Nedra System?"

It was Grant's turn to look surprised. "The Forbidden system? It is near the heart of the Corvus Commonwealth of star systems. Once we began to take to the stars, I AM forbid us to go there. He has never said why. All nations among the stars have agreed to the Sakar Pact to never travel there. The Corvus Commonwealth was formed by the wisdom of I AM to help enforce that Pact." Grant looked at her confused. "These are things that used to be common knowledge and should be readily available to someone like you. I'm not sure why you needed me to tell you."

She continued to measure his responses. "There are some that think the cult of The Way has actually setup a base of operations in the Nedra system. That the cult has done this to avoid taxes and accountability to the rest of the nations. It is rumored that the Nedra system might contain untold wealth being hoarded by the people of The Way."

Grant couldn't help but laugh. "I assure you, these are fairy tales. There is no way the people who follow I AM would find refuge in a place that is strictly forbidden by him. And for the record... we are not a cult."

Faith gave no emotion that Grant could read. The man was paying attention to her changing terms and observed his physical mannerisms were only slightly riled up by it. "There is also a rumor that the rebel group called the Remnant may have begun to hide out in that system as well. A rumor I more inclined to believe."

Grant's smile faded. It took him a moment to respond. "I doubt the Remnant have taken refuge there. It would be unlike them. Is the intelligence community so desperate to find an excuse to go to Nedra despite the Sakar Pact?"

Faith smiled as she turned her head slightly to the side, "How do you know the Remnant wouldn't do such a thing? Do you have dealings with the Remnant?" She watched him like a hawk.

He was breathing a little heavier. She noticed his hands were getting fidgety. "I've seen news vids. They are in support of the old ways, like the founding fathers of the Corvus Commonwealth. Just as the current Magistrate is. From that I assume, naturally, they would never do such a thing."

"It's said that your god has put terrible mist creatures to guard the way to Nedra. Is this true?"

"I've only heard the stories. I have no clue if they are true or not. The only thing in the holy writings is that it's forbidden to go there. Nothing more, nothing less. Believe me, I've never been there. I don't know of anyone who has been there. No one, and I mean no one, should go there for any reason."

"Does your god protect his followers?"

Grant swallowed hard and his face went pale. "He has. Particularly those who stay very close to Him. Sometimes we die as martyrs, standing up for our belief in Him."

"Does he protect you now?"

Grant just stared at her. Seconds seemed like an eternity.

"I have need of you yet. Probably not the way you would like though." With fluid motion and speed, as if her life depended on it, her pistol was out. Three shots of slug rounds pierced Grant's body in rapid secession. Two into his chest at the heart, and one to his head. His body stumbled backward and fell.

"Guess not," she said as she lowered the sidearm. "Agent Olsen," Faith yelled out.

A uniformed intelligence officer came running into the area. "Get anything good from him?"

"Not really. He was a poor lier. He practically admitted he had been working with the Remnant. His death will be more valuable. Make sure this gets utilized well. I want it all over the Commonwealth that the Remnant killed this innocent believer, a leader of a peaceful people." She tossed the pistol to the officer that caught it. "It's a Remnant weapon we rounded up yesterday. Make sure it gets planted at the scene where I told you to set up."

"Got it. Cleaners are on standby. Crime scene has been prepped and can be ready in two hours with Mr. Robinson."

"Don't screw this up, Olsen. High-profile killings are a tricky business. This has to cause division among the people, the Magistrate and his Remnant. Understood?"

"Yes ma'am," Olsen said.

Faith left the warehouse to her shuttle craft. She strapped herself into the pilot seat and began flight checks. As she waited for the checks to complete, she contemplated what she had just done. She realized she felt void of emotion about killing the man. She had killed many people over the last few hundred years while working for the Intelligence agency.

A thought struck her. Had she just become some cold-blooded killer that didn't care about human life anymore? It was so mechanical killing Grant. Once upon a time she believed that she only killed bad people.

Grant Robinson didn't really fit that mold, if she were to be honest with herself. He was a simple religious man that honestly seemed to help desperate people. His god didn't impress her. Couldn't even stop a slug, let alone three. Yet something he said nagged at the back of her mind. This god of his had warned him something was about to happen to him... and he had peace with it.

Faith shook her head. It didn't make any sense. Yet... he had something, a spark of life, or something. Something in stark contrast to her, highlighted with how mechanically she killed an innocent man to further goals set for her.

She shook it off as the flight controls register, ready for flight. She engaged the engines and lifted off to space. Within hours she had landed the shuttle on the flight deck of the Cerberus Hunter. It wasn't an enormous ship, but it was fast and had a lot of bells and whistles typical of government agency ships. She was grateful she hadn't been given command of a military vessel. It would have just made things slower for her to get the jobs done she needed done in a timely manner.

She exited the shuttle and was greeted by the Bay Manager. "Anything special?"

"No, just refuel and prep for the next mission."

"Yes, ma'am."

Simple. She like simple and straightforward, she realized. She thought of all the webs of entangled intelligence she was handling. She looked at her time piece strapped to her wrist. She would have to wait to get something to eat and changed for duties aboard the ship. She went straight to her quarters.

She grabbed a particular bag before heading off to the special communications room. Once at the room she entered in a pass phrase into a computer terminal and then put her hand up to a scan pad. The computer accepted and unlocked the door for her.

Once inside, she reached into the bag and pulled out a device to scan the room for anything that might be out of place to spy on her. The room scanned as clean. She put the scanner back in the bag and pulled out a device that she put over her throat. It powered on as soon as it detected her pulse.

"Test," she said. The sound of her voice was completely changed to a digitized voice that would be untraceable to her. Next she pulled out a mask and cloak that would conceal her entire body. She stashed the bag out of sight and accessed the terminal to login to the meeting.

She turned around and five other figures appeared in life-sized hologram form. All of them were dressed the same. A number floated above each member.

"Ah, Six has joined us. We are all here then," the digitized voice numbered four said. "How did the task go?"

"The task is complete. Evidence should be apparent in a few hours," Faith said.

"Very good," said Three, "Are we set to begin the next song and dance?"

The one labeled Two spoke, "I know of someone in the field already. I hear rumor they have candidates that are desperate enough to do the deed. I will let this council know when movement has been made."

"Timing will be of the essence," Five said, "The Usurper and his rebels must be stopped soon so the carcase of this current government can be finally laid to rest. It must be discovered that the people of The Way are working with the Remnant and that one or both are operating out of the forbidden place. It should be enough to finish off this movement and turn the people against them in an all out civil war. If we are not careful and this blows up into a war with our neighbors, we may all be doomed."

"Always the dramatic one," Three said. "I do agree that we need to advance the time tables as fast as possible. Even if we have to endanger ourselves to do it. We don't want society to collapse before we can establish the new government. History has proved it takes a very long time and a lot of bloodshed to reestablish power after a fall. Five, will the truth be ready to be released when discovery is made in the forbidden system."

"It will be. If visuals could be captured of the traitors occupation in the forbidden place, it would be very helpful."

Four spoke, "I will see what can be done. It will depend on what happens with the candidate that actually does the task and what information Two can provide me."

"The next course of action is now in play then," Five said. "We will meet again once it's fulfilled."

One by one, the members disappeared. Faith switched off her connection. She plugged in a device to the small terminal and made a copy of the log and the video she had secretly captured of the meeting before deleting it from the main computer. She was beginning to have some doubts about what she was doing. If she betrayed them, she would be dead at the hands of the most dedicated of assassins.

What then? She always assumed everything would fade away to nothingness after she died. Somehow, there was now doubt about that in the back of her mind. She shook her head. What was this madness she was thinking? It must have been something to do with Grant Robinson. Maybe he put a curse on her or some such thing.

She had seen a lot of weird stuff working in intelligence over the last several decades. He didn't seem the type though. Could it be his god, I AM, was making her feel guilty about killing one of his people? Would his god get the last laugh as she went mad?

If she were to continue on the path of helping establish a new government, would she feel guilty about the death of tens of thousands that were going to happen because of her actions? It was a hell of a moment to start growing a conscience about such things. She had never been superstitious before. Being superstitious was starting to overcome her whether she wanted it to or not now that she had killed Grant Robinson.

Return

Sonja did another passive scan. "I'm still not detecting anything. No one seems to be following us."

"I'm not detecting anything over here either. Looks like we might not have to scratch and claw our way out of a system after doing a delivery for once."

"Don't jinx it!" Sonja said as she got up from the pilot's seat. "I'm off to get ready for the pearl."

"I'll meet you there in a few minutes. I just want to keep searching until your ready."

"You're actually going to come and watch me take the plunge this time?"

"I keep thinking I need to learn more about that system."

"See you in a few minutes then."

Roger really wanted to check his account to see if he had been paid for the job yet. The Fold Space Generators for comms in this system only engaged periodically, so he would have to be patient and wait. It would take at least a day for the low power relays here to get his delivery confirmations sent.

Slow communications speeds had a flip side. The raiders couldn't send word that reinforcements were needed quickly enough to catch them. There would have to have been ships in the system already to catch the Pedlar's Omen. At the moment, there didn't seem to be anyone around that was searching for them.

He ran another systems check on the Phantom Drive as

well as making sure the capacitors were completely topped off.

After a few minutes he got up and went to where the pearl was installed in the center of the ship. The room wasn't very big, like every other room on the ship. Space was a premium thing.

The pearl was a large pink colored sphere nearly three meters in diameter. It was completely sealed with a single entrance at the top. The doors to the hatch sealed from inside the pearl so that no one could open it from the outside once the pilot was inside. It ensured the pilot had the maximum protection from anything that might harm them from outside, short of destruction of the pearl itself.

Roger went to the terminal to access the pearl's internal computer. He checked that it had everything it needed to maintain the fluid that filled the pearl.

"Everything good?"

Roger turned to see her. What she was wearing hid no curvature to her athletic, fit body. The two pieces she wore were skin tight, top and bottom. "Uh, yeah. It looks good. I mean, mix looks right and plenty of supplies."

She just smiled at him and went to the ladder that got her to the top platform of the pearl.

"Is that really that comfortable to wear for that long?"

Sonja laughed at him, "You were serious when you said you didn't know much about the pearl system! You honestly don't know?"

"I'm still having to learn a lot about owning and maintaining a ship. There has been way more to it then I ever would have realized. Even after months of doing this. The pearl is one of those things I can't operate, and so I haven't given it much time to learn yet."

"Well," she smiled at him, "what pilots choose to wear is a matter of preference. Largely because it doesn't matter. Once the pilot is in the drink, anything they are wearing has to come off."

Roger's face turned red. "Oh," was all he could say.

She laughed at his embarrassment. "Some of the more exhibitionist pilots come to the pearl with nothing but a robe, which they promptly shed before entering. The rest of us with some ounce of modesty wear something that is easy to get off and put on again while we are inside the pearl."

"I see," Roger looked at the pearl's pink surface. "So what's it like getting into it after you seal it up?"

Her smile faded. "That's a part I never have gotten used to, and I dread it every time. It's like drowning your self. The pearl will help you get the remaining air out of your lungs as gracefully as it can. It will also get rid of the air pocket as soon as it surfaces to keep a person from being tempted to try and breathe it in again out of panic. But it is very much like drowning. There is plenty of oxygen in the fluid and you do eventually get used to it. Just like being a baby in the womb again. Course once the pearl attaches all the fiber attachments to you, you essentially become the ship. You can feel your body in the ship's pearl, but you loose awareness of being in your body."

She took a deep breath. "And I'm stalling. You need to get to the bridge." She smiled at him just before she slipped into the pearl and activated the seal from inside.

Roger heard the pearl hatch squeeze shut and air evacuating from the top. "I think you have job security there. I don't think I could ever bring myself to do that." He walked to the bridge and sat in the navigation and weapons seat, as was his custom.

He pulled up the passive scanner. It still showed nothing. After a few long minutes, he heard her voice over the speakers.

"I'm ready when you are captain."

"Let's go."

Sonja put large amounts of power to the Phantom Drive to transition the physical ship from one realm of existence to the other. The thrum of the drive could be felt throughout the ship. The black star filled scene outside the front window changed to the white mists. The thrum dissipated and the entire ship took on a feeling of surreal stillness.

Roger still had a hard time imagining how this whole thing worked. For him it was like entering a white fog that had even brighter white clouds in it that moved around. And somehow in this fog the ship could traverse massive distances in a matter of days. Until he had gotten his own ship, he had never seen the mists in the little traveling he had done.

Roger just stared at the tranquil scene for a little while.

"You need me for anything?"

"Nope."

"I think I might catch up on some sleep then."

"Good idea."

She never was very talkative when she was navigating the mists. She told him once that things move around and a pilot has to pay very close attention to what was happening or they could lose their way and get lost.

She once tried to explain navigating the mists to a blind man reading a physical book. It was done by reaching out and sensing where physical things in the universe were placed in relation to each other. Then moving and checking you were still where you needed to be. It had the added complication of those same things moving. As if in an ocean, loosely tethered to a specific place, but it could be anywhere nearby in the flow of shifting currents.

She also told him that pilots had to be careful about reaching out carelessly. That there are some sort of creatures in the mists that could attack and try to feed on the life of the pilot in the pearl and those on the ship. Touching one of these creatures through sensing around would draw them in. Roger had never seen one. Wasn't sure if he even could.

The next six days were quiet. Sonja rarely spoke, and Roger made sure he didn't break her focus by distracting her. He cleaned up and repaired his body armor, did minor repairs to the ship and the mini truck that had taken a few shots to it. He also did a lot of cleaning.

Roger was pouring over information, weighing the decision on the wisdom of skimping on engine repairs to use the money for a targeting computer upgrade instead. Roger knew just enough to patch the engine, hopefully not doing more damage to it in the long run.

Course it wouldn't take much, he realized, for that patch to blow apart. Then they would be without an engine, potentially under dire circumstances. On the other hand, a really good targeting computer that could shoot better than he could, might prevent such a dire circumstance in the first place. Not to mention save him a fortune in needed repairs later.

Roger exhaled forcefully as he rubbed his forehead. An

experienced ship captain would know this stuff. The stray thought of selling the ship and going back to being a prison officer passed through his head. He rejected it quickly. He would rather take a chance on getting killed on one of these missions then go back and die inside doing something he had come to hate.

"We're almost there. Give me about fifteen minutes or so to find a clear spot to safely drop back into real space."

"Got it," Roger strapped himself into his desk chair in his quarters. With a wave of his hand, he slid the current analysis information away from the center view of his projected display. He tapped on the virtual keyboard on his desk surface. He pulled up several items that he wanted updated as soon as they hit real space and communications were possible again.

"Dropping."

The Phantom Drive began to thrum more and more as the ship transitioned out of the mists and back into the physical realm. The stillness of the ship slipped away as the subtle sounds and vibrations of the ship's systems came back into awareness. Roger had at one time been told why that happened years ago. The super technical explanation was so far over Roger's head, the words might as well have been the droning sounds of a rattling engine.

The display before him was static, waiting for a communications link to update. It happened. Floods of information came in. The computer sorted it all and refreshed the information that Roger was looking for first. It pulled information that he would want to look at later and flagged it with a lower priority.

Roger looked at his account balance and clenched his teeth. "Six days was more than enough time..." he muttered. He looked to his messages next. There were no messages from his past co-worker, Kris Barron, either. Roger rubbed his head. No payment. And Kris hadn't given him a list of assignments to choose from so he could plan the next run. He shut down the terminal, too pissed off to look at anything else.

He got up and grabbed a large towel from the laundry for Sonja before heading to the pearl. He could hear her puking out the fluids and gasping for air from down the corridor. He walked into the pearl room to see her propped up by her arms at the opening of the pearl. She was breathing heavy. Her long hair was a wet mess around her. Her eyes looked heavy and a little dark.

She looked at Roger when he came in. "I think I might actually need your help." She coughed out more fluid, then spit into the pearl.

Roger climbed up the ladder and helped hoist her out of the fluid so she could sit on the edge of the platform like she had several days before she slipped herself in. Roger wrapped the towel around her.

"Thank you," she said. She coughed up more fluid and spit.

"I don't know that doing six days at a time is a good idea anymore."

"I know that I can manage eight. I've done it before. Doing six days now and then isn't going to kill me." She took a deep breath.

Roger helped her stand up and get down the ladder. He walked with her to her quarters.

When they got to her door, she gave Roger a weak smile. "I'll be fine. I just need a shower and some sleep. Then I'll be right back to being a pain in your posterior."

Roger laughed. "Alright. I didn't hear anything from Kris for our next run, so I need to track him down and find out what's going on anyway. So no need to rush on getting you back on your feet."

"Thank you. See you later." She stepped into her quarters and closed the door.

He knew she would end up sleeping at least a day and a half. She was looking pretty ragged, so it might even be two days. Roger went to the bridge thinking about the missing payment. Before he even got to the bridge, he could feel the thrusters engage and gently accelerate the ship. "Of course you did," Roger said with a smile.

When he got to the bridge, he confirmed that Sonja had already communicated with Lestat Station, arranged for docking, and setup for autopilot to the station, and automated docking. Roger wasn't going to have to pilot the ship at all, even as she slept. Roger was relieved.

Hours later the ship was landed in one of the many bays setup for passenger and cargo transfers to smaller ships.

Roger exited the ship and secured it.

A bay management droid drove up to him as soon as Roger was on the deck. "Greetings, sir. Can I be of assistance for the transfer of cargo or contacting a repair engineer today?"

"Yes, I need a repair estimate. An estimate ONLY. Repairs are not to be started until I approve. Understood?"

"Completely. Your request has been filed."

"There is still crew aboard my ship that need to not be bothered with requests. Flag the ship for do not disturb."

"It is done. How long will you need this space?"

"Estimate four days."

"There is a five percent increase in price per day if the date of departure is not listed. Continue anyway?"

"Yes."

"Anything else I can do for you?"

"No."

"Thank you for your business." With that, the droid spun around and sped off to another ship that was just entering the bay.

Roger began to make his way to the business district. As he walked along he tried to call up Kris at three different numbers. All three gave a message that the contact for that number was no longer available. Roger began to fear something might have happened to Kris on his latest rotation working with the industrial prison work crews.

Roger went to one of the buildings where Kris was renting a space with a couple of employees that handled his side delivery business. When he came to the door it was sealed as a crime scene. Roger took a deep breath. This was not a good omen.

Busted

Roger left the office building. Not knowing what else to do, he made his way to a place to get something to eat and hopefully some information. He had made friends with the owner of The Ugly Unicorn Bar & Grill, discretely handling a few gang related problems that regular station law enforcement didn't seem to have time for.

Roger came to the eating establishment. Outside, the picture of what was probably some little kid drawing of a vicious dinosaur head with a single curved horn protruding from near its one eye, hung from the establishment entrance. Hardly an award-winning design, Roger guessed the owner must have lost some sort of bet and just rolled with it.

Inside, the light levels were low and focused on individual tables and the bar. Music played in the background just loud enough to make it really difficult to listen in to the conversation of others. Each of the tables had a speech scrambler that also made private conversations possible. It made The Ugly Unicorn the best place on the entire space station to do business. Not to mention the food was above average.

Roger went to the bar. It was made of actual wood, a luxury on a space station like this. The owner happened to be working today.

"Roger, my man! Been a long while since I've seen your face. How ya do'in?" Fermin said. Fermin stood on the other side of the bar from Roger. "And how's Sonja? She still working out for you?"

"I'm still alive, I guess. Sonja is doing good. Getting some well-deserved rest after a long run. She's been working out better than I deserve. I owe you one for sending her my way. I'm not sure I could have found a better pilot."

"That's what I like to hear!" Fermin poured himself a drink and offered a drink to Roger. He accepted. Fermin raised his glass, "To excellent staff that are so damn hard to find."

Roger raised his glass, and they both drank.

"How's business been?" Roger asked.

"Good, very good. And for you?"

"Not sure. Just finished a job and haven't seen payment yet. Have you heard anything about Kris Barron and his business office ending up a crime scene?"

"Ah man, you weren't still working for him, were you?"

Roger took the question as another bad omen. "What happened?"

Fermin leaned on the bar closer to Roger. "Hope you had good working relationships with the other delivery facilitators already. Ten days ago Kris was taken into custody. Heard he got nailed with running drugs, and not the light recreational stuff." Fermin eyed Roger really hard, "Krystalite, and lots of it."

Roger's eyes got wide with shock, "You've got to be kidding me!"

"Nope," Fermin said, "Take it you didn't know? Hope to high hell you weren't running it yourself."

"I had no idea. I would have never guessed in all the years I've known Kris he would fall to doing such a thing. He was giving me jobs running medical supplies, food, and weapons for outlying Corvus law enforcement outposts." Roger rested his elbows on the bar and buried his face into his hands.

"I believe you. Kris probably kept you out of it. Might have even used you as an example of legit work being done on the surface. He's done and gone though. Civil Defense Service seized everything that had anything to do with Kris and his side business."

"That explains why I didn't get paid."

"Sorry to hear that man. Let me get you something to eat at

least. On the house."

"You don't need to do that. I'm not looking to be a charity case."

"Not at all, man. You took care of the thug problem I was having a year ago. You also took on Sonja and it sounds like you've been taking good care of her. You may think that was just me helping you, which it was a little. It was actually you taking care of another debt I owed. A favored owed to a friend of a friend. So me giving you a meal is a mere token of my appreciation for all you've helped me."

Roger spent the whole next day meeting with delivery facilitators. One by one, as they discovered who he had been working for, they wanted nothing to do with him. Word seemed to spread like wildfire that he was looking for work. He was starting to get rejected as soon as he walked up to them. He didn't even get a chance to introduce himself.

Roger took refuge between buildings after just being rejected by his last hope of gaining any work. His datapad signaled that he had received a message. The message was the estimate of how much the repairs would cost. Roger looked over the estimate. He wanted to throw his datapad against the opposite wall and shatter it into a million pieces. The repairs were three times as much as he guessed they would be.

He was trying to think of what to tell Sonja. He didn't even have enough in his account to pay her for this last run, let alone repairs.

Another message signal. Roger really didn't want to look at it. He wasn't sure he could handle anymore bad news. Or worse, Sonja wanting to know what they were doing next. He was really dreading his next conversation with Sonja. He looked at the datapad anyway and was surprised.

It was Fermin Levine asking him to meet him at The Ugly Unicorn in an hour for an urgent meeting. Roger replied that he would be there. Perhaps Fermin had another "issue" that needed taking care of. Or he might have a lead on a job.

It nearly took Roger the whole hour to get there. It was nearly after hours for the establishment. He noticed only a handful of people remained when he walked in.

Fermin Levine got Roger's attention and motioned with his

head for Roger to come join him. Fermin exited from behind the bar to talk with him. "Hey man. You look like you could use a little pick me up."

"Hasn't exactly been a productive day."

"Hmmmmm. Well, let's see what The Ugly Unicorn can do for a man like you," Fermin laughed. "Come on, I have someone I want you to meet."

Fermin lead him to a back corner table where a man had nearly finished a meal. Fermin ushered Roger to sit across from the man. Roger took the seat. Fermin turned to the man that had stopped eating his meal and seemed to be sizing up Roger. "This is the man I told you about. He's legit."

The man nodded, and Fermin patted Roger on the shoulder just before he left.

Roger looked at the man.

"Captain Roger Vance," the man said, "Tell me what you see."

"Mannerisms suggest a government employee. You don't seem to have a broomstick shoved up your rump, so your not military. Boots and haircut are typical for a LEO. Clothing that are not a uniform, yet nearly so... I would peg you as some sort of intelligence officer or investigator of some kind."

"Not bad, Mr. Vance! Very well in deed. I am in fact an investigator with the Civil Defense Service. My department specializes in smuggling of illegal items. I'm Inspector Daniel Byrd."

Roger started to feel a little uncomfortable.

"I was the lead investigator responsible for taking down your friend Kris Barron." Daniel seemed to wait for something. After a moment, he raised his eyebrows when Roger remained quiet. "You have nothing to say about that?"

Roger leaned back and put one arm over the other across his chest. "Why would I. If you believed I was running whatever it was that might be illegal he was shipping, you would have picked me up yesterday."

"That's true. We had Mr. Barron under surveillance for a long while. We know what got shipped where. Mr. Barron wanted to keep you out of the illegal loop because he knew you wouldn't go along with it. We even have him on record saying you would more than likely turn him in. From all the evidence we have, you're just an innocent bystander in the whole thing."

"So why did you call this meeting?"

"I didn't, actually. Mr. Levine over there reached out to me. I'm still not sure how he managed it but, it seems Mr. Levine has proposed a possible answer to a very dire need he could not have possibly known about. A possible answer to a problem that has been right in front of me the whole time and I didn't realize it."

"So long as it's not flirting with the illegal, or so dangerous, it will get my crew killed."

"Sounds like something you would say from what I've read about you. I've taken a deeper look at your records before this meeting. A very respectable and distinguished career as an officer in the Corvus prison system. Reports from the delivery jobs you have been taken thus far show you are always on time, or early.

"I was a little taken back by how few raiders seem to survive an encounter with you. That caused me to dig a little more to find out why. When I linked it back to the cruise ship, I understood. Had I walked in your shoes, I probably would be no different."

"So what are you asking of me?"

"This is my proposal. You don't have to do it and are free to walk away if you wish. The deal is this. The civil war that has been growing in the shadows of the public eye has put a huge strain on the resources of all law enforcement agencies. My department has recently received intelligence that a smuggler has established a base of operations in a very out of the way star system. We need to know how much of a weapons cache he has there. To find it, we need a deep space probe deployed in that system that won't draw a lot of attention from whoever might be there watching. The agency doesn't have any small ships available to do that anytime soon. Finding a private reputable ship and crew that can do this with integrity and speed are extremely hard to find at the moment.

"I'm under a lot of pressure from higher ups to get this done ASAP. I'm authorized to utilize any assets that I need to get it accomplished. So my question to you is how much will this cost for you to go to this system, and drop off a probe,"

Daniel slid a datapad across the table that had a chart of how far he would have to travel and what was close by. "Once the probe is deployed you leave. We do our thing and search, you come back and get paid. Simple and straightforward."

"I'm not familiar with the Nedra system," Roger said while he pulled out his own datapad and did calculations.

"Like I said, it's a very out of the way system. No one ever goes there. Perfect place to hide a weapons cache."

Roger quoted him a price.

Daniel looked at him and laughed. "You obviously don't do government contracts. That has to be barely above cost." Daniel leaned forward, "You're an honest man, and this galaxy needs more people like you. Tell you what. I've been told you can't even get a job in this place because of what happened to Mr. Barron.

"I will pay you double the quote you just gave me if you take the job. In addition to that, I'll pull some strings and make sure your last contract gets paid from the funds we confiscated. You did the work, and it was an honest cargo that helped good people, so it's only right the contract gets legally honored.

"Upon completion of dropping off the probe, I will get you hooked up to run some supplies to our remote assets out here. When people see you running supplies for the Civil Defense Service, rumors will start that you were more likely working undercover for us and not smuggling for Mr. Barron. That should put you in a position that the delivery facilitators here will actually hire you. Then you can continue to haul for us if it's mutually beneficial. Or you can haul for the locals here. How does that sound?"

"Almost too good to be true. Why so generous?"

"I'm just trying to help an honest guy out. Besides, you have no idea how much heat we are under to track down all the rebel weapons that seem to be moving around. We are trying to get a handle on things before an all out civil war starts."

Roger thought it through. "You have a deal. I've got an estimate to repair my ship. It's going to take four days. Is that a problem?"

"That's not a problem. Contract for the probe will come your way here in a couple of hours. I'll also work on getting those funds for your last job to you as soon as I can so you can make good on those repairs. Let me know when you are ready to receive the probe."

"I will. I greatly appreciate this."

Daniel nodded, got up from the table and left the establishment. Roger made notes of the conversation and information he would need for planning the details of the run.

Fermin stopped by the table with a hot plate of food and something to drink. He put it down in front of Roger. "Well... Did the Ugly Unicorn deliver? How did it go?"

Roger looked up and smiled at him. "It went good. I'm going to help him with his problem, and he's going to help me. Thank you for that."

Fermin laughed loud and hard, "Ah man! You are really good for business. You just did me another favor. Keep this up and I'll have to make you a partner." He collected the other man's dishes and left Roger to enjoy his meal.

Roger got to looking at his charts. The Nedra system wasn't listed anywhere. Yet, it was on Daniel's charts. Daniel said it was a system that no one ever went to. Something was starting to bother him about it in the back of his mind.

Roger's desperate circumstances made him push back on the sense that something was wrong with this. His mind recalled other times when he ignored that sense over the centuries. Most often he paid a real price for it. He had a sense of feeling trapped. It was a bad omen, and he knew it.

The Probe

Roger arrived back at the ship. The main station lights were dimmed low and the small path marker lights turned up to give some indication of night. He pulled out his datapad and went through the layers of security to get the cargo area ramp and door to open up. It would have been easier to just call up Sonja. If she was still sleeping, he didn't dare wake her up.

The ramp pistons hissed and the ramp edge thudded against the steel deck plate. Roger quickly climbed the ramp and passed through the door. He secured both once inside. He walked to his quarters and noticed when he came to Sonja's that the marker showed she wasn't there. He called out to her and did a quick search of the ship. Not finding her, he went to his quarters.

He sat down to his desk and pulled up his messaging system. The contract was there already, just like Daniel said it would be. Roger looked over it carefully, looking for issues. It was more straightforward than most government documents he had dealt with in the past. It also gave the cargo space requirement for the probe. He made note of it and needing to reserve a storage space to store his mini truck and trailers. Roger signed the contract and submitted it. He hoped he didn't regret doing so later.

He moved onto the next message. This one too was from Daniel. It let him know that payment had been made for the last job. Roger switched over to his financial screen. The money was there... finally.

He switched back to his messages and found the one for the estimate. He more closely looked at the terms and what it said needed to be fixed. He rolled his eyes when he found out his patch job had in fact ruined other parts of the engine.

The benefit of hiring a ship engineer was obvious. An actual full crew would be nice. The Pedlar's Omen had the capacity for a mist pilot, pilot, engineer, weapons specialist, navigation and communications officer, and a cargo handler, and the captain. His cash flow simply didn't allow for him to hire more than the mist pilot.

Doing this business looked so much easier than this on datapad. He wondered how other captains managed a money flow to keep on full crews like that. Roger was having a hard time seeing how it could be done. He followed the link to the station service ticket system. He paid for the parts and the 50% deposit required for labor.

He received a new message that his payment had been processed and accepted and repairs would commence first thing in the morning. He would need to be there when repairs started to give the work crew access to ship systems so repairs could be done in a timely manner.

Roger went through the rest of his messages, which were mundane at best. He caught up on some of the highlights of local and Corvus wide news. Thinking about the civil war Daniel mentioned, he took notice of a news vid that showed some faction called the Remnant gunning down some sort of religious leader named Grant Robinson. Apparently there was a massive outcry.

Roger had never really paid attention to such things. Maybe he needed to. He had just taken a job that was related to some group smuggling weapons. If a civil war was in fact coming, he wondered, how might that change things for him? What side would he be on? Roger realized he didn't even know who were taking what sides for what cause.

The thought of added complexity to an already difficult job... jobs, he corrected himself, made his head hurt. He shut it all down and went to bed.

Early in the morning Roger heard the distant sound of the

ramp lower. He just laid there in bed and listened. The ramp closed again. His senses sharpened as something didn't set right inside of him. It sounded like Sonja was stumbling along in the corridor. There was a faint groan of pain and the sound of her body collapsing to the floor.

Roger scrambled out of bed and rushed into the corridor. Sonja was there on the floor. She was leaning on one arm, trying to prop herself up. Her head slowly wobbled. Hearing Roger's door open, she looked up at him. Her right eye was red and turning black. Her right cheek was swollen. Blood dripped out of the corner of her mouth. Her right hand was holding her left side.

Roger rushed to her. "Who did this to you?!" He helped her up.

She just looked at him, "Don't ask. It's my problem, not yours."

Roger noticed the blood around her hand at her side. "It's my problem when you come back to the ship like this. We need to get you medical attention."

"NO! No records."

"I might be a stumbling idiot when it comes to running a ship. I'm not an idiot when it comes to investigations and use of force. Tell me straight up, are you involved in something illegal here?"

"No, it's not like that at all." Her eyes pleaded with him on the verge of tears.

Roger looked at her, drawing on experience. He measured her response and what she said very carefully. "Alright. I believe you. For now, I'll leave it alone. The ship's basic medical kit isn't going to do squat for your side. What's your plan?"

"I have something to help in my quarters."

He helped her get into her room and lay on her bed. She had him get a bag out of her closet. He set it on her desk and opened it up. He recognized a few of the devices. One was used to treat serious stab and gunshot wounds, and another one for broken bones. He wasn't sure about the other three. All of them looked like high grade equipment. He grabbed the one for stab and gunshot wounds. It had Corvus Military markings.

"Where did you get these?"

"A woman that was assigned to help me. She was a combat field medic."

Combat medic? Assigned to help? Roger was putting pieces of information together that he knew about her and running the probabilities of what Sonja was involved in. He would keep his promise to not actively investigate. Passive information collection was still on the table. He wouldn't tell her that though. He would definitely see if something happened to turn up in the local news tomorrow that might have more leads that he could follow up on later.

Roger turned back to the bag and got out a pair of cutters for her clothing. He had her keep pressure on the wound while he carefully cut apart her shirt around the wound big enough for the device to rest against her skin. He removed the device from its casing and turned it on.

Sonja let her hand slip away from the wound to her side and let Roger remove the cloth. He put the device over the wound and it secured itself to her. Sonja flinched in pain as it started its analysis. It gave her a shot of some drug to deaden the area so it could work on repairing the flesh.

Roger went and got clean wash rags to clean up the blood on her hands, arms, and face.

She had been watching him the entire time without saying a word. Roger checked the progress of the device. It was about a third of the way done.

"I think I'm going to have to move on. I don't think it's safe for you if I stay."

Roger crossed his arms and looked at her. "You think I'll be safe just because you leave?"

"These people that are after me, they hunt people down and kill them. This isn't like supervising inmates in a controlled environment. Or even getting into chance starship encounters with raiders. Killing other people in ships is different than having someone hunt you in person."

Roger laughed.

"It's not funny! I'm serious. I'm constantly having to watch over my shoulder." She was on the verge of crying. "Have you ever had to kill someone in person? Or watch someone die? You wear a ring, so I assume you might have a wife or ex-wife.

What about her? Kids or future kids?"

Roger stopped smiling, and he looked down at the ring on his right hand. He looked back at Sonja. "In person kills that I've done... I stopped counting decades ago."

Sonja got a shocked look on her face, "What?!"

"I know its different, person to person. I know I don't talk about it. I do what I have to do and I don't dwell on it. I've seen dozens of officers killed in the line of duty. I've had a few die in my arms. I don't take you with me on the deliveries for a reason. Just this last run I ended up killing a half dozen raiders just outside the outpost."

Sonja's face was in utter shock. This wasn't the glorified baby-sitting stories he had told her about before. He never mentioned killing anyone on the job deliveries they did. She had assumed he just subdued them all for arrests later. Roger looked down at the ring again.

"As for wife and kids... A long time ago, in my last job, I was supposed to be scheduled for vacation. I was supposed to go with my wife and three daughters on a cruise ship to the Magical Gorathan Forests. I got mandated to stay because a riot broke out in the prison I was at. Four officers killed and over a dozen wounded when it all broke loose. So none of us were going anywhere soon until it was all over. I convinced my wife and daughters to go without me.

"Later I found out raiders made a bold move and attacked that cruise ship, intent on taking as many as they could alive for human trafficking. Local authorities responded and put up a good fight. The raiders, realizing they couldn't get their prize, destroyed the cruise ship instead. No one on the cruise ship survived."

"I can't even count the number of death threats I've received over the years from inmates and their families. I live a life constantly looking over my shoulder. It's nothing new. Maybe one day that will change, most likely not."

She finally looked away and at the ceiling. "I had no idea."

"These are things I don't share with others. I ask you keep what I've told you to yourself."

"I can understand that, and I will." She seemed to be thinking as she stared at the ceiling. "You make a bit more sense to me now."

There was a long moment of silence between them. "So you still thinking you need to leave?"

"No," she said softly, "Now that I know what you just told me, I'm probably safer here than anywhere else at the moment."

"Glad to hear it. We have an easy good paying job to do for once. I'll fill you in after you've had a chance to recover. Might get a little noisy around here. Repairs are supposed to take four days."

"Okay."

The device beeped that it was finished. Roger removed it from her side and put it on the table. Aside from a bit of redness, you couldn't even tell she had been stabbed. He gathered up the bloody rags and left her quarters, shutting the door behind him.

The next few days flew by. Sonja stayed in the ship and out of sight of the repair crew. Roger paid extra to have someone pickup his mini truck and trailers to take to storage. Now that he had found out someone was probably hunting Sonja, he made an effort to stay near the ship.

The repairs were set to be completed within a few hours. Roger had the ship restocked completely for the next run. He didn't want to have to stop at another station to do anymore than refuel the ship. The probe was loaded and secured.

The next several days were uneventful as Sonja moved them through the mists to their eventual destination. Roger again did a bunch of cleaning and he looked through the Lestat news articles he archived. There was mention that two men had gotten in an altercation and both had mortally wounded each other. They had both died at the scene. It was the same night that Sonja had come back to the ship. He made note of it for a possible follow up later.

They refueled at a system that was not far from their destination. Roger found a remote location near an asteroid belt to hide the ship to give Sonja time to rest from the latest mist jump. She would need to be fresh for the next round of jumps.

While she rested, Roger made use of the available communications system. Daniel had sent him a potential list of jobs pending completion of deploying the probe. Roger looked over the list and analyzed them. The jobs were all easier and paid much better. Roger flagged the ones he could do and sent the request back to Daniel. He then put together the plans to do each run.

"Hey, want to get your nose out of that terminal and get this job done?" Sonja said from the speaker.

Roger was caught off guard. "I didn't even hear you get out and about."

"I was kinda quiet. I'm ready to go as soon as you are."

"Go for it. I'm really curious about this system that seems to be unlisted."

"I'm curious, but at the same time concerned. It still seems odd to me that this place isn't visited."

"Maybe it has a dead star."

The thrum of the Phantom Drive started up. Roger could feel the transition take place.

"That's a good point. I guess we will find out."

Roger spent the next several hours pouring over reports of raider activity for the destinations that they were going to be delivering to.

"Whoa. I think I found it. Um... there's something there."

"What do you mean?"

"There is something massive huge just sitting on top of that system. It doesn't seem to be moving. I've never sensed anything like it. I can't get into the system without brushing up against it."

"What does it look like?"

"I can't see it anymore than you can. I can only sense objects, movement, and intent in the mists. I don't like this. It's like it's sheltering this system. Maybe hiding it intentionally?"

"Do mist creatures always move? Or can they rest in one place?"

"They are always on the move. As far as anyone knows, they never stop in one place for very long."

Roger considered it. "All we have to do is get in there, drop the thing off and get back out again. Although I told Daniel I would not risk the death of my crew for a job. Is there a chance you will get hurt if you try?"

"Having never come across something like this before, I have no idea. Creatures attack with something like claws and teeth. So as long as there isn't something like that, we would probably be fine."

"It's your life on the line. You make the call."

"If I get killed out here, you will die too."

"I know. Your call."

"I'll get as close as I can and see what it does. If it moves, I may run for it."

"Go for it."

Sonja moved the ship to what she felt like was near the edge of whatever the thing was. Nothing happened, so she dived down along a curvature she sensed down to the system. She was nearly there. "AGH... it's moving!" Sonja poured on the speed and dumped the ship into the physical realm.

Roger could feel his heart pounding in his chest. "Sonja?"

"I'm here. I'm fine. I think I might have peed in the pearl... a lot."

Roger hadn't considered that aspect of things. "Gross."

"Yeah, the filtration system will take care of it. But... yeah."

A feeling like a wet blanket came over Roger. It was a feeling of him being in violation, that he shouldn't be here.

"Roger... I'm still sensing things in the physical world like I do in the mists. This isn't right. I shouldn't be feeling anything, especially a serious sense to leave. We need to get out of here!"

"I think I might be feeling it too. We need to dump that probe and leave ASAP." Roger got up from his seat and ran to the cargo bay. He went to the probe and activated it. The computer systems started up and acknowledged that it was launch ready. Roger stepped over the cargo bay control panel and activated the atmosphere shielding. He opened up the belly protective plates and lowered the floor into the vacuum of space. The pistons were fully extended. He disengaged the floor magnetic locks that held the probe in place.

"Go ahead and back away from it."

The Pedlar's Omen backed away, leaving the probe floating in place. After the probe was clear of the nose of the ship, Roger retracted the lift and sealed up the belly before returning to the bridge. Once there was enough distance and the probe was clear of collision risk, its thrusters fired and propelled it towards the center of the system.

Roger made sure to record everything the ship was seeing for future records. The system wasn't dead after all. It had a vibrant star and at least two possible habitable planets. There looked like there might be a rich amount of resources in the system as well. Yet, there remained the sense that no one should be here.

"How are you feeling? Think you might be able to outrun whatever that thing is in the mists? Or are we stuck here for a while?"

The engines fired up and he could feel the ship turn around. "We are not staying here another minute more if I can avoid it. This place gives me the absolute creeps."

"I know. Yet it has a beauty to it. It's weird."

Sonja engaged the drive to transition. The blackness of space gave way to the white of the mists. "It's not moving," Sonja whispered.

Roger could hear the engines rumble at full throttle. The stillness of the mists kept him from feeling it. Roger could sense something in the distance behind them growl and he felt like it was looking at him. He nearly wet his pants when he sensed it come closer to him.

"Ahhhhh..."

Roger sensed it pull back and become almost invisible. Roger was breathing heavy. "What the hell was THAT?!"

"What?"

"The feeling of something growling, it looked at me, and then it just disappeared."

"You sensed that?! That's even more freaky given you were not in a pearl. That's what I sense when I come too close to a mist creature. NEVER on that scale, though. That thing was immensely huge. I never want to come back here again."

"I'm with you on that one."

Jobs

Roger was cleaning in the tiny room that served as a dining area and conference room for the crew. He faintly heard Sonja cry out from her room, "OH GOD... OH GOD... WE'RE SO DEAD!"

They had just parked the Pedlar's Omen at a massive asteroid upon getting halfway back to Lestat station. Supposedly Sonja was going to shower and rest after the four days in the pearl. Roger was a little surprised to hear hollering instead.

He stopped wiping the table down when he heard the door to her quarters open. "ROGER!"

"I'm in here."

He heard her bare feet hit against the metal plates of the floor as she ran. She arrived at the doorway of the room Roger was in wearing a pair of shorts and a tank top. A towel was wrapped around her head, concealing her hair. She was breathing heavy.

"What's the matter?" Roger asked, confused.

"I was just doing a little homework. Do you know why the Nedra system wasn't in our charts?"

Roger just shrugged his shoulders, "Someone slipped up on their chart making? It wouldn't be the first shoddy thing I've been suckered into purchasing. Just look at our targeting computer."

Sonja just closed her eyes and slowly shook her head, "Your ignorance is amazing. NO! It's not because it's a shoddy chart.

It because the Nedra system is the FORBIDDEN system! Do you know what that means?!"

Sonja slapped her hands against her face and dragged them down. "UNBELIEVABLE!!! How do you NOT know about the forbidden system!?"

"How is it you don't know basic hand to hand combat given your circumstances?"

She put her hands on her hips and gave him a look of, oh really.

"I'm serious. Pretend for a moment I'm a noob to space, and barely know anything about the mists or someplace called," he did air quotes, "'the forbidden place'. Honestly, it shouldn't be hard for you to do. I've already given you lots of practice by now."

"Okay, you at least know what the Sakar Pact is, right?"

"Never heard of it."

"My god... isn't there some sort of test or something you have to take to purchase a ship?"

"If you've got enough money to put down for a ship, what you do with it after that is your responsibility. How do you not know this?"

Sonja was just dumbfounded as she looked at the ceiling. Eventually not knowing what else to do... "Okay... from the top. One of the first things drilled into everyone's head at the Academy of the Mists, is that we can travel anywhere we want within our galaxy, except for one place.

"Some god, who's name I can't even begin to remember now, supposedly forbid all mankind from this one star system in all the galaxy. It's location was supposedly given. As we moved out and came to control the space all around this forbidden place, the nations at the time formed a pact with each other to guard this forbidden system and keep anyone from accidentally, or otherwise, from going there so that this god didn't get pissed off at humanity and kill us all.

"The pact made it punishable by DEATH anyone that might get too close to it, let alone enter it. The Corvus Commonwealth was later established to enforce this pact. The name of the forbidden system is Nedra. Does that now make sense?"

"So you're telling me, we just went into, and came out of

a system, an act that by international law is punishable by death?"

"YES!"

"Shouldn't there be some warnings, broadcasts, or something to warn people like me, mist pilots like you from accidentally going there... if say because it wasn't on some chart?"

"Mist pilots are all taught about the warning beacons that..." Sonja just stopped and looked like she was searching.

"What warning beacons? I don't remember hearing or seeing any beacons."

She looked confused, "That's because they weren't there. They are supposed to be there. Beacons are placed at dangerous systems, and mist pilots can feel them and stay away. They had practice ones at the academy, so I know what the forbidden ones feel like. But they weren't there. None of them."

"Is it possible you just missed it?"

"There are supposed to be seven beacons around it which makes it absolutely impossible to miss."

"Could someone have turned them off?"

"I don't know. I didn't think so. Maybe that wasn't the Nedra system. Maybe another system with the same name?"

Roger cleared the dining items off the table and activated the interactive star map. Sonja came in to the room and stood at the table. She pulled up a side screen that had information from her schooling she had been researching. It gave coordinates for the forbidden system.

She accessed the map of the floating and spinning galaxy above the table. She entered in the coordinates for the forbidden system.

The computer highlighted a cube chunk of the map and zoomed into it. Sonja gave it the command to keep zooming. It did until she commanded it to stop. A red circle was around where the undocumented system they had just been to was.

Sonja looked at Roger. "I don't like this!"

Roger considered what he had just learned. "Do the beacons do active monitoring or are they just warning systems?"

"Beacons are only passive. The Corvus security fleet monitors everyone coming and going around that system."

"What fleet?"

"I just told you, the Corvus security fleet!"

"Sonja... there were no Corvus security ships in any of the systems we were in around there. Only local security. Where they in the mists?"

Sonja was about to argue before she thought about it. "I didn't feel any other ships nearby. I guess I should have."

Roger brushed his goatee with one of his hands. "No warning beacons, no ships, no one stopped us to arrest or blast us to pieces going in or coming out. Aside from the creature, we were able to waltz right in there and out again. Oh, and no god struck us dead for trespassing. At this point, I'm not sure what to think. I don't know if I should be relieved or worried."

"I'm not sure anymore now either." Sonja just quietly watched Roger for a while. "What do we do now?"

"At this point, I'm going to do an investigation on Inspector Daniel Byrd. The results of that will dictate what I do from there."

"Well, you have fun with that. I'm going to attempt to get some sleep." With that said, Sonja removed the wet towel from her head as she walked back to her quarters.

They were located in a well-populated system, which meant there was a Fold Space Generator here. Communications would be near instant across the galaxy except for those out of the way places. It was just a matter of paying for the data transfers, which wasn't overly hard on the pocketbook. An easy thing to do considering there wasn't any ship repairs to save up for this time. He shutdown the table and went to his quarters to look into Daniel Byrd while Sonja slept.

The next day Roger, wearing a t-shirt and shorts of his own, was in the empty cargo bay exercising. Sonja had walked barefoot to the cargo area and leaned against a wall and just watched the captain. She was still in her shorts and tank top, her light brown hair was braided up this time.

He got up from what he was doing on the floor when he noticed her watching him with a smile on her face. "And how long have you been standing there watching me?"

"Just a couple minutes."

"You want to start learning hand to hand?"

Roger started her with the basics of how to stand, block, punch, and kick. He showed her some basic moves for getting out of a few holds. She took the lessons seriously and seemed to be a quick study. Towards the end Roger started to teach her how to escape when someone had her back to the ground and was on top of her.

After the tenth round Roger was exhausted and sore from her hits. She finished the maneuver, using leverage to put him on his back with her above. Only Roger knocked one of her hands out of place and she ended up flopping on top of him instead of breaking away.

The two of them laughed.

"I'm spent and I'm pretty sure I have a dozen new bruises. Lessons are done for the day," he said.

She positioned herself so their faces were close to each other. She had that heart-warming smile he found he was starting to really like. She looked into his blue eyes. "Thank you for this. It means a lot to me." She let her head dip down and kissed him lightly on the lips. She quickly backed away and headed to her quarters.

Roger just laid there for a minute on the cool steel plate floor. *I promised myself I would never do this again.* He had to admit he was thinking about her more often. Taking notice of how she moved when she walked. The revealing outfit she wore when she went to the pearl.

"Oh, knock it off man," he whispered to himself. He picked himself up off the floor and went to get cleaned up. He put his focus back on the things they were facing. He had sent a message as a small test to Daniel to get a feel for where his involvement of things were. He expected to hear back from him anytime.

He checked his messages after having gotten a shower and getting dressed. He had gotten a reply from Daniel. He read it carefully. It was consistent with his other findings. Roger asked Daniel to meet him at The Ugly Unicorn at a date and time he knew they would be able to make.

Only a few minutes later he got confirmation that he would meet him. He got up from his desk and went to Sonja's quarters. It showed she was in. He knocked on her door.

She opened it. She had changed into something that looked

more like a semi-casual uniform that she liked. She took a deep sniff. "You stink pretty."

Roger didn't even know how to respond to that and apparently is showed.

She laughed.

"We have a meeting with Daniel Byrd." He told her when.

"So in other words, I need to get ready for pearl duty. I see how you are."

"Yeah, we need to find out from him how dire things are. I'll see you at the pearl in a few."

She gave him a coy smile. "I've noticed, when I first started working for you you couldn't hardly get to the pearl to help me. Now you never miss it."

Roger's face turned red.

She laughed and closed the door. Roger wasn't sure if he should go there now or not. He went to the pearl and checked all the systems as quickly as he could. She hadn't arrived yet, so he left for the bridge and took his normal seat.

A bit later he heard her voice. "Was it something I said?"

"No... I'm just a little preoccupied with how short my life might be if I'm wrong about Daniel."

"May I come with you this time?"

Roger thought about it. "You might as well. Both of our lives are on the line."

Sonja transitioned them into the mists and began navigating her way to the system where Lestat Station resided.

The next few days were quiet. When she told Roger they were close, he setup communications and information updates he wanted as soon as they entered the system. The ship dropped back into the physical realm gracefully.

The informations systems began to update. He checked his account. The probe must have worked because he had been paid already. The next cargo run was setup and ready to be delivered to his ship. There were other messages in replies to information he had requested. There was nothing that struck him as a red flag that he should abort his meeting with Daniel.

Roger could just barely hear Sonja puking up the pearl fluids. He went and got her a large towel before heading to the pearl. When he got there she was sitting up on the platform, her arms bracing herself against the platform as she spit more fluid back into the tank.

"Hi," she said just before coughing some more.

"Brought you a towel. Noticed you've stopped bring your own the last several times." Roger smiled at her.

She just smiled back at him. Eventually she got up and climbed down the ladder. She dried herself off as best she could. She then used the towel to wrap up her hair around her head. "How long before the meeting?"

"Nine hours. First thing in the morning."

He walked with her to her quarters. "The probe must be functional. Payment for the job showed up. I've transferred your payment already. Feels weird not to have a mountain of repairs that need done."

They got to her door. "I was thinking you should keep my payment and put it towards a better targeting system."

"You don't need to do that. I've already placed an order for one. They are going to get it installed the day after tomorrow."

"Cool. That should help a lot." She turned and face him and just smiled.

He stood close to her. He gently touched the side of her face with his right hand. He started to kiss her lightly. She wanted a little more and he let her. When they came apart, she backed into her room. "You need to stop, or I'm not going to get any sleep at all!" she said smiling big. She closed her door on him.

The next morning the two of them exited the ship and headed down to The Ugly Unicorn. They were shown to their seat. Roger sat down with his back to a wall so that he could keep an eye on people's movement around him.

Daniel joined them a few minutes later. At first, he was hesitant to sit down when he looked at Sonja.

"She's my mist pilot. The other half of my crew."

"Ah," Daniel said. It seemed to put him more at ease and he sat down. "So what can I do for you Captain."

"Tell me what you know of the Nedra system."

"Interesting turn," Daniel said. "Not much, actually. Higher ups gave me a task, gave me the information I needed to use to get the task done. I'm told the device is operational and has made some interesting discoveries but, beyond that you probably know more than I do at this point."

"Do you know about the Forbidden system?"

"I've heard of it. It's protected by the Sakar Pact, a responsibility taken very seriously by the Corvus Commonwealth."

"Are you sure about that?"

"Have you seen something to suggest otherwise? If so, you would do well to report it if someone is attempting to break into it."

Roger leaned forward and whispered, "The Nedra system IS the forbidden system. And you sent us there with a probe."

"That can't possibly be! There is no way," he looked to Sonja as if she could confirm the possibility.

Roger looked at Sonja as if to say, go ahead.

Sonja looked at Daniel, "I looked it up afterward. It's true, that's where you sent us. The thing is, all the warning beacons aren't there. The only thing that is protecting that place is a massive huge mist creature that has decided to camp out there. I hope your boss doesn't plan to send us back, because we won't do it!"

Roger put a hand over Sonja's. "Inspector, the Corvus ships that are supposed to be there weren't there at all. I did some checking. Those ships haven't been around for the last three standard decades."

Sonja shot Roger a surprised look. Roger didn't take his eyes off of Daniel. "So with regard to the Sakar Pact. What are your intentions with us?"

Daniel was in shock about the whole thing. "I would say keep your heads low and don't mention it to anyone. If what you say is true, I'm in the same ship as you. I've had someone from the Magistrate's office contact me. They suspect the head of the Civil Defense Service might be working against the Magistrate. You wouldn't happen to have anything besides your testimony that I can pass on to them as evidence, would you?"

Roger looked at Daniel carefully. After a long moment, he reached into his pocket and slid a small metal device across the table. It was a data storage device. "It's not much. It's the few ship recordings and images we were able to get before we hightailed it out of there."

Daniel took the device and hid it away in his jacket. "If

there are pictures, that alone should be proof enough. I will leave your names out of this unless they absolutely force my hand. I'm serious that you two need to lie low for a while. I've got your jobs setup, complete with auto payment upon the field agents confirming delivery. You still want to do them?"

"Yes, we need the cash flow."

"Alright. I'll leave it alone then. Best of luck to you two." With that, Daniel got up and left.

Roger just continued to stare off in the direction Daniel had left. "I hope I'm right and that wasn't some huge mistake that gets us killed."

Discovery

A man put on a face mask, complete with cloak to cover all of his features. He tested the device attached to his throat. His voice was completely sterile digitally to hide his identity. He stood alone in a special secured room for communications. He tucked away a now empty bag beside the computer terminal. He pulled back the cloth around one of his hands enough to check his time piece.

He put the required information into the terminal to join the meeting. He covered his hands with the long cloth again and turned around. A projected number two hovered over his head. Numbers one and three appeared before him, having already joined the meeting. They all wore the same plain face mask and covered in the same cloak. They all stood still and quiet.

Soon Numbers six, four, and finally, five joined within minutes.

"Let us begin," Three said with a digitized voice. "What progress has been made towards first contact?"

The man in the room labeled Two answered, "I hear that an agent was able to secure someone to go to the place and drop off a special package. I suspect the agent will get a debrief in person and receive any documentation they were able to acquire there."

Number Four chimed in, "It would be interesting to find this agent and see if the documentation is something that would be of interest. For someone to fabricate evidence wouldn't be too difficult. How long before this debrief happens?"

"Be mindful and do not speak of specifics in this channel!" Three said.

Both Two and Four nodded.

Two looked at the floor. "I saw on the news vids the death of a friend of ours. It was most tragic." He turned to Four, "Did you see the jasper rose?"

Four looked down at the floor. After a moment he looked back at Two, "I did. It was a nice touch. I will be sure to thank the preparer personally."

"The old must pass to give way to the new. If you two are done, we need to move forward. Six, I hear an opportunity comes your way," Three said.

"I will look for it."

"Five, when you have what you need, you should run with it. Pieces are moving faster than we anticipated. I've heard the troublemaker has struck again. It will be made public in short order, I suspect. A move needs to be made and soon." She turned to number One, "Have the documents been modified?"

"It has been done... long ago, as suggested," One said.

"Two, this one that helped for the greater good with a package. It would be fitting for such good deeds to be rewarded. Perhaps they might help again. Great risks should be met with proper reward. Whatever it takes, whatever they want, my hope is that it will be done for them. With fortune on our side, they will be on the way to help with the other item before bad news breaks. After they are done, the tables might turn."

"Understood," Two said.

"I have seen that a tourist droid has been misplaced. I will try to find it and see what it turns up. We all have things that need our time. Good day," Three said.

One by one the images of the other members disappeared until Two was left in the room alone. He turned and terminated his own connection. He entered in his security code and deleted the log file of the meeting and the log entry of himself entering the room. He took off his mask and the voice modulator from his throat. He wrapped them both up in the long cloth and put them in the bag.

He exited the secured room and into a brightly lit office building hallway. Few people actually worked on this floor. The security camera in the hallway had been "accidentally" knocked out-of-place so that it didn't see from the door of the communications room to the closet. He walked over to a closet space and stepped into it.

The broad-shouldered man turned sideways to get past the narrow shelving to the back of the closet. At the back of the closet, he accessed a rarely used service corridor. Like so many of the design choices of this building that he came across, he swore this building was designed by a short person intent on punishing the tall. He managed his way through all the plumbing and cabling, taking a number of turns.

Eventually he came to a locker room service access. He cracked open the door to see if anyone was in eyesight of him entering. The room was vacant at the moment. He slipped in and secured the door behind him. He accessed a locker that had a larger bag with exercise clothing in it. He buried the small bag in the larger one and walked out of the area.

He went up several floors and to an office that was labeled Director Dewey Maddox. He opened the door to a small reception area. A sharply dressed woman manned a desk. As the door opened, she looked up from her screen and stopped typing. "Good afternoon, Mr. Maddox. I have a package that was delivered for you about 20 minutes ago."

She opened a drawer and pulled out a small rectangular container. She got up and offered it to him as he walked to his private office door.

"Thank you, Claire. Has Inspector Byrd called in yet?"

"I'm afraid not. Shall I try and track him down to contact you?"

"No. There's a lot going on out in the field. I'll be a bit more patient. Thank you." Dewey stepped into his office and closed the door. He dropped his bag near his desk and plopped down in his plush leather chair.

He looked at the package. It was marked by one of his informants which caused him to raise an eyebrow. He opened the package and removed a metal cylinder with large end caps on either end of it. He turned it to see the micro screen on it. He touched a pressure-sensitive switch on the device that activated a virtual keyboard. He entered in a passcode and the end of the cylinder popped open.

Dewey tapped the tube to get the small piece of paper to come out. He unrolled it and read the contents. Dewey's face got red and the vein in his forehead popped out as his teeth clenched. He cussed softly so his secretary wouldn't hear him. His gaze shifted to the floor as he considered what course of actions he would now have to take.

He looked at the paper one last time, then rolled it back up and put it back in the tube. Once it was back inside, he reattached the cap. He unscrewed a top piece of the cap, which revealed a button. He pressed it and the micro screen turned red and the cylinder got warm in his hand. The screen turned green, and the cylinder began to cool.

Dewey removed the other cap top and held that end of the cylinder directly over the trash can. He pressed the button a second time and a tiny puff of ash discharged into the trash. He got a small piece of paper out of his desk and wrote a message on it and setup the cylinder to receive a new message. With the message placed and the cylinder put back together, he replaced it in the box.

He gathered his bag at his desk and the package and headed out the door. "Claire, please have this returned to Mr. Evans."

She received the package again. "Yes, sir."

"I'm going to be out of the office for the rest of today. I need to check on some things. Depending on what I find, I may need to visit some of our field offices."

"I will be sure to reschedule your meetings."

"Thank you. I'll let you know tomorrow morning what the plan is."

Dewey left the building and went to a public shopping place. He found an access terminal and went to an information board. He logged in to post a public message. It read: "Overheard a strange story. A child finished his homework. But instead of giving it to his teacher, he gave it to the principle's secretary. Strange. I'm thinking of taking a hunting trip before it gets busy at the office. I could let my coworker go instead, but he would need a few days to get ready."

He posted the message and waited. After a few minutes there was a reply from someone going by the moniker

RoseOfTheWishMaker. It read: "Happy hunting."

Dewey nodded his head and logged out. He went to his residence and gathered traveling clothes and moved his small bag that had his concealment items to his traveling case. After a few comms connections to cover himself, should someone being paying attention, he left the building and hopped on a transport that was heading to Lestat Station.

Several days later, he stepped out of the transport onto Lestat Station. He checked in to an Inn and got himself situated. Dewey logged in to the local Civil Defense Service information systems. He pulled up the caseload for Daniel Byrd. He then accessed all the files Daniel had been depositing into the system. He didn't find what he was looking for.

Dewey was pleased to find Daniel had followed instructions at least that far. Dewey researched the station to find out about it and the problem areas that the people here were facing. He found a location that he liked. He left his room to see things in person. He came to a low sub level of the station that was becoming neglected.

It was known locally that a local gang was taking up residence down here. The gang had made sure to keep their crime level below the threshold of demanding time and attention from other crimes the Civil Defense Service was having to deal with.

Dewey watched from the shadows for a couple of days. Long enough to find out there were only eight of them, and they followed a very predictable pattern. At first he wondered why this small band hadn't been dealt with. Until he started to ID them all. Dewey was about to do the local Civil Defense Service a favor.

Today he watched and waited from the shadows of the abandoned corridor. The thrumming of the air handlers down here were obnoxious. The listening device he had planted yesterday yielded enough information on their meeting for today for him to get something rolling. He had sent a message to Daniel about an hour ago requesting his help on a new case.

One by one, all eight members of this child's play of a gang assembled in what used to be a large room across from him. They had turned it into a pathetic sort of lair for their little gang.

The place had piles of debris all over the place with filthy cloth looking flags dangling in a crisscross from one end of the room to the other. Broken furniture was arranged in some sort of circle with broken shelving that had been shoved into something that resembled a circle around them. The only thing that was in good shape was the vid projector in the center of the room.

Dewey pulled his laser pistol from its hiding place and silently made his way to the doorway. The room was poorly lit, just like the corridor, when Dewey peeked into the room. They talked like they were a bunch of kids.

He looked where each of the members were positioned. Only two of them had an actual gun. The others relied on bunt weapons to intimidate people with. As far as he knew, their guns had never been discharged, and might be inoperable. He wouldn't take the chance though. He looked at his timepiece. Daniel would be along soon.

Dewey spun from cover into the broken and wide open doorway. He made controlled aimed shots. The first gun owner didn't stand a chance. His face was filled with shock as he slumped over with two steaming holes burned in his chest. The second gun owner looked like he was spasming as his panicked hands had trouble finding his weapon. Then when he did find it, he jerked repeatedly trying to get it loose from his clothing.

Three aimed shots hit him. He fell backwards on the pile that he was on. His body slid back behind the pile. Two of the members just stood there and screamed in hysterics. Another was frozen with fear. The remaining had the fight end of the fight-or-flight response. Only one had a bat like weapon ready. He charged at Dewey.

Dewey had taken the split second to reassess threats in the room. The man with the bat like weapon was gunned down first. Followed by the others that had found, or were still in the process of finding their weapons. Dewey gunned down the screamers next. He ended with the fear frozen one that was still just standing there.

"Bunch of amateur idiots," he muttered. He went around and checked all the bodies. One of the women that had been reaching for a weapon groaned when he turned her over with his foot. He pointed at her head and fired. The groaning stopped.

Dewey holstered his own weapon as he went over to the leader of the gang that was slumped over in the center chair. He grabbed the guy by the hair and lifted up his head to get a better look at his face. "Your daddy ain't going to be happy about this. Might be best for all of us if your never found again."

Dewey pulled the leader's weapon from the nearly falling apart holster at the guy's hip. It was definitely a cheap laser weapon. He pointed at the back of the room and attempted to fire it. It spewed laser fire like a shotgun. The blast had eaten up a third of the clip charge. The fragmented small bolts dissipated at a short distance, barely scorching the metal wall ten meters away. "That's a dumb modification. Absolute amateur hour."

Dewey went back out to the entrance and waited. He put the modified weapon in his jacket pocket. Dewey leaned up against the wall, putting his foot against it to easily push off if the need should arise. He pulled out a datapad to review some information while he waited.

After a while he saw movement out of the corner of his eye. The noise of the place had masked Daniel's foot falls.

"Inspector Byrd," Dewey said as he put his datapad away.

"Yes, sir."

"Did you catch up with Captain Vance? I'm assuming the probe has been delivered to the requested system?"

Daniel looked concerned, "The probe has been delivered as instructed. I have him running jobs as was requested as well."

"Very good. Did Captain Vance give you anything, any data or objects, he may have collected from that system?"

Daniel just stared at Dewey for a moment, "Did you know the system you had me send him to was the forbidden system protected by the Sakar Pact?"

"You didn't answer my question, Inspector."

"And you're not answering mine."

Dewey chuckled. He just looked at Daniel for a moment. "Yes, I did. The smuggler I sent you after stole Corvus military weapons and a whole lot of government supplies. He was hired by the Remnant to deposit those things in that system to make it look like the Corvus Commonwealth is the one violating the Sakar Pact."

Daniel looked away as he considered the implications of such a thing in light of what he had recently learned. "That doesn't make sense."

Dewey was loosing his patience. "Think, man! If Corvus is violating the Sakar Pack for its own interests, it could put us at war with all of our neighbors. If the Remnant, and those in Corvus government that are helping them, convince our neighbors with proof this is happening it makes a place for them to say they will overthrow the current government and establish a new one in its place. If they ask for help from our neighbors having told this lie, our current way of life ends and who knows what corrupt blood thirsty government we will get in its place."

The words made sense to Daniel.

"So I ask you again, did Captain Vance give you anything? Anything he gave you could be used as evidence to kill our nation and millions of our own people."

Daniel seemed to hesitate. Eventually he reached into a pocket and pulled out a small data storage device. He tossed it to Dewey.

Dewey caught it and looked at it. "What did he manage to get? Have you seen it?"

Daniel looked defeated. "There're images of the star. A couple of the planets there and something dark orbiting what looks like a habitable planet that has life on it. There are some systems readings and analysis. That's it. They didn't stay very long at all."

Dewey looked like he approved. He put the device in a secure pocket. "To the matter that I called you down here for," Dewey motioned with his head to the open doorway. "Another smuggling stash that needs looked into."

Daniel seemed relieved for the change in subject matter. "Anyone we know?" he asked as he walked over and into the doorway.

Dewey heard Daniel sniff the air and stop just inside. He pulled the modified pistol from his pocket and pointed it at Daniel's head.

Daniel turned around. His face went white.

"Going to the Magistrate's informant with the data was a mistake. You should have followed the instructions I gave you for evidence handling and brought it directly to me." Dewey fired. Daniel's body fell to the ground.

Dewey leaned over his body and searched him for anything else he might have been hiding. He pulled out Daniel's datapad and entered in a supervisor's override authorization code. He transferred the contents of Daniels datapad to the data storage device that Daniel had given him. He then erased the message requesting the meeting with him.

He accessed the text messaging service next. He addressed it to a coded address. The text read: "Cleanup at device source. Gang bust gone bad. Officer down. High-profile death, station mayor's son, body not to be found."

A few seconds later he got a message: "Confirmed". He erased this last set of messages and did a double check for any other messages that might need to be deleted. Not finding any more, Dewey dumped the datapad and modified pistol on Daniels' body and left the area.

Weapons

The lights began to gradually and noticeably dim as the path marker lights grew brighter in the docking bay of Lestat Station. The bay was mostly quiet. The service crews had packed up for the night already. One or two ships departed just as one more late comer came in. Automated services for managing basic docking requirements were the only thing still running. Everything else would have to wait until morning.

The Pedlar's Omen was docked in one of the many bays. Her cargo lift was down against the deck, packed tight with crates. Roger checked over the last of the containers and marked off the containers as being received. He entered in a bio-signature on the datapad. "All accounted for," Roger handed the datapad to the Civil Defense Service officer that was waiting.

"Thank you, sir. I have a good friend stationed where these supplies are heading," the officer received the datapad, "They need it very badly. From what I've heard, they are in good hands. Godspeed, sir."

Roger nodded, then looked up into the cargo bay. "Cargo secured. Pull it up."

Small rotating amber lights on the cargo lift switched on. The pistons hissed as they pulled on the floor of the cargo lift gradually into place. Roger watched as it ascended to make sure there were no issues.

He was taken aback when he noticed there had been

another Civil Defense Service person standing on the other side of the cargo lift. When the lift had cleared enough for Roger to get a full view of the man in the dim light, he realized this wasn't just some officer. The man was broad shouldered and somewhat tall. He seemed to be the stiff type that may have been past military at one time and never shook it off. Roger had met plenty of those kinds on both sides of the prison fencing.

"Something I can help you with?" Roger asked loud enough to be heard over all the mechanical noise as he continued to watch the cargo lift for potential problems. The pistons stopped, and the locks snapped into place. The armored belly plates slid across and locked when they slammed into each other. He heard the automated systems check for pressure seal. Then all fell quiet.

The man who had been watching the sealing up of the ship, and waiting for all the loud noises to end, finally looked to Roger. "Good evening. You are Captain Roger Vance, correct?"

"I am."

"My name is Dewey Maddox. I'm Daniel Byrd's supervisor. There have been some developments that we desperately need help with. I need to talk to you in private, please. Can we do so aboard your ship?"

"My only other crew member is aboard. Will that be an issue?"

"Ah yes... Sonja Brock. That will not be a problem at all."

Roger gestured to the ramp and open door. Dewey moved quickly and was up the ramp in no time. Roger followed him.

"If you would please secure the ramp. We don't need prying ears or eyes."

Sonja, who was still in the cargo area having just finished locking things down inside, watched the stranger enter the ship. She gave Roger a look of, 'what's going on?' when he entered the ship. Roger just shrugged and activated the controls to raise the ramp and close the door.

Dewey looked around a little of the ship. "The Pedlar's Omen... interesting name for a ship. Did you choose it?"

"No. The name was already registered when I bought it. Too many other things need paid for before I can squander money on changing the registration." Roger moved to the small dining and conference room. Dewey followed. Sonja hung back from them, following at a distance.

Roger took a seat at the table and Dewey took a seat across from him.

"Is this a private party?" Sonja asked.

Dewey locked eyes on Roger. "My business is with the Captain of this ship. As it involves his crew and I'm unsure of the depth of your relationship with him... I will defer that to him if you listen in or not."

Roger was watching Dewey like a hawk, trying to get a feel for what he was dealing with. This didn't have a feel at all of two people here to negotiate some sort of mutually beneficial deal. It had the same feel he had in dealing with supervisors in the prison system.

In a typical prison system, it was a dangerous political game played against three other players. Officers on the front lines, verses the supervisors that would do anything to get promoted, verses clueless bureaucrats that often made things worse as they lined their own pockets, verses the inmates. To the public, the bureaucrats, supervisors, and officers were all on the same side. The bureaucrats and supervisors claimed that all were on the same side to help the inmates. Reality in practice, out of the public's eye, was much different.

Roger could tell that his every word and deed would be weighed and measured by this man. "She can stay if she wants. If there are any questions about the mists, she can answer them better than I can."

Dewey considered that. "That is a good call captain."

"Can I get you anything to drink?" Sonja asked. She gave him options.

Dewey leaned back and seemed to relax ever so slightly. He gave her his pick. Roger stuck with water. Sonja drank a fluid she normally drank a day or so before getting into the pearl in preparation.

"I don't have a lot of time, so I will get right to the point. There was a death of a significant religious leader not too long ago. The result of that was like kicking a hornet's nest and has lead to outbreaks of violence all over the Corvus Commonwealth. That has created a couple of issues that need to be taken care of as soon as possible.

"Inspector Byrd shared with you that evidence had been found that a smuggler working for the Remnant rebel group was stashing weapons and other goods in the Nedra system."

"The Forbidden system," Roger said. "He didn't seem to know that the Nedra system was the Forbidden system. Did you?"

Roger read the expression on Dewey's face that he didn't like being interrupted. Or was it the truth being brought out?

Dewey just looked at Roger a few seconds, "Yes, that was discovered after the fact. A few days ago that smuggler was caught and for violating the Sakar Pact. He has already been executed from what I understand. The first person in recorded history to be executed under the Sakar Pact."

Sonja started to breathe heavy.

Dewey's eyes remained on Roger, seeming to ignore Sonja.

"Your two issues. We were in the Forbidden system. Are we to be executed as well? Did you come here to collect us?"

Dewey chuckled, "No. Far from it. A few hundred years ago the Sakar Pact was amended. A provision was added to allow searching of the system in the event of a breach. Also in that provision is a means of correcting that breach." Dewey reached into his pocket and pulled out two thick cards that were sealed to prevent modification. He slid them across the table to Roger.

Roger picked up the one that had a picture of his face on it. It was an identity card for Sakar Pact Law Enforcement. It had all his identifiers and listed the Pedlar's Omen as an official Sakar Pact approved vessel to enter the Nedra system. Roger glanced at the other card. It had a picture of Sonja and all of her details as well as the ship information.

They both also had effective dates. The limitation didn't surprise Roger as much as the actual dates listed on them. Roger looked at Dewey. "What's with the dates?"

"They are back dated so that you are covered for going in and dropping off the probe. That was official business in trying to catch the smuggler. What you did was allowed under the amendment of the Sakar Pact. The Sakar Council didn't exactly approve of Corvus going about things the way they did. However, once everything was explained, they voted on the matter and decided that they would cover the two of you this way, despite Corvus' actions. You two are the first and only ones to be granted this access for the purpose of enforcing the Sakar Pact."

"These are good for another standard month though..."

"Yes, the two other issues I spoke of. The Interior Intelligence Division has informed the Sakar Council that the manifest of supplies stashed in the Nedra system is in the hands of the Remnant. They plan to go before the people and claim that Corvus has violated the Sakar Pact to claim the Nedra system. Their evidence is the manifest. We need you to retrieve those weapons and supplies and eliminate all evidence of the smuggler's presence there."

Sonja just looked at Roger. Her face was pale. He knew she didn't want to ever go back there.

"I don't know if you realize what you are asking by sending us back there. After having been there, we both vowed we would never return. It's extremely dangerous to even approach the place. Then... there is something in that place that doesn't want ANYONE in there. I doubt these," Roger dropped his identification card down beside Sonja's, "are going to make any difference to whatever it is that's in that system. You need to find someone else."

Dewey took a deep breath. "Do you realize the Remnant believe that doing this will have one of two results? It will cause an all out war between Corvus and her neighbors. At which point they will sweep in and take control by force in the midst of chaos. Or they convince the Corvus neighbors to back them and overthrow the current government and replace it with one that they say will honor the Sakar Pact. Either of which would bring a war that would kill billions, disrupt profitable trade, and leave the Nedra system unprotected from being invaded. No one, but the Remnant, wants this."

Dewey let his words sink in before continuing. "So... you two, and only you two, have been authorized to go back into the Nedra system and remove that cargo. After removing the cargo, the probe that is already there can verify that no cargo exists. If the cargo doesn't exist, the manifest the Remnant has is invalid, and there is no reason for a war to be started. The Sakar Council will not allow anyone else to be in there.

"These people are extremely superstitious. They believe

some god has promised to destroy the universe if anyone where to go there. Yet, you went in there and came out and the universe didn't end. They think you might have some sort of blessing from some god to fix a wrong and give us all a second chance. They are unwilling to gamble with anyone else and will let war happen if you do not go.

"Don't get me wrong. The council doesn't want war either. They've directed me to make you this offer." Dewey accessed a port on the table and plugged in a data device. The amount being offered along with the terms popped up above the table.

The amount was substantial. It would allow Roger to buy a very respectable sized cargo ship outright without any debt and outfit the ship properly to keep everyone safe. Even after that he would still have funds to finance a full crew for a good couple years he guessed. It would give him enough time to find and get good-paying jobs that were much easier and paid better. He wouldn't have to struggle so hard for scraps anymore.

He read over the terms. There was nothing there that was surprising. Not even what was essentially a gag order for the rest of his life. Neither he nor Sonja were allowed to say a word about going to the Nedra system, or what the Sakar Council was proposing in conjunction with the Corvus Commonwealth in activities done there.

He looked at Sonja. He could see the fear all over her face.

Dewey leaned forward. "I understand the risks. If I could go instead of asking you, I would in a heartbeat. I know of hundreds of people that would step up and put their lives on the line if there was a way.

"However, if anyone else tries to go, it will be in violation of the Sakar Pact, which could mean the end of the universe if the story is true. More likely it would mean an all out war between nations. A war that would kill billions of people between fighting, starvation, disease, and all the other causes of death that arise in the aftermath of war. If you choose not to go, it will mean a growing threat of war can't be quelled, and billions of people will still die."

Dewey was quiet for a few seconds. "I know it's a lot to ask. Yet, I'm pleading with you... Please do this for the sake of us all."

Roger looked at the offering displayed in front of him. He looked at Sonja. She almost looked depressed as she stared down at the table. Eventually she noticed that Roger was looking at her.

"Your thoughts?" Roger asked her.

Her eyes welled up, and a tear rolled down one of her cheeks. "There are no good options here. What if whatever is there attacks and kills us? If we get killed doing this, the wars will happen anyway." She wiped away the forming tears and sniffed. Her eyes drifted from Roger to the table. "If we don't go... I would probably have a hard time living with myself." She eventually looked back up at him, "I'm with you in whatever you choose."

A small amount of relief came to Roger when she had voiced her decision. He really didn't want her to have to do it against her will, as it would just strain their working relationship. He had already made his decision.

Roger looked at Dewey. "We will do this on one condition."

"Name it."

"We go there to get this cargo, it will be a one-shot deal. When we come out again, that's it. We are never going back in there again for any reason. If we can't get all the cargo hauled out in one trip, I'm going to jettison the cargo on a vector into the star so it burns up. We will not be going back for anything else or any reason."

Dewey smiled. "I don't think anyone is going to have a problem with that. I will pass on your condition. The probe is exploring other parts of the system and is set to inspect the site again after your temporary authorization expires." He started a transfer of information from the data device to the ship's storage. "I'm giving you as much information as I'm authorized that has been collected from the probe. Hopefully, it's helpful to you so you don't have to be there any longer than you need to."

Roger pulled out a datapad and laid it on his thigh so he could just see it from the edge of the table. He quickly accessed a number of commands on the device. He looked back up to Dewey and waited.

"You should really invest in some better computers. Your system is very slow," Dewey said.

Sonja looked confused, "I thought the computer bank that got hit was fixed the last go around."

Roger just kept his eyes on Dewey and tried to look bored. "I'll have to check and make sure their replacement was the right one. Maybe it's defective. If it is, I'll have them fix it after we drop off our current run and before we go to Nedra system."

After Dewey was done transferring the information, he disconnected his data drive. "I know it's not much data. Still, I hope it's helpful."

Roger slipped his datapad into a pant pocket and got up to show Dewey out.

The Guardian

Several days had passed. The Pedlar's Omen had completed its cargo run that it was loaded up for the night that Dewey Maddox showed up. With the delivery complete, they had moved on to get the Nedra system job done and over with.

Sonja's voice came over the intercom system, "That creature is still here! I've never heard of a mist creature hanging around in one place like this before. It's almost like it's picked this spot to be some sort of lair or something. I really don't like it."

Roger sat in the pilot's seat and just stared out the window at the white fog like substance. His eyes tracked the even brighter "mist" that ebbed and flowed around the ship like silent wandering clouds. "Has it seen us yet?"

"Not that I can tell. Honestly, I'm afraid to reach out and feel if it's just waiting for a potential meal to get too close or if it's asleep or something."

"We have to get into that system."

"I feel like we are flirting with a death sentence. I don't like this!"

"The more I think about all this, the more I starting to think we've been manipulated. Death has become the price for freedom."

"Do you think they will leave us alone after the end of this job? Assuming we live to tell about it?"

"The more I think about it, the less I trust Maddox. Worst

case, if we are still being strong armed into taking jobs like this after we get paid, I might be able to stage our deaths. We lie low for a while, pickup a couple reforged ID's, get a new ship, and live a normal simple cargo hauler life."

There was a moment of quietness.

"I trust you," she said softly.

The weight of that statement fell on Roger. He always had assumed responsibility for Sonja's safety, as he would for any crew member. She had an obligation to perform all duties pertaining to piloting the ship per her contract with him. Her confession made him question himself. He realized he trusted her with his life as well. Perhaps more than that? He didn't dare go there. Especially not right now.

"I just hope I worthy of it." Roger continued his brainstorming until he had a solid idea. "If we divert enough power to the phantom drive to keep it topped off, how often can you pop in and out of the mists?"

"It really depends on the person. I've never tried to do it a lot in a short period of time. Naval combat mist pilots are conditioned for it so they can do it something like a dozen times or more before collapsing from exhaustion. I doubt I could do that many times."

"How long does it take for a mist creature to typically loose interest?"

"Anywhere from a few minutes to a couple days or so in normal space. Are you suggesting playing a cat-and-mouse game with this thing?"

"Only if we can get close enough like last time and you don't get hurt by it this go around."

"You realize we will have to hang out in the Nedra system for a long while so I can rest, right?"

"I know. I would rather chance that, then take a chance of you getting seriously hurt by that thing. Or worse."

"Let's try it. You ready?"

"Whenever you are. I'm in your hands in this place," Roger said. He could feel the engines power up and move the ship. "I trust you too."

The ship jerked to evade something Roger couldn't see. He sank into the pilot's seat as Sonja hit max speed. He had the sensation of ducks, dives, and rolls.

"Damn… This thing is a lot more feisty this time!"

Roger got the sinking feeling accompanied by dropping back into normal space at a much faster rate than normal. He pulled up the star charts to get his bearings for where they were at in the void of space. He diverted power from other systems to recharge the capacitors for another jump into the mists.

With this many jumps pushing the generators so hard, he was going to have to find a source of fuel to refine. He figured it would be fine, given Sonja would probably need a couple of days to rest before they attempted to get out of there.

The computer returned the results of their location. "We have a long way to go yet. How are you doing?"

"I'm fine for now."

"Ten minutes and capacitors will be ready for you. Is there anything else I can do to help?"

"Just stay strapped in. It's going to be a rough ride all the way if this first encounter is any indication. I suppose you could pray I don't get killed out here. If I die, you'll die out here alone, slowly."

"I could always try my hand at climbing into the pearl and navigating the mists."

"You wouldn't last thirty seconds in there. Without experience, just getting yourself into the mists might kill you. Course that might be better than starving to death slowly."

"Such cheery thoughts."

Roger did busy work with the ship systems that wouldn't interfere with Sonja trying to fly the ship.

Without warning, the Pedlar's Omen transitioned to the mists. Immediately the evasive maneuvers continued.

"AGH!"

"What happened?"

"That was too close."

"You okay?"

"I'll be alright." They dropped back into normal space. "That thing is so damn huge."

"Are you hurt?"

"Just grazed. I've suffered much worse from other mist creatures that have managed to catch up with me before. I'll be alright."

Roger rerouted power to charge up the capacitors again. They had gotten somewhat closer. Roger was starting to wonder if this plan might fail. If it took too many mist jumps, the generators might eat up all the fuel before they could get to the system to try and find more. He kept his concerns to himself.

Sonja jumped into the mists again, and again, and again. Each time making more and more progress.

"I'm getting the impression this creature really doesn't want us here. It's like it's actually guarding the place. I think we might have just had dumb luck getting past it the first time."

"We're really close. Maybe only one more jump to go? How are you feeling?"

"I'm damn near spent. I think I can get us there in one more jump if I push hard."

"Okay. Once we are there, I need some time to hunt down some fuel anyway. You can rest as much as you need."

"This place really gives me the creeps. I don't want to stay here any longer than we have too. I'm only going to rest long enough to escape this place again."

"I don't blame you. I don't want to be here any longer than we have to be either. I'll round up some fuel, find the smuggler's stash, and get what we can recovered. We'll see how you are by then. Capacitors are ready when you are."

"I'm going to need a few more minutes. This last one is going to be a bit taxing."

"Take as much time as you need. I think I will go ahead and suit up."

Roger unstrapped himself from the pilot's seat. He hated being stuck in that seat for such a long period of time. It felt good to stretch his legs. He moved to the armory and put on his former law enforcement body armor. He also equipped a full array of weapons he might need in close combat.

The smuggler had supposedly been captured and executed. Working for the government for a long time had taught him things the decision makers at the top said, didn't always match with reality on the ground. He had witnessed too many officers killed in the line of duty because of managerial arrogance.

Once he was suited up, he returned to the pilot seat and strapped himself in again. "Ready when you are. No rush."

"Last push." The phantom drive powered up again, and Sonja used it to transition to the mists once again. "Hmmm... the creature is not moving."

She pushed the ship hard and fast to the destination, which was just right there. "Oh crap! It was just waiting!"

The ship violently shuttered. Roger's hands did a death grip on the arm rests of the seat.

Sonja screamed in pain. Roger felt absolutely helpless. Sonja was the only one who could do much of anything in the mists.

The Pedlar's Omen tumbled out of the mists and back into the physical realm. The ship rolled on all three axis. Roger saw what looked like a beautiful planet repeatedly pass in front of the window, along with something else that was dark that passed too quickly for him to identify.

"Sonja?!"

He heard her voice groan over the speakers. He triggered the controls to extend for piloting. "I'm taking over flight controls for a minute."

Roger fought with the directional thrusters to stop the rolling. "You make this look so easy..." Roger managed to get the ship under control enough to resemble something of a wobble in one direction.

"That was painful," Sonja finally said.

Rogers controls deactivated as Sonja took over again. The ship leveled out and slowly drifted toward the large darkened object high in orbit around a planet that was beautiful to the eyes.

"I'm just glad you're still among the living. How bad did it get you?"

"I will heal with time. I need rest very badly. I'm going to stay in the pearl for a while yet. The fluids I'm immersed in should help me with the pain for now."

Roger closed his eyes for a second now that things had calmed down. He noticed something. "Sonja, do you still feel that sense of 'Go Away' we experienced the first time?"

"Only faintly. I wonder why it's different this time."

"I don't know. I'm not sure I like it either." Roger got out of his seat and stood as close as he could to the sloped window. He gave a command to his helmet computer to enhance the light on the dark object. "Is that the site we were supposed to find? That's no rock with a stashed container. That looks more like an actual space station."

"It's the right location. That thing is massive. There's no way some smuggler set that up by himself."

"I've never seen anything like it. If this place is forbidden, I wonder who built this?"

"I'm starting to think we may have been lied too."

"It looks like it might be a derelict station. No lights, no movement, looks like holes from explosions at different places on the surface of it."

The ship shuttered and lurched forward, causing Rodger to stumble backwards to the floor.

"That's not me, Roger! Something has gotten a hold of the ship and is pulling it toward that station. I can't get free of it!"

Roger climbed into the more familiar navigation and weapons seat. The turret weapon made its normal sounds as it lifted into firing position. Using the weapon camera, he zoomed in on the station. He couldn't find anything to really shoot at to make it stop pulling them in.

"It's slowing us down and repositioning our approach."

"Approach to what? The business end of a barrel?"

"I don't think so. A docking station maybe? Maybe we triggered something like an automated docking sequence?"

"If that's true, then this space station may not be as fully derelict as it looks. Maybe the smuggler found this place and managed to get some of the station's systems back online."

The Pedlar's Omen gracefully drifted to the side of the station's dark form. A large section of what looked like a wall split open, revealing a functioning energy barrier to a landing bay. The ship was spun around and backed into the bay.

Sonja lowered the landing gear. The ship gracefully touched down onto the deck. "Whatever had a hold on us has let go. I hate this place already. Let's get what we came for and get out of here!"

Roger got up and checked his personal weapons as he walked to the cargo bay door. "No argument here. I'll see if there is fuel stash here too. Everything feels wrong about this place. Like death cloaked in lies or something." Roger made his way to the cargo bay exit of the ship.

"The cargo bay actually has breathable air. Gravity is slightly under 1G on the station. There are no computers for me to interface with that, I can tell."

"Any indication that someone else is in here with us?"

"Not that I can tell."

He pulled out his sidearm and opened the door. "I feel like I'm walking into a nightmare." He took a deep breath, "Let's get this over with."

He gradually moved into the dark bay. Interior lights didn't seem to function. Or maybe they just didn't work automatically. He walked slowly down the ramp, carefully looking over his surroundings for potential threats. He planted his first foot on the deck of the landing bay and lights began to come on inside the bay if only dimly.

Off to the other side of the bay there was a loud crackling snap. Roger turned and took aim. One of the lights shorted out on the ceiling that sent showers of sparks raining down to the floor.

Roger took some more deep breaths. The floor was now lighting up with lines and some markings he figured were some written language for warnings or labels.

There were also dots that seemed to mark something like paths between marked off areas. Everything looked so alien, yet familiar. His eyes traced one of the paths to a doorway that was outlined with blue lines.

Roger looked around for some crates that might have the cargo he was looking for. No such luck. Aside from some control panels, there was nothing else here except empty space for about three more ships.

"I guess we take door number one." He kept his sidearm at the ready and made his way to the door, constantly looking around for a threat. "Sonja, secure the door and ramp. We didn't come for passengers."

He heard the door seal and the pistons pull the ramp up into place. Normally she would have acknowledge and reported she had done it per required communications.

He didn't fault her for not doing so right now. The woman had pushed herself, probably to the brink, to get them here.

He felt guilty for asking so much of her. He would have to find a way to make it up to her somehow.

He approached the doorway and looked to either side as far as he could without exposing himself anymore than he had to. The doorway lead to a hallway. He noticed that the doorway was massive in size. Probably for machinery to move cargo and supplies, he thought.

The left was blocked by debris from some structure above that crashed through the wall and ceiling. It looked to be too much effort to get through that way anytime soon.

The other direction was clear and dimly lit. Smooth slightly rounded walls. Not a single place to take any cover for a long way. Roger raised his pistol and began walking down the hallway. There was a fine film of dust coating everything. He stopped dead in his tracks part way down the hallway when he realized there were no foot prints.

He considered going back. Everything in his gut told him to turn around and run and never return. Perhaps the smuggler had a bigger ship and the automatic docking put him in a different bay. Roger thought about the size of this station. It could take him days to search it.

No cargo, no pay. No pay meant no larger ship for them to run, or respectable jobs. Top it all off with a potential war if he failed. Assuming that any thread of what Dewey had told them was true. He needed to stop putting Sonja in so much danger. He needed to put an end to this. He pressed forward to the end of the hallway.

The hallway emptied into a large room that looked similar to a hub of sorts to other places of the station. The same markings he saw on the floor in the docking bay were all over the place in here. He started to notice patterns in things that looked like they might be furniture and how high most of the writings were. He started to feel like whoever had made this place may have been two to three times his own height. He suddenly felt really small.

Questions came hard and fast. In all the expansion mankind had done in this galaxy, of all the life forms encountered on other planets, we were the only beings in the galaxy that exercised intelligence beyond being mere animals.

"Roger, why is your heart racing all of a sudden? Are you

alright?"

"You wouldn't believe what I'm seeing right now."

"You don't have a helmet cam in that bulky thing you wear?"

Roger had forgotten about that function. "I haven't used it for that since I quit my last job. Let's see if it still works." He gave the command to activate it. He had to make several setting changes to allow the Pedlar's Omen to have access to it.

"I got access to... Holy crap!"

"Yeah... not sure this was built by humans." Roger looked for evidence that someone had been here recently. The dust remained undisturbed, like an undefiled tomb.

"Roger... That itch to get out of here is getting worse for me."

"For me, it's well beyond an itch. More like a red hot poker."

"Maybe we should leave. Forget the job."

Roger considered it. "I want to look around for the cargo just a little more. If I can't find it soon, then yeah, I agree that we give up and get the hell out of here. This already isn't what we were told we would find."

The Fall

Roger looked around the large room for where the other doorways would take him. He picked the one that he thought might take him deeper into the station. Perhaps to a central hub that might lead to some place that made sense as a storage area. Of course, if this place was built by some aliens, who knows what really made sense from their perspective.

Roger came to the doorway and looked. This hallway was like a gradual ramp downward. With his pistol still raised, he walked down slowly. His eyes were pealed for evidence of disturbed dust or movement. Nothing.

The downward ramp ended in an even larger corridor. Dim lights revealed something else he recognized. The corridor was torn up. Burn marks that ended in smooth surfaces ripped open by a focused discharge of energy. The desperate assembly of loose items used to create cover in firefights were scattered about here and there.

Roger suddenly felt like he was being watched. Nothing moved as he looked and listened.

"Roger, I've seen vids before of wars. Do you think this looks like some sort of fighting happened here?"

Roger was still looking around the room carefully. "Most definitely there was fighting here."

"Be careful."

"Pretty sure the fighting was over a very long time ago. But yeah, I'm keeping a careful eye out." Roger moved in the direction that might take him to the heart of the station. If he didn't find what he was looking for there, he would call this search a bust.

He cautiously continued down the massive corridor. He found it curious that there were no side rooms. Unless, he realized, they opened up like the docking bay did. Either he never got close enough to trigger a sensor for the rooms to open up, or it could have been they simply had no power for the doors to even open.

At the end of the corridor he came to an area that was so large the Pedlar's Omen could fly around in it. Most of the room was darkened. At least one fight had also taken place in this room as well. He realized that he never saw any bodies, weapons, armor, or anything that had been engaged in any fighting lying around.

At the center of this massive room was something that looked very much like a tree. It was black, laced with silver threads all over it. Also on its surface was something that looked like veins that were thick at the base and branched off into smaller and smaller veins. The veins themselves were an iridescent blue and seemed to pulse as if it had a heart beat like a living thing.

"Bet that is breath taking in person."

"Yeah, it sure is." Roger thought he glimpsed movement and heard something slide on the floor near the tree. The tree then seemed to sway ever so gently. It's movement somehow put his mind at ease and caused him to disregard what he had just seen.

He continued to look for danger as he got a little closer to the tree. The closer he got to it, the more the bark of the tree looked like carbon fiber that was laced with silver threads. The more he looked at the tree, the more mesmerizing it was to him.

"Roger, are you okay?"

"Yeah, it's just... I've never seen anything like it. It's so beautiful."

A soft blue light began to form in front of the tree. Roger stepped back and raised his pistol. Not that it would have any effect on a floating light, he realized. It gradually grew in size. It began to gracefully flow outward and into the form of a human woman of normal stature, clothed in flowing robes. She was very detailed and lifelike, composed of varying shades of blue light that gave her depth and form.

She hovered just above the floor, her head down and arms hanging at her sides, feet pointed to the floor. It looked almost as if she had been pinned to a wall and hung there lifeless. Her robes gracefully stirred around her like an unfelt breeze swirled all around her.

Her eyes fluttered open, and she lifted her head. Her eyes found Roger, who was still holding a gun up in her direction. She spoke a few words in languages that sounded familiar to him. None of which he spoke.

"Galeric?" Roger said.

She gave him a heart-warming smile. "You are welcome in this place traveler." She spread open her arms and slightly bowed her head. Her form gently descended to the floor and her feet responded as though she could stand and walk on its surface. "Welcome to Reemdoran Station, keeper of the Sacred Tree of Illiad. How may I be of assistance to you?"

Roger lowered his weapon to a ready position. "What are you?"

"I am the one who assists all who come here. I help beings find where they need to go and answer questions about the facilities here."

"How did you learn to speak Galeric?"

"There was a device that was left behind in this star system not long ago. It drifted nearby, and I was able to learn from it."

"Impressive. So who built this station?"

"This station was built by the Keepers of Truth."

"And who are the Keepers of Truth?"

The image of the woman seemed to glitch for a split second and a long thin tongue, forked at the tip, slipped out of the woman's mouth for a brief second before retracting. "They were the mighty servants of I AM."

"Were?"

"Yes. There was a war among the servants long ago. The Keepers of Truth were defeated."

"What happened to the other side?"

"I'm sorry, I do not know."

"When did this war among the servants happen?"

"Before the passing of time was established. Well before this current age of mankind started."

"How long have the servants been gone?"

"Before the passing of time was established. Well before this current age of mankind started."

"How many travelers have been here since then?"

"You are the first."

"What?! Are you sure?"

"I am sure. Where you expecting to meet someone here? I can assist with making sure you find each other."

"No. I was told someone had been here already and left some stuff for me to pickup."

"I'm sorry. There has been no one here except you. Can I assist you with something else?"

"What's with the tree? It's special somehow?"

The image of the woman glitched again and the thin forked tongue slipped out and back in. "The tree is very sssssspecial. It is sought by many travelers. The Ssssssacred Tree of Illiad is an access point to the reservoir of infinite knowledge. For every problem, disease, creation, health, or wealth... whatever you have need of, the knowledge for it is freely available."

"Roger, I don't like this. Something is wrong. I can feel it, something is moving like in the mist but it's in real space. We need to get out of here!"

Roger didn't respond. "How does the tree give the knowledge? How do you get the knowledge you want?"

"It's child like simple. There is a tube here. Ask in your mind and take a drink of one drop from the tree. It will channel the answer you seek to your mind. Would you like to try? Surely there is something you need to know. Something to help mankind? Wisdom to overcome a seemingly impossible challenge? A cure that plagues society?"

"Roger, come back to me please. Something is happening. Something very bad!"

Roger hesitated.

"It only takes a couple of seconds. One drink and you can quickly be on your way."

"Sonja, I'll be right there." He thought of his question, his life focus at the moment. He holstered his sidearm and reached for the tube the woman had pointed to with his right hand while lifting his helmet up enough with his left hand to put it to his lips. He sucked up the drop of blue fluid. The moment he took it in, he couldn't believe he had done such a thing on impulse. His lack of common sense and self control in this moment was frightening to him.

The fluid was sweet, like a ripe fruit or honey. It dissolved in his mouth and flowed into his bloodstream and passed to all of his body. Then it hit him.

Roger's body fell to his hands and knees. He was screaming at the top of his lungs. He had an out-of-body experience. His body was still alive and his spirit was still tied to it. As his body screamed in agony, so too did his soul. He became aware of three realms of existence. The physical realm, the mists, and another realm he was not familiar with.

A burst of incredible power exploded from within Roger and rippled throughout all the universe. In the blink of an eye, every human being in all of creation was screaming out in pain with one voice with him. The screams of all humanity felt like a set of piercing spikes being driven through his head and mind. His human body collapsed, unable to bear it all.

Above all the screaming of every single human, thundered a voice of unmistakable authority and power, "Why have you disobeyed me?! Lawlessness of all has born its fruit and has brought death upon all mankind. Restoration will come, but at a cost you can not possibly comprehend."

Something had changed in every man, woman, and child. A sense of death came. The sense was of natural unending life being cut off like a string severed by a razor blade from eternity that sustained everyone. Human life was now measured and would decay like a fruit from a tree once it had fallen.

The screaming died down to whimpering and crying from the pain. Roger felt himself fall back into his body. His eyes were open, and he was still breathing. He was having a hard time getting up. He heard movement from behind the tree. The glowing woman was gone.

Something behind the tree was saying something in a language he couldn't understand. Its voice sounded rather hissy. Whatever it was, it sounded really excited as it dragged itself across the floor just out of Roger's sight.

In the shadows behind a makeshift barrier Roger saw two

small red reptilian looking eyes staring at him. There was a flash of bright white light from somewhere at the corridor entrance. A man covered with what looked like armor made of light, kind of like the image of the woman he had seen in blue, ran past Roger.

The small red eyes got wide at seeing the man. With a sword drawn and a shield up, the man shouted at the creature and laughed at it. The two of them exchanged a number of blows out of Roger's sight.

He was still struggling on just getting up off the floor. He needed to get back to the ship. To get back to Sonja. "I should have listened to you Sonja. I'm so sorry." She didn't reply. He continued to struggle to just move.

"Roger, are you there?"

"I'm here. I'm trying to get up. I'm trying to get to the ship."

"Something is terribly wrong. I want out of the pearl!" Roger could hear her panic. "I can't get out, Roger. Help me, please!"

"I'm coming," Roger managed to move one of his arms enough to drag himself a few decimeters.

"I don't want to be here anymore. Please hurry."

A tear rolled down his cheek as he fought to drag himself a couple of more decimeters.

He heard the sound of a blade pierce some form of plating. It wasn't steel bone perhaps. There was a declaration of victory and more joyful laughter. Heavy footsteps approached him from the battle.

"Sonja?"

No response.

The man came to where Roger could easily see him and squatted down. The man no longer had the armor, the sword, or shield. His eyes were full of life, his hair and beard were white as the purest of snow. His smile was so full of joy it would have been impossible to be cranky around him.

Roger gave up moving for a moment and just stared at the man. "Who are you?"

"Someone who knows all about you, every deed you have done and will do. And I like you anyway."

"How can you possibly know me?"

"Roger Dale Vance, only child to Oscar and Patricia Vance.

You are 594 standard years old. You treasure straight forward honesty and justice.

"Your afraid of not being able to pay your debts for your current ship and are in a position to lose what little you have left. You're beginning to believe you have been lied to about why you are here. Your afraid your actions have seriously hurt Sonja.

"You feel the crushing weight of what has just transpired and your not sure you can live through it. You are afraid that the One who forbid mankind to come to this place might actually be real and sitting in front of you. Your afraid you're going to be tortured for eternity for what you have done."

Roger looked at the floor feeling ashamed. His whole life seemed to be laid bare before this guy. "Are you telling me you are God?"

The man slowly waved a hand to get Roger's attention until he looked back up from the floor. "I AM." The words carried such unmistakable authority. The same as the thundering voice he heard when all of mankind cried out.

"How can you possibly like me after what I just did?" Roger couldn't come to grips with it.

"If you really knew me, the question would be how could I not like you." He was still smiling at Roger. His eyes were filled with compassion. "I want to help you. I would love for you to get to know me. I invite you to do so, if you are willing. I am here for you. I want a rich and fulfilling life for you, like any good father wants their child to be rich in all aspects of life. To live to your fullest potential." I AM reached out a hand.

Roger nodded and took His hand.

"Great," I AM stood up and hauled Roger up with him, putting Roger's arm around His neck. "Let's get you back to your ship. The Fallen Ones have awakened and you don't want to be around here when they start looking for a meal."

They moved quickly through the station.

"What about Sonja? Is she still alive?"

"Yes. For now, she is trapped in the pearl. She will live. Continue to help her. You both will need each other in the coming months."

Roger could feel strength returning to him in a way he couldn't explain. Just being around this I AM was bringing clarity of thought, healing to his body, and strength to carry on. By the time they got near the ship, Roger was able to start running on his own.

I AM placed the palm of His hand on the bottom of the hull of the Pedlar's Omen. "Awaken Sonja."

"Roger!? I think I blacked out. Where are you?"

"I'm here. Open the cargo ramp."

The ramp pistons hissed as it lowered and the door opened.

"Who is that with you?"

Roger laughed, "Would you believe me if I told you it is I AM?"

"Under normal circumstances, no. In this case... maybe."

"You two need to leave here now. You have enough fuel to get yourselves out of the system. Sonja has enough strength to jump. Leave this place before you get caught by the Fallen Ones."

"I can't out run that mist creature like I am. I'm in such bad shape, I don't have the endurance for it!"

"I will take care of the creature for you. Now go!" He looked at Roger with that bright life filled smile, "I will catch up with you. I will never abandon you... ever!"

Roger ran up the ramp and turn to secure the door and ramp. He looked down where I AM had stood last. He was gone. Roger hit the switches to close things up and ran to the cockpit.

"Get in your seat. I'm lifting off already."

Roger plopped down into the navigation and weapons seat and strapped himself in. The Pedlar's Omen shot out of the docking bay.

"I'm picking up movement coming from the planet's surface. Looks like maybe a ship?"

"I'm guessing your right. I don't know what these Fallen Ones are, and I'm not to eager to find out at the moment. I AM mentioned something about me not wanting to be around for meal time. Guessing they will eat people."

Roger topped off the capacitors for jumping. "Phantom Drive is juiced up. Whenever your ready."

"I think that ship is following us already. I hope I can lose them in the mist. Assuming I don't get killed by that creature." Sonja made the transition to the mists.

Roger felt the ship's engines kick on hard. "Well, is the creature still around?"

He heard Sonja laugh. "You're not going to believe this. I can feel that I AM guy here somehow. He's playing with it. Like some kid playing with his puppy."

"Well, don't slow down. We don't know what that other ship can do yet."

Sonja pressed hard to get distance from the forbidden place and back to known systems.

"I AM is all of a sudden gone. The creature is back to guarding. And there is another presence in the mists I've never felt before. It's dark and jagged."

"We need to get back to civilization. We might need help to get you out of that pearl."

"Something is wrong with me. I don't feel the same anymore. Something very bad has happened and I can't tell what it is."

Roger was searching the ship star chart database. "Dakkas Station is the nearest place with Phantom Drive and pearl repair services. Dakkas Station it is, then. Fast as you can manage."

On the Run

Roger kept wanting to check sensors to see if the dark ship was following them. He would immediately get frustrated when he would remember that sensors didn't work in the mists. Or weapons, for that matter. He hated feeling helpless in the midst of danger.

Part of him wanted to go take his body armor off as something to do. Yet, in the face of a potential fight, there wasn't a chance he was going to forgo having the armor on. Especially given the body armor also did double duty of working in the vacuum of space.

He pulled up the information on Dakkas Station. It was a bit of a distance from where they had left. It was also a long distance from Lestat Station. How long it took to get to the system that had Dakkas Station would depend on Sonja and how well she navigated the mists.

He checked the fuel supply. It was nearly depleted. With what the engines would consume, Roger guessed they would be running on fumes when they got to where they were going. It would be fine so long as they didn't have to prematurely drop back into physical space.

"Have you lost the dark ship yet?"

"No. Unfortunately, they are gaining on us. I'm not sure if I can make it to Dakkas before they catch up with us."

Roger drummed his fingers on the side of the console. What the station assistant in front of the tree replayed in his mind. His years of experience as an officer kicked in. His hands stopped drumming, and he swiped away the current information screen. His mind had found something familiar that he knew how to do well.

He documented everything that he had seen and heard for later. Memory would fade with time. It was important to get it down while it was fresh. He had a realization. When he activated his helmet to be used by the Pedlar's Omen, he had to specify where to dump the recording. The software in his armor was designed for evidence collection for future prosecutions.

He went to the computer system where he specified for recording dumps. The video, audio, and other information tied in with his armor was all there from the moment he activated it until now. He deactivated the Pedlar's Omen from monitoring and the recording ended.

He continued his documentation of everything he saw and did up until that point when the recording started. Several hours later, he finished. He replayed the video and audio of the station assistant over and over again. He wished he had asked a lot more questions now.

One thing was clear. They had been sent to get a cargo that didn't exist. The probe had been by that station, and so Director Maddox should have known. Why he would lie about this, Roger couldn't begin to guess.

Roger installed some of the software from his armor to the ship's systems to better handle data collection. Next he modified his helmet functions to include control of when the Pedlar's Omen would begin and stop recording activity.

Using the new function, he activated the Pedlar's Omen monitoring of his armor again. He got up from his station and went back to the conference room. The two IDs were still on the table. He picked up each one and used his helmet to document them as he was trained to do such a long time ago.

He deactivated the recording session. Figuring out who was manipulating them would likely be a dangerous operation. He considered his options. Faking their deaths might be a necessary solution after all. Assuming they weren't killed by this ship that was giving chase.

Roger closed his eyes. He considered his recent actions. He

had only meant to gain wisdom to help them out. Knowledge that would make things safer for him and Sonja. His head dropped down. Instead, whatever he had done had changed every human in the universe. Sonja was hurting somehow and couldn't get out of the pearl. And worse, something had been awakened and unleashed in the Nedra system. Something that felt dark and terrifying.

Roger sat in a seat at the table. "What have I done," he whispered. The weight of what he had done hit him like an invisible, heavy wet blanket. He closed his eyes again and whispered some more. "I've killed us all. I AM, I'm sorry for killing every person that was alive, or cutting their lives short, or whatever it was I did that I don't fully understand. Maybe it's just as well that we end up dead by the aliens. I deserve to die for what I've done. For Sonja, it might be an act of mercy for whatever I did to her."

"I don't agree," a familiar voice full of authority and power said.

Roger's eyes popped open as he looked up. He still sat in the chair at the table. I AM sat in the chair next to him. The whole rest of the ship was gone. A scene like what he had seen in the mists outside the window was all around him, as if he sat in the midst of it.

"Why don't you take that thing off your head for a few minutes."

Roger hesitated as part of him wanted to hide from I AM inside of it. The thought seemed stupid he realized. He disconnected and removed the helmet, setting it aside on the table surface. He nearly felt overwhelmed with guilt and shame as he looked at I AM. He was struggling to keep his composure.

I AM leaned forward. His eyes were still full of compassion. His smile was disarming. "Listen to me carefully... I do not hate you. Very much the opposite. I knew from the very beginning that this day would come. I knew the terrible price that would have to be paid to satisfy My own laws. What it would take to set my children free again. I've done it for everyone, past, present, and future... I still would have done it, even if it was just for you."

"I know I messed up badly. Not that it's an excuse but, I'm

also pretty sure I had a lot of help by people that lied to me to get me to do what I did. Supposedly there was a smuggler involved in this mess too but, the station said I was the only one to have been there."

I AM took a deep breath. "Son, you have no idea how deep the deceptions run. What has transpired started with an orchestration of a few powerful men. It has since grown to include many people in governments among the nations of peoples. Most of whom don't know the whole of what is going on."

"It took that much to arrange sending someone like me there?"

"You are a small, but key piece of what they needed."

"It actually started long ago with a probe dropped from the mists into the Nedra system. They thought that by not having an actual human explore the system, they would be safe. It didn't take them long to discover the remnants of the Fallen Ones. The Fallen Ones reached out to them and promised them power beyond their wildest imaginations. They required a price.

"You were not the first human to go to that place. I had come into the physical realm in the flesh as a mere man years ago. One of the many things I was doing was calling out those who were persecuting My people. They didn't like that much. I was rounded up and smuggled into the Nedra system. The people in power handed me over to the Fallen Ones as the first part of their price nearly a standard month before you entered. I was the 'smuggler' they lied to you about."

"What did the Fallen Ones do to you?"

"They quickly figured out it was Me when they received Me. They have been doing unspeakable torturing of Me this whole time."

"Why?"

"Before the time of mankind, they were once my servants. One of them embraced pride and moved to overthrow me in my own kingdom. He convinced a third of my servants to join him to become something they could never be. They engaged in war against My kingdom to take my place of authority. They were driven into the physical realm and imprisoned here. They have chosen to forever become my enemy, and to this day they still dream of taking my rightful place. They hate me with an unbridled passion."

I AM chuckled, "I made mankind in my own image, which includes a desire to rule. I gave mankind the physical realm to rule in my stead so they could rightfully exercise that desire. When the Fallen Ones found out, they burned with hatred of mankind." He looked more serious, "And that is why I issued a warning for mankind not to go to the Nedra system. It was to protect you all from a very dangerous threat."

I AM continued, "The other part of the bargain was they needed another human to partake of the tree. That was why they sent you. They needed someone who would be tempted by what the tree offered. After you partook of it, a seal was broken. They had my body in place the as soon as they found out you arrived in the system. Once the seal was broken, they sacrificed my physical body and used my blood to break the shielding over the planet that kept them trapped there."

The face of I AM became sad. A tear rolled down the side of His face. "And now they are loose. Soon they will move against mankind to kill, steal, and destroy all."

It was so much to take in. There was so much intensity with I AM. "Is there any hope for us?"

I AM looked back up at Roger and that smile of His returned. "YES! They do not know it yet, but... by breaking the shielding the way that they did using my blood, they've been stripped of their physical immortality and great strength. My sacrifice has not only provided a means of forgiveness for mankind, it has also leveled the playing field in the coming fight.

"You need to understand this. I gave the physical realm to mankind to rule over. So I will not intervene unless I'm asked to. Those people who reject and hate Me I will leave them be, which also means I will not protect them either. I only dwell among those who desire me in their midst."

Roger raised his hand, "Please count me in with wanting you around... always."

I AM stood up and walked over to Roger, "I promise to never leave you or forsake you." I AM laid a hand on Roger's forehead. "To all mankind, I promise this. For anyone that accepts me as their God, I will receive them back as my child. As proof of My word, I give of My Spirit to you." A glowing light began to emanate all around I AM. It flowed down around his arm like a mist. From there it flowed into Roger's eyes, ears, nose, and mouth.

Roger couldn't see anything but the light for the space of several breaths. Deep inside he felt a reconnection of life to that which was eternal again. What the tree he had drank from destroyed was once again repaired. Yet, there was more that wasn't there before. Roger could actually sense I AM dwelling inside of him somehow.

"It is my joy to bring restoration to you. To dwell with you, to give you life in abundance." He could sense that I AM was so full of joy at Roger's restoration. "I want this for all mankind. I call all mankind back to Me, to choose life, but only those who come to Me will receive it.

"One more thing for you, Roger. I have provided another ship for you. It won't be what you expect. It will be what you, Sonja, and others will need. When it's offered to you, accept the gift."

After what seemed like several minutes of light filling his senses, Roger blinked and found himself back on the ship, still sitting at the table. The depression was gone, replaced with hope and a fullness he couldn't explain. He looked and his helmet was still on the table. He grabbed his helmet and the IDs and went to his quarters.

He accessed his terminal and typed up everything he had just experienced and what he was told so that he would have a record of it for later. When he got done a half hour later, he wasn't sure anyone would believe him.

The ship shuttered as if struck by something.

"ROGER! They have a weapon that works in the mists!"

Roger got up from his chair only to get knocked to the floor with another shuttering. He heard an explosion outside. Whatever it was that hit them, hit harder than the first time. He got up again and ran to the small bridge of the ship.

When he got there, he grabbed his normal chair just in time to catch himself from another impact against the ship. Roger could feel the subtle shifts in directions. The mists dampened most of it.

"I'm going to drop into this closest system!"

Roger had a sense they shouldn't go there, but the next one

she found instead. "Whatever one your going for skip it and go to the next one!"

"Are you serious!"

"Yes! Do it! We might be grateful later!"

Roger got strapped in. He extended the ship's one turret.

"That won't work out here!"

"I know. Getting it ready for when we drop."

Another hard impact. Roger heard a grinding like noise come from the back of the ship. Sonja screamed in frustration through the speakers. "If we have to fight that thing, we're probably dead."

"Such the optimist. What got hit back there?"

"One of the main thrusters!"

Sonja was making noises as if she was straining with exertion. The Pedlar's Omen dropped into the physical realm just as another impact hit it. The star in the system was dim. Roger pulled up information for where they were at.

The system had binary white dwarf stars with three dead planets in orbit around them. There was also an unusually large asteroid belt between the second and third planet. Sonja had managed to drop in between the belt and the second planet.

"Go for the belt. Maybe we can hide out there long enough for you to get some rest."

Sonja just groaned as if she was exhausted to the point of collapse. The ship thrusters engaged. The one thruster that had been damaged before revved up. There was a loud clank followed by a small explosion. Roger could feel the thruster sputter and die as it rattled the entire ship.

Roger just sat there, irritated that he couldn't do anything to help. He pulled up the scanning system and looked for anything that might be around. The chart database listed the system as not conducive for habitation and of little value. There were also no official listings of anyone or organization that had established itself here.

They had nearly gotten to the asteroid belt when Roger picked up a large ship on active scanning that just dropped into real space. Roger quickly shut off everything that would put out a signal from the Pedlar's Omen and hoped it wouldn't be too late. "Sonja, I think they followed us here."

"I'm almost there."

Roger watched the passive visual screen. It was the same ship that ascended from the planet at Nedra system. It turned in their direction.

Betrayal

Faith stood at a large wall in a conference room. Holographic images and displays were all around her. Sorting through the information and images, she linked some of them together. On occasion she made staffing orders to go out into the field and collect information, do surveillance, or monitor certain accounts that she had flagged.

A soft tone sounded in the room. "Yes?"

"Director, there is activity on the account for Roger Vance. You ask to be notified as soon as anything moved. All information for the transaction is in the file."

"Thank you, Trisha."

Another soft tone ended the communications.

Faith swiped away some of the information she had been working on and called up the file for Roger Vance in the space she had made. She looked at how the information related with other bits. She called up other information from her databases.

She smiled, "The missing piece." She called up the captain, "Captain Yao, real in any resources that are deployed and get us to Lestat station as soon as possible. Quarry likely to run."

The captain acknowledged. A few minutes later, he contacted her. "Assets will be stowed within the hour. Travel time looks like two days."

"Very good captain." She went back to her analysis.

The Cerberus Hunter didn't waste time getting to the

station once it entered the system. The mist pilot had brought them in dangerously close, as protocol dictated when a target could make a run for it.

Faith updated her information she needed to deal with first. Roger hadn't returned for the other cargo runs yet. She wasn't disappointed. It gave her time to deal with her other personally selected target. After reviewing her information and confirming her other target was still here, she closed down her terminals and went to her quarters to prepare herself.

Faith disembarked from the Cerberus Hunter. She checked different places of the station for setups and considered her options. She had found out her target wasn't scheduled to leave for another three days.

Further research revealed the contact used to hook Roger into serving them unaware had been killed in a gang bust gone bad. She reviewed the case. It didn't look right to her. It had a few characteristics of scene prep. Something she was all too familiar with.

The face of the religious man came up in her mind again. It made her feel guilty. The killing of an innocent man for a political agenda. She tried hard to shake the thought. She had a plan, however faulty, to help rectify what she had done. It wouldn't bring Grant back to life. Just settle the score a little. Maybe enough for the guilty feeling to go away.

Which brought her thoughts back to her personally chosen target. She decided to wait until her target left his apartment. The next morning she stood in the shadows between structures and watched the entrance of the living spaces. A large man stepped out and looked all around him. She kept herself still. This one knew what he was doing.

Eventually he moved on down the station street. She continued to stand absolutely still until she knew he was gone for sure. People were beginning to show up in greater frequency as they started to make their way to jobs. She just watched, taking in what she saw, looking for potential problems in her plan. After the initial throng of people had left, she decided to make her move.

She went to the building that her target had come out of. She navigated her way to the corridor where the living spaces were. The target's housing rental was nearly halfway down the corridor. She pulled out her datapad and pretended to look down at it as she walked, just in case someone entered the corridor.

Two doors away from her target's apartment, she stopped and leaned against the door entrance. Her hand reached into one of her pockets and retrieved a device no bigger than a contact lens. As she pushed herself away from the wall, her hand with the tiny device reached up and stuck the device high on the edge of the entrance.

She started to walk slowly. Her datapad accessed the device and she could see down the corridor to the entrance. The image was crystal clear. She setup her target's face to be watched for and to notify her as soon as it recognized him.

When she got to her target's door. She reached into another pocket and pulled out a card. She waved it in front of the security pad. It responded by turning green. The screen documented a fictitious name followed by Building Maintenance. The door slid open. She reached into the same pocket as the device and popped a pill looking thing into her mouth.

She took a deep breath, then bit down on the pill. She exhaled a long breath, aimed at the floor and up to the ceiling. Once the chemical was several inches from her, it billowed into a semi transparent smoke.

Not seeing any laser lines, she stepped into the door and stood still. The door closed behind her. The room was tiny, even for a studio apartment. It was only slightly bigger than a hotel room. It was quieter and more private than a hotel room, and she probably would have picked a similar setup for a short term living space.

Out of another pocket came a thin circular device that just fit in the palm of her hand. She held it out flat and activated it with her datapad.

A rapid moving laser formed a flat vertical plane that slowly swept from one side of the room to the other. It also gave off a sort of pinging sound. On her datapad, she could see a number of things that would have been otherwise hidden from view. For her, the room was laid bare.

The scanner would reveal objects in the closets, aged thermal scans of where her target had been last and left significant heat behind, traces of blood and other identifiable fluids, possible explosives, and other potential traps that had been set.

There actually wasn't much in the room. A larger suitcase that looked to have another bag in it was the only real item of interest. She went to the closet near the bed and pulled out the suitcase. She lifted it onto the bed and pealed it open.

Nothing unusual jumped out at her as important. She pulled out the smaller bag and set it aside. After doing a detail search of the suitcase and all the items in it, she came up with nothing. Anything important he must have kept on his person.

She opened up the small bag and looked inside. There was a large bundle of black cloth. She pulled out the cloth and felt a hard surface underneath. The cloth was familiar and her hopes rose. Her hands unveiled the solid object hidden within. A smile crested her face.

A plain mask that was attached to the cloth, just like hers. Faith turned over the mask and found the voice modulator. "I've found you. Now the question is, which one are you?" she whispered.

She thought about her plan and decided to be a little more dramatic. Her new plan would protect her identity as well. Picking up the voice modulator, she applied it to the surface of her throat and tested it. It worked, just like her's did. She shifted her tools around on her to make them easier to access for her modified plan.

She threw the small bag back into the suitcase and stashed the suitcase under the bed against the wall so that the target wouldn't see it when he walked into the room. The mask fit just like her own and the cloth draped over her, hiding her features. She waited for the camera she setup outside to go off.

Several hours later, her datapad pinged a warning.

"About time," she muttered. The datapad was quickly stashed into one of her pockets. She got out a weapon for each hand. She hoped she wouldn't need the pistol. Once she had what she needed, she got into the closet and almost closed it, intentionally leaving it ajar.

The door slid open and she could hear him take off a jacket and toss it on the table along with something else. His movement stopped. She heard a weapon being pulled from a holster. She made sure the first weapon was clear of the robes. He might actually kill her if she was too slow.

The closet door jerked open. The man's eyes went wide with shock. Faith took advantage of the delay and fired off her first weapon. The prongs pierced the large man's thin shirt and made his whole body arc and shutter as the massive amount of voltage ran through him.

He thudded to the floor, still spasming. She pulled out a chemical injection system and put it firmly to his neck. Pressing a button, a dose was delivered. She considered the man's large size and opted to give him a second dose to make sure.

The taser had done its work and now the large man just groaned there on the floor. Given a few more minutes and the drugs would start to do its job. She dragged his body up onto the bed and fastened his hands to the bed anchors on the wall. She also tied his ankles to the legs at the end of the bed.

The man's head was a little wobbly as he struggled to focus. "Who are you?" he slurred.

Her digitized voice responded, "Someone who is going to have a little chat with you. You are going to tell me everything I need to know."

"Not telling you nothing."

"Oh, but you will in just a few minutes. Let's start with easy stuff. Tell me your name."

"Told you, I'm not telling you anything."

She looked at a time piece on her wrist. After about ten minutes had passed, she quizzed him again. "What's your name?"

The man looked to be in a happy stupor and smiled at her. "Maddox... Dewey Maddox."

"Who do you work for Dewey?"

"I'm... uh... I'm a director of Civil Defense Service. I help catch smugglers."

The answers were correct so far. Faith asked a few more to be sure. Dewey answered correctly. She ran him through the typical gamut of questions after that. Passwords, security codes, anything and everything she might need to unlock information he might be hiding. She got him to unlock his datapad, and she took a copy of all the contents it had access to.

She searched his person and removed a couple of data storage devices. He was happy to give her the encryption codes for them both. She took a current DNA sample, blood sample, copies of his finger prints and scans of his eyes. By the time she was done, the drugs were starting to wear off already. She didn't want to give him another dose if she could avoid it. It would make his memory slushy and worthless for longer than she wanted to hang around.

"Few more questions, Dewey. You've been very helpful so far. You're a member of the Council of Six?"

"I am, how did you guess?"

"Do you know who the other members are?"

He seemed to have to think about it, "No clue. They look just like you though."

Dewey was starting to break out in a sweat already. She was going to run out of time soon. "Do you have any guesses or information that might lead to who they are?"

The happy state he was in was beginning to fade. "No, I don't have a clue."

"What number are you in the Council of Six?"

"Two."

"Do you know where Captain Roger Vance is?"

"Not since he left for the Nedra system. He should be back soon?"

"Do you have orders concerning him?"

"No."

"Any plans for him when he returns?"

Dewey had to think about it. "I think I'll kill him for what he did." He laid there and blinked his eyes repeatedly as if waking up. He furrowed his eyebrows, "Who are you?"

"I think we are done here for today."

Dewey pulled at his hands and feet and became aware of his state. His face was turning red and mean. "Who the hell are you!?"

"I came here to help correct a wrong." She pulled out her laser pistol and turned the power down to be quieter. It would be less destructive, but still lethal. Faith shot him twice in the chest and once in the head.

She waited a few minutes. Her burden didn't feel any lighter. Perhaps it only would if she killed the one who carried out the deed that killed them all.

Faith took off the mask and voice modulator. She threw the modulator on his limp body and put the mask over his face. She draped the cloth to cover him as if he might be wearing it. She reached into another pocket and pulled out a small cylinder. She unfolded the base for it and set a timer on it for two hours. She set it down in the middle of the room and left.

Two hours later station fire crews responded to an apartment that was reported to have smoke coming from the door. They found the insides of the apartment to have been incinerated to the point the metal in the room had started to seriously deform.

The Slip

Roger got a calculation of how far away the ship was from them. It was still a long way out. The Pedlar's Omen banked to the right as it dived into the midst of the floating debris of rocks. Roger tried not to watch as larger stones when flying past the front window. He could see the multitude of ripples of the shields getting pelted by smaller stones.

Roger managed to get one more sight of the alien ship. It had adjusted its course to follow them. The image of the alien ship was lost in a sea of asteroids. Sonja popped out of the other side of the asteroid belt and banked hard the other direction.

"Smart woman!"

She didn't respond. The thrusters that remained pushed as hard as they could go. She went on for some time, then slowed as she dived back into the asteroid belt. Eventually she came to a small grouping of asteroids that were easily ten times the size of the Pedlar's Omen. She flew into the midst of them and stopped.

"I can't go any further. I have to stop. I'm sorry, Roger."

"You don't need to apologize to me! You've put out a heroic effort as far as I know."

"How long will you need to sleep? And how do I wake you up if the aliens manage to find us?"

"I can't sleep in here, remember. The best I can do is just be still and quiet."

Roger thought about it. "If I can find some sort of sleeping agent, can I add it to your food supply?"

"Oh, Roger... I'm in a tank full of fluid. Any drug you add would have to take into account that kind of dilution, not to mention the filtration system. You would have to inject such a high dose you might kill me in the process. Besides, we don't have enough of anything like that on board that I know of."

Roger groaned. He couldn't come up with any other ideas to help her. "I guess I go on a mineral hunt. I can only imagine how many parts need to be made up to patch us back together again. This ship was not designed for this kind of thing."

"I'll let you know if I spot anything."

Roger walked to the small walk-in closet where his weapons and body armor were normally stored. "Thanks. I'd be grateful to not be left behind."

He reached into the closet and pulled out an attachment back piece. It had thrusters, and a sealed breathing system. It was designed around the concept of needing to get on the outside of a prison station in the event a section of the station was compromised. Officers could get to the vacuum of space and evacuate or invade to take back control of a section from the outside.

Roger slung the thing to his back and lined it up. The armor registered the attachment and locked it to his back. The ports to the pack sealed and gave him access to the air supply and filtration system. The suit sealed off access to oxygen from everywhere except the attached pack.

He made his way to the cargo bay and accessed a large tool chest. He pulled out a hand-held scanner and a laser drill that was awful to wield due to its bulk and weight. At least he would be using it in zero gravity, he thought to himself. Another thing on his list of wants, one of those ship drilling packages that could be put in place of a turret. It would make life so much easier in times like this.

He setup the cargo space to 'catch' physical items with something that resembled an energy net of sorts. He activated the atmosphere seal over the floor of the cargo area and retracted the belly plates of the ship. The pistons hissed as the floor of the cargo area descended into open space. The faint blue lines of the 'net' could just be seen against the darkness of shadows outside.

Roger dropped through the open area, avoiding the net as he exited. Short, powerful bursts from his pack brought him to a stop just in front of the cargo area. Roger remembered to tether his tools to his suit. Something he should have remembered to do before he exited.

He let go of the drill and began scanning for minerals in the surrounding rocks. He found small pockets of what he needed. Some of it deeper than he wanted to have to work for. There wasn't much choice though. He worked as quickly as he could. Every so often he would check his field of view for any signs the alien ship might be around. He didn't really like mining by hand like this anyway. It was worse feeling vulnerable while a predator was around, some place, hunting them.

He was hoping to find more Aurin crystals than he did to resupply the ship's fuel system. They would have to look more in another location. What he managed to gather would only get them by for a few days.

He drilled out the other deposits and cast the chunks of minerals at the cargo bay net. Each pieced stopped where it got caught in the net. Gradually small vibrations in the net caused the stones to gravitate to the middle in a cluster on the cargo bay floor. Doing this made room for more items to be caught.

Roger kept at it for several hours. The cargo area was nearly half full. Most of it would be refined out and the worthless bits would be ejected back into the vacuum of space. Roger had done all he could do. His nerves were shot constantly, looking for a ship he never did see. His body's energy was spent with physical labor.

He returned to the ship and pulled in the cargo. He buttoned up the ship again and setup the mini refinery and fabricator to start processing all the raw ores he gathered into usable materials. He was going to need a lot of plating to patch up the damage done outside and prevent hull ruptures should they get hit again in those same places.

Roger couldn't bring himself to look at what it might take to get the engine back to functional again. Or if he even could. He thought about what happened the last time he tried to repair the thruster, and the cost made him cringe. Of course if it was nearly destroyed anyway, he was going to have to replace it. He could practically feel the credits fleeing from his account, abandoning him to a life of hardship working for scraps.

He removed the jetpack attachment from his armor. After cleaning the filtration system and recharging the propellant in it, he put it away. He felt exhausted. He dragged himself to his quarters and laid down. He felt kind of guilty. He could actually sleep. It was his fault that she couldn't. It was his fault that she was stuck inside of that pearl.

"Roger!" she whispered harshly.

"What?"

"They're here!"

Roger moved his aching body to the bridge. He plopped down in his usual seat. He turned off the automated targeting of the turret and took manual control. Last thing they needed was for the gun to go off and give away their position.

"Where?"

Sonja told him where she had seen movement last. He caught movement out of the corner of his eye through the main window. In the small space between the close asteroids where open space once was, the hull of a ship could be seen slowly drifting by.

A green light from the ship pierced its way into the darkness between the cluster of asteroids. It did a fast sweeping search. The light just missed the aft end of the Pedlar's Omen. The light was cut off as the ship continued to drift past. Roger slowly exhaled.

The green light appeared a few more times as the alien ship circled around. Sometime the light came close to the Pedlar's Omen, other times it didn't. Eventually Roger saw the light of their thrusters facing their direction.

The alien ship was very large. Roger thought back to the station and how it looked to be made by a species much larger than himself. There was no way to really know if the ship he was looking at was small or medium in those terms. "Looks like they didn't see us. We may have to hang out here for a while."

"Fine by me. I'm still too exhausted to hardly move. There's no way I can get us to the mists. Besides... the ship is still beat up really bad. You have a lot of work to do before we can even attempt to get out of here."

Roger set the turret back to automatic targeting. He got up and went to his quarters and plopped onto his bed. He would have to sleep in the armor, just in case. As much as he hated the idea, it wouldn't be the first time.

Roger woke up and swung his legs off the bed. His body was still tired and felt like he'd spent the night on the floor. He took off his helmet and carried it at his side while he went to get something to eat along with some coffee. He would need it today.

"Oh, your finally up. You lucky dog."

Roger pulled up the date and time. He immediately felt guilty. "I didn't sleep that long intentionally."

"Yeah... well, you were asleep for so long that I went ahead and moved us. I found another cluster of large asteroids back the way we came."

"Kinda risky. What would you have done if they decided to double back?"

"In my current state of mind... probably turned around and rammed them."

That was not what Roger wanted to hear. "We need to get you to Dakkas soon."

"Well, maybe if you would quit napping for twelve hours at a time, we could get moving."

"I'm sorry, Sonja. I'll work harder to help you."

"I..." there was a long pause, "I don't mean to... I think I'll just shut up for now."

Roger could only imagine what she was going through. He quickly ate and then got to work on making repairs. While he was outside he used, the hand held mineral scanner and found more Aurin crystals. There was enough there to get them to Dakkas and still have just a little fuel to spare. He also picked up more of the other minerals that were there. Again, he underestimated how many parts they needed to get the ship patched up enough to just get by.

The process of refining and manufacturing the parts was taking forever. It didn't help when he ruined a few of the parts because he installed them wrong, damaging them or the devices they were supposed to connect too. Roger's temper was getting shorter and shorter as the hours dragged on. More than once he moaned about needing an engineer for this.

He unstrapped the jetpack and followed his routine before putting it away. The repairs were complete as best he could do. He had even managed to get the one damaged thruster to work at a limited capacity. It was better than nothing, he figured.

There was no way he was going to get away with not replacing it when he saw how bad the damage was. There was nothing to lose in attempting to fix it. Even though it was such a hack job, no engineer would be willing to touch it.

Neither of them had seen the alien ship again.

Roger cleaned his hands with a rag, "Are you sure your ready for this?"

"I think so."

Roger moved on to the bridge.

Sonja moved to the edge of the asteroid belt before attempting to jump into the mists. The thrumming started and the scene outside the window transitioned. "We made it," there was such relief in her voice.

"Well done!"

Roger was looking forward to getting back to some form of civilization. It hadn't really been that long, but it felt like forever. More than anything, he wanted to get Sonja help. He would do whatever was necessary, even if it broke his account to do so.

He felt the ducking and diving start. "Your kidding?!"

"No... I think they may have been in the mist waiting for us!"

"Damn it." Back to feeling powerless.

"Never wanted to find one before... Now that I want one, there doesn't seem to be any around..."

"Any what?"

"Ahhhhh... I feel you. You're a big boy, too. Come here you. You know you want a piece of me!"

Roger was getting concerned. "What are you doing?"

"Come on... that's it. Oh yeah!!!"

Roger felt the ship rattle a little with a hard banking maneuver. The thrusters thundered at full power. The thruster he had repaired did not sound too good at the moment. "What are we doing? It sounds like my patch job on that thruster is going to blow apart!"

"I'm going head to head with the alien ship!"

"Have you lost your mind entirely!?"

"Maybe..." she laughed. "And dive!"

Roger got a slight sinking feeling in his guts. He really hated not knowing what was happening.

"Oh yeah... you have fun with that alien ship. Chew on them all you like!"

Sonja shifted directions again as if to make a run for it.

Roger pieced together what she was saying. He relaxed just slightly. "The two of them going at it?"

"Yes, I can feel the two of them fighting with each other. That mist creature was a pretty good-sized one. Hopefully it can kill their mist pilot and knock them out of the mists."

"Good work!"

"Yeah, well... we'll see if I can even make it to Dakkas. Keep praying."

Roger got up and checked on the supplies for the pearl. Everything looked normal. The filtration system looked like it was going to be due for having its consumables changed out soon. Probably sooner than normal, given Sonja was still in there. He wasn't sure if they could even change those out with her still in the pearl. He figured he would find out soon enough.

"Damn aliens..."

"Chasing us again?"

"Yes. They are struggling to catch up this time. I think their ship might have taken a pretty good beating."

"I sure hope so. Can you get to Dakkas before they catch us?" Roger asked while walking to the room with the conference table.

"I think so. It'll be close. I think I can get there in about another day."

Roger pulled up information about the Dakkas system. It was a decent hub of activity that was important enough to have a couple of actual smaller warships assigned to protect it. The local authorities had a large number of ships to enforce the law as well.

"If we can just get to Dakkas, there's enough firepower there they should be able to do something about that alien ship." Roger considered it, "If they can take down that ship, maybe we can start working on putting our lives back together."

"That sounds so good. I can't wait to be able to sleep again." She was sounding nearly exhausted already.

"I AM," Roger quietly muttered the words so Sonja wouldn't hear, "please help her make it."

Respite

Sonja strained to make the last stretch as the alien ship fired off more shots. The Pedlar's Omen was hit in the back corner. The already damaged thruster burst in to flames as it made a lot of noise. Sonja lost control, and the ship went into a horizontal spin. "I'm going to lose points for being graceful on this one!"

The Pedlar's Omen tumbled back into the physical realm, still spinning. Roger cut off the fuel to the damaged thruster. The flames extinguished in the vacuum of space. The metal parts of the thruster that were never intended to get hot, groaned as it twisted and snapped under the stress of going from super heated to freezing cold.

Sonja managed to get it back under control and made like a shot for the Dakkas station. "Thank god there isn't anyone in this space. That could have been even more messy."

The alien ship dropped into physical space not too far behind. The ship slowed and veered away. It seemed to go the other way into the outer reaches of the system.

"Looks like they're afraid of crowds." Roger made sure to capture as many images of the ship as he could. He looked over what he was able to get. Looking at enlarged pictures of the ship and comparing them with others they were able to get, he noticed some differences. "Looks like it did take a bit of punishment. Not near as much as we took though."

"Yeah, well, they're probably an actual combat vessel. Not

civilian cargo ship."

"Point taken."

Roger took initiative and made arrangements for landing. He was also put in contact with an independent engineer for a repair estimate. It never failed to surprise Roger that with all the regulations to make things consistent, every station he visited seemed to be very different in how they handled things.

He also updated all of his news feeds and checked on his account. He was shocked to see that the full amount that Maddox had promised was in his account already. He was not expecting payment for a week more at the soonest, if at all. He felt something get very hot in his pocket to the point it might burn him.

He reached into the armor storage where he had the two IDs still and pulled them out and let them fall to the floor before they burned his finger tips. The ID's in their secured case turned to ash. The heat was so intense it warped the security casing that held them.

"That's probably not good."

"What?"

"The IDs that gave us authorization to be in the Nedra system just burned themselves up as soon as I connected to the comms relay."

"So we have no proof anymore to save our skins."

"Something like that. It's possible they may not have been real anyway. Just a forgery done up by Mr. Maddox. I have legal documentation of the IDs. I also have a load of files I managed to pull from Mr. Maddox's data device he plugged into the table when he gave us the information on where to go. It's all encrypted so I still need to figure out how to deal with that."

"Oh... Is that why our system seemed to run so slow for him. You sneaky man you."

"I've worked with too many people like him. He's the type that will stab you in the back the moment he's done using you. A felon is more trustworthy."

The ship docked in a very large bay that could house nearly forty small cargo ships like the Pedlar's Omen. Nearly two thirds of the bay had such ships currently docked. The place was busy with activity. Repair crews and cargo handlers were everywhere. This station was considerably larger than Lestat station, and it showed.

Roger changed out of his body armor and into something more normal. Normal for a former officer that was trying to look more like a ship captain. He dropped the ramp to the cargo area and opened the door. He was expecting the engineer to show up soon.

He walked down the ramp and saw a very thick and muscular man that looked like he could wrestle trees to the ground without much effort. He was poking his thick sausage fingers into a new gash of the Pedlar's Omen. His whole right arm, from shoulder to hand, was a massive industrial looking prosthetic. He had a permanent control device attached to the right side of this head to match. Both devices looked like they attached to a spinal device that could be clearly seen under his thin shirt.

"Hey," he said with a deep husky voice. "You Roger Vance?"

"Yes. You the engineer I messaged, or the station bouncer?"

The man roared in laughter. "Name's Randall Turner. I'm the engineer that picked up your request." He pointed at the gash and motioned around the rest of the ship, "You been taking this thing into combat zones? Or are you just a piss poor pilot?"

"Combat seems to be a difficult thing to avoid when making deliveries to desperate people in remote places."

"You should get a different ship for that kind of work. This kind of ship isn't built for that. One day it could get you killed. Just say'n."

"Understood. For now, I have to work with what I have. Thing is, I need this ship fixed up like new. It's really important to me it happens soon."

Randall and Roger went over the ship, and Randall made a list of everything that needed to be fixed.

"She's a pretty little ship. Gunna take a while to get her fixed up though."

"I might be stuck here for a few days anyway. I was put on a waiting list for a pearl technician. Apparently they are in high demand lately. No one could tell me when one would be available."

"Oh, man. Don't you be getting into that pearl or let'n anyone else get in it. I hear pilots are get'n stuck in them and can't get back out again."

Roger thought he could feel the blood drain from his face.

"By the looks of ya, I take it you got someone in there already."

"How hard is it to get someone out?"

Randall just shook his head slowly. "I don't know nothin official. Word spread'n at the shops is, no one has been able to get out. Not alive anyway. Somethin seems to happen on first jump after get'n in a pearl. Pilot gets stuck. Somethin bad ends up happening to the pilot. News is spread'n everywhere to ship crews. No pilots should be get'n in pearls until a fix is found. People say'n it has somethin to do with The Event."

"The Event?" Roger swallowed hard.

"Yeah, man. Didn't you experience what happened last week?"

"My pilot and I both did. We were in a remote place when it happened."

"Man, everyone, and I mean everyone experienced it. It was right after that people started get'n stuck in pearls. It's all over the news vids. Crazy stuff. Just like some peoples hair turning gray or sometimes white. It's nuts. I'm sorry about your pilot, though. How they do'n?"

"Exhausted. She needs sleep in a really bad way."

"Ah, man. She just a hire or someone close?"

"Started out as a hire. I'm pretty sure it was becoming more than that." Roger looked down at the floor, "It's my fault that she's stuck in there."

"Hey man, there's no way you could have known. I totally understand why you want the ship fixed up quickly. Tell you what. Normally to fix this much damage would take about a month. If you would be will'n, I'll move all my shop into your cargo bay and stay in one of your ship's rooms. I'll work on the ship day and night until she's fixed. Might have it done in a couple weeks or so. I'll also knock of ten percent of the labor cost too."

"What about the thruster?"

Randall put the back of his mechanical hand up level and activated a terminal that was built in. He flipped through the screens, Roger guessed, using his head controller. "Sorry, boss. Nothin available to replace it outright. Parts are startin to get scarce with the whole pearl pilot problem too. I'll need the money for the parts up front. I'll need to get them all before things run out. I'll have to rebuild what you got."

Roger cringed. "Don't look at the past repair job too close. It might hurt."

"Patched it yourself did ya?"

"It was that or the possibility of getting shot out of the sky. I had to give her every chance possible."

"I get it, man. I'll get her back up and run'n. That is, if we have a deal."

"It's a deal. Thank you for your consideration of her."

Roger set him up to have temporary access to the ship to make repairs. After Randall left, Roger went to talk to Sonja. He told her of all he had learned so far. She was quiet.

"So it's not just me. In some twisted way, that's a small piece of relief. To just know I'm not alone in my struggle. Maybe after a little rest I might reach out to some of the other ships and see how many here are in the same fix. Maybe they have found something that might help cope until a real fix is found."

"That sounds like a good idea. I think while you recover and the ship gets repaired, I'm going to see if I can't get some more concrete answers and sort out our next move."

Roger had learned several things the hard way when it came to owning and operating a ship. He intended to be wiser this time. Jumping in with both feet and getting what he thought he needed from a ship dealer didn't prove to be the best of decisions in getting started. Kris had told him who to go see and talk to about getting a ship the first time. Thinking about it now, Kris might have had ulterior motives.

As he went into the different districts of the station, he noticed a whole lot of people had hair that were some degree of changing color to a white or gray. It was surreal. More than that, he also noticed some people began to look weak and frail. It was like their body was deteriorating. He overheard many conversations of people talking about hospitals and med bays being over run with people having all manner of physical conditions.

Roger picked up on a lot of fear people were having. He started to slip into that state of hyper awareness that was so familiar to him. People often did stupid things when they were afraid in mass.

Roger looked for the places that ship captains hung out. He offered to buy a few of them drinks in exchange for advice. An offer that with more often than not quickly accepted. He found out a lot of things he had never considered before. A couple of the captains mocked him, telling him he had no business being in the business with no more than he knew. Others had compassion for a new guy starting out and tried to give him good advice.

He learned more in three days than he had in months. He also found out in talking with shop keepers that pre-built ship parts, add-ons, and tooling where quickly disappearing from warehouses. It was something one captain had mentioned to him as well. For all the additions that Roger knew he would need for a new ship, he began to purchase the blueprints for them. He also tried to get plans for building the tooling as well but, he was denied. Turned out an engineer's union had the legal rights to those locked down so that only engineers could get them.

He purchased what he could get a hold of. A couple of captains had shared with him how to best locate raw materials and where he should go for them. When it was done correctly, it was much more cost effective than purchasing. Some of them even sold extras off to help with their profits. Things like that helped Roger understand how these captains were able to hire the crews they did and still pay the bills.

When he shared with them the ship type and size he was running, he quickly got the impression he would forever struggle to make it. It was just too weak and small to be practical. His ship was considered more of a glorified shuttle than a true cargo ship.

He also found out that what Randall had told him about most pilots getting stuck in their pearls was true. Many of the captains were very concerned about it. A couple had also shared that the few pilots that had their pearls broken into so they could be rescued, died within minutes of being removed.

No one had any answers for that problem.

One thing was unanimously agreed on. Cargo running business was going to start booming in a big way. There wasn't a lot of mist pilots that wanted to commit their lives to potentially becoming a permanent part of a ship. Those who were already stuck being a part of a ship were struggling with how to deal with exhaustion and not being able to sleep. Both factors would drive up the costs of shipping.

Roger considered that too. It might also make it difficult to buy a new ship that he really needed in the short term. There was the other issue he needed to work out. He didn't know when Director Maddox might come calling again. He was still considering how and when he would stage his and Sonja's death. With her being stuck in the pearl, he wasn't sure how he could pull it off. Until a solution could be found to get people out of the pearls, a new and more practical ship was out of reach.

Loose Ends

Faith was still catching up on the last round of information that had been sent to her before they left for Dakkas station. Two of her teams had failed to turn up any more information. One agent was MIA and probably dead. One team had gotten lucky and sent her a trove of information that solved a critical link. She put together a report for her superior about the critical link.

"Director Jerin?"

"Go ahead, Captain Yao."

"We have arrived. We are within a four-hour shuttle flight time as requested."

"Excellent. How is our mist pilot holding up?"

"He says he's feeling strong enough to get us to the next destination. He'll probably need three days of rest before he can go anymore."

"I have a meeting in a few hours that will dictate our next course of action. Have him try and rest until I find out more."

"Aye."

Faith sent off her report and checked that Roger Vance was still on the Dakkas station. The Pedlar's Omen was under extensive repairs still, and apparently he had spent most of the money that Dewey had paid him with. She shook her head. The man had to be a stupid captain to continue to put so much into that ship, when he could have gotten something better. Suspicion crept in. She would have to take a closer look at his purchases as something struck her as odd all of a sudden.

She studied up on the station, looking for places to suit her purpose. A plan needed to be put together to interrogate Roger and then kill him off. The feeling of guilt crept up on her again. Was she actually feeling guilty about planning to kill the man that had caused people to start dying? It didn't make sense. She felt like something was restraining her, causing her confusion as she tried to focus on how to do this needed action.

"AHHHH... Why is this happening?!" she put her hands to her head in frustration. A thought passed through her mind. 'You are wrestling against I AM.'

"I don't know if this I AM is even real," she whispered. She sat still, not moving, yet fighting to regain clarity of thought. "WHAT DO YOU WANT FROM ME?!"

'I want you.' A gentle thought came.

"Prove to me that you are real. Make it so I can't kill Roger Vance. Stop me from doing it. If you can stop me from shooting him, you can have me. I will believe in you and you can kill me however you want."

The mental struggling stopped and clarity returned. Another thought came, 'According to your word.'

She looked at the station and got an idea on how to deal with Roger. She thought about Grant Robinson and then about Roger Vance. The Council of Six had set him up, sent him in that place with the intent that he mess up. Her impression from the message boards was that none of the council had dreamed this would be the outcome. She would find out soon enough with this first meeting after the disaster in Nedra.

She looked at her time piece. The meeting would be soon, so she grabbed a small bag. She headed down to the secured communications room and entered. Protocols were followed as before, minus the unauthorized recording she was doing of these meetings. She opened up the bag and put on the voice modulator, mask, and black cloth. It was nearly time. The codes for the meeting were entered before she turned around.

A holographic six appeared above her head as the link established to the meeting. Her heart raced a little, knowing that two would be absent from the meeting and she alone would know why.

One by one the other showed in the meeting, with the exception of two.

Three spoke, "Two will not be joining us. This meeting will be short."

"Has something happened with Two?" Five asked.

"Things have changed so drastically that we can no longer continue with our plans. I suspect a traitor among us. Two has been killed, and-" Three was cut off.

A noise that sounded like a door opening followed by two military soldiers appearing into the video and taking down One. They shouted at him to stay down.

Three did something to cut One from the meeting. "We've been betrayed! The Council of Six is disbanded! You better pray one of you is not the traitor!" the video link ended.

Faith turned and secured the video and log onto the data storage device. She erased the logs from the ship's computer and pulled off her mask, modulator, and cloth. She stashed them back in the bag and exited the room. She went to the where the ship had a small incinerator and dumped the small bag into it. She stood there a minute and watched the contents become nothing but fine ash.

The words last spoken by Three echoed in her mind. 'Better pray one of you is not the traitor!' Yet someone had tipped off the military to One's location. Someone knew about the meetings, knew about the council. Three might try to have her killed if Three could figure out it was her that killed Two. Faith didn't have anything to do with the capture of One. There was at least another player in the game. Her life might be shorter than she realized.

She moved with a purpose. If nothing else, she would carry out her plan to kill Roger Vance. Perhaps it would be him that killed her if this I AM actually intervened this time. She got to her quarters and packed up as much as she dared. She got out all the data storage devices that contained files and documentation she had gathered from before the Council of Six was established.

Perhaps if she survived killing Roger Vance, she would work on a plan to take down all that was left of the council. Burn the whole thing down. Maybe then the guilt feelings would stop. Maybe then memory of killing Grant could be satisfied and finally leave her in peace.

As she threw in a few more items, the captain responded to her call.

"This is Captain Yao."

"Captain, as soon as I depart, head off to the next objective. Once you get there, there is no rush for you to return for me. I will probably be at least a week here under cover to deal with a sensitive matter. Make sure the mist pilot gets plenty of rest."

"Understood director."

She grabbed both of her suitcases and made her way to the small shuttle bay. Only three workers were here at the moment. Two technicians worked on one of the four shuttles. The bay manager was at the control station for the bay. Locking mechanisms clanked and the bay doors rumbled as they shifted out away from the ship and then split, half going up and the other half sliding down over the outside of the hull. The bluish energy barrier kept the atmosphere in the bay.

"Number two is primed and ready for you, director," the bay manager said.

"Thank you. See you in a week or so."

She made her way to the shuttle and stashed her bags in the back. Climbing into the pilot's seat, she strapped herself in while she ran through the checks. All checks came back positive. She hit the thrust hard and shot out of the bay. It was only a split second of a thrill and nothing like her early days.

She regretted not having Captain Yao put the ship near an asteroid belt. She enjoyed any chance she got to go full throttle, ducking, diving, and rolling her way through it as fast as the shuttle could go. She knew the captain hated it when she did it too. He wouldn't tell it to her face, but she had heard that he had mentioned one day she might get herself killed doing it. For her it was a recapturing, a thrill of a long forgotten life. She questioned why she left that life. At the time, it seemed the right thing to do. Now she wasn't so sure.

The time seemed to drag on until she got to the station. Once there, the pace picked up until she docked. She got settled in on the station and began checking things out to make sure her plan was in fact workable.

She found Roger and watched him from a distance. He was

hanging out with ship captains and buying some of them a drink, which seem to get them to talk. He also went to some shops and attempted to make some purchases. She talked to some of the people after he had visited them to see what he was asking about and trying to purchase. The mist pilot issue was starting to cause some real supply problems already.

After finding out what he was up to, she refined her plan. She would hang out in the district with the captains tomorrow and take it from there. Until then, she would gather what she needed to make the plan work.

The next afternoon she watched the movement around the Pedlar's Omen from the docking bay. It was in the afternoon before Roger left and headed for the district to do his brain picking again. Faith made sure to get ahead of him and find out where he would land today. He made his way in to a couple of the shops first. She had to work at being patient. Eventually he made his way to one of the pub like establishments. She followed him in and lurked in a dark corner.

She let him get in a few drinks to other captains before she made a move. The time came as the captain he was talking with bid Roger fair well and left him alone at the bar. Faith ordered up the same drink Roger had ordered yesterday and today and one for herself. She walked up to Roger and asked if the seat was taken and if she could pick his brain about keeping a ship secure in exchange for a drink.

He chuckled. "I actually didn't come here to give advice. I was actually looking for it. I do have some experience with security, so I guess I could try."

"Any help would be much appreciated. I just came out of being in a remote system for a long time and problems seem to have exploded recently. Just trying to find ways to stay safe," Faith offered him the drink, which he graciously accepted.

They talked for a little while. Roger looked at his time piece. "Hopefully that's helpful to you. I hate to cut this short but, I need to be getting back to my crew."

"Not a problem. Thank you for the advice."

As soon as Roger got up from the bar he had a hard time staying on his feet. He put a hand to his head. "Whoa," was all he said.

Faith wasted no time and put one of Rogers arm around

her neck. "Little too much to drink? I'll help you get to where you need to go." There were some chuckles at the scene from around the bar. No one really seemed to care too deeply about it as someone was obviously already at his side to help him out of the establishment.

Faith walked him out. Roger was stumbling along and looking confused. The two of them walked to the end of the business district where they went to a service elevator. "Where are you taking me?"

"Someplace safe," she said as she tapped the control box to summon the lift.

"This isn't the way to my ship."

Faith didn't say anything. The lift arrived, and she dragged Roger along with her. She could see it in his eyes, he didn't like wherever they were going. The lift descended to the garbage processing level. The workers had left for the evening, leaving just the necessary automations running with a few droids to do manual tasks. The place smelled of rotting organic materials that were being processed. The place looked clean despite the nasty smells.

She dragged him to one of the large recycling rooms that was currently empty. It smelled more like burned plastic, which Faith found better than the organic smell that made her want to gag. She took Roger to the center of the room and pushed him to his knees. It was all he could do to stay upright, so she didn't bother to bind his hands and feet.

She stood facing him, nearly two meters away. She pulled out her laser pistol and turned up the power to full. She pointed the weapon at his chest. "You're the one that ultimately got us all killed. Nothing personal, I'm just needing peace of mind."

Roger just sat there on his knees trying to keep his balance.

"Any last words?"

Roger swallowed. "Just... I ask your forgiveness for what I have done."

The request threw her off, "What?!"

"I sincerely ask for your forgiveness for what I did. I don't blame you for wanting to kill me. When I AM approached me, I was shocked He didn't kill me. He forgave me for what I did. Now I ask your forgiveness. I don't fault you for wanting to kill me."

Her mind reeled. This was Grant Robinson all over again. How could she go through with this? She had been a part of the group that set him up. Not only that, Roger had spoken with I AM, and been forgiven. What would that say of her if she shot him now? She remembered the promise she made. She struggled inside. She wanted peace of mind again.

Her finger squeezed the trigger as she held her aim at Roger's chest. Click. Nothing. She squeezed the trigger again. Click. Nothing. She brought the weapon up close to her to examine it. The weapon looked fine. She aimed at a distant section of the room and pulled the trigger. The weapon fired and the searing energy bolt exploded against the steel wall, creating a jagged hole.

She brought the weapon back to Roger and aimed for his chest. She squeezed the trigger. Click. Nothing. Click, click, click, click. Tears formed in her eyes and she felt herself loose emotional control. "So... I AM truly is real." Faith got within arm's length of Roger and fell to her knees before him.

She took hold of the barrel of her pistol and held the grip end of the pistol out to Roger. "I AM is real, and my life is forfeit. He won't allow me to kill you."

Roger was starting to regain his strength and balance. Though not as fast as he wanted it. He took hold of the pistol grip. Faith let go and closed her eyes. She heard him move. What sounded like the pistol sliding against the metal floor far away wasn't the sound she was expecting in the last seconds of her life.

She opened her eyes, and he just shook his head at her. "Yes, I AM is real. He doesn't want you dead. He wants you to live, and not just live, but live fully. He wants you to get to know Him. He wants you to find peace and joy in him."

"You have no idea what I have done," She managed to say through crying.

Roger laughed. He spread his arms out, "You can't possibly have done worse than me. Because of me, all humanity has suffered eventual death. Because of me, something terrible has been unleashed that threatens all humans."

Even though she felt on the verge of loosing it, that last bit of information perked her ears up. Unleashed what?

"He forgave me of all that I have done, and even of what

mistakes I will make. He wants to do the same for you if you will let Him."

She felt a sense of peace in her. A sense of invitation. She didn't know what to think or say. The man she had brought down here to kill wasn't going to retaliate. Instead he asks for forgiveness. Her whole world seemed to turn inside out and upside down. She got up and ran out of the area, leaving him behind. She needed to get to a place to think.

A Move

Roger's closed eyes flinched with the loud banging down the hallway. He rubbed his head as if it would ease the now forming headache. He wasn't sure if it was because he had too much to drink, or if it was whatever that woman had drugged him with.

His mind went back to the events of what had happened yesterday evening. It was so bizarre to him. He had to work at piecing it back together. A woman had essentially kidnapped him to kill him.

Then she couldn't kill him because of I AM. So then she asked him to kill her and he ended up saying things to her that he didn't have a clear enough mind to say. She eventually ran away and Roger spent hours trying to find his way back out of that place.

He had a strong sense that he would see her again one day. Not only that, but he would need to be accepting of her. He rubbed his head and thought to himself that it wouldn't hurt his feelings to never see the woman again.

The banging started up again. "He had to start inside the ship?" he muttered.

"Just be thankful your not stuck in a waking state around the clock."

Roger apparently forgot to turn ship comms off to his room last night. He wondered what else he might have said that she overheard. "I can only imagine what it's like to feel the ship and have it being worked on." He thought about the grinders and torches that Randall would naturally have been using. "It doesn't hurt you when he makes cuts, does it?"

"It stings some. Nothing like when I'm being shot. That hurts a lot."

"That I can relate too."

"It's interesting, though. Until now, I've never been in the pearl while repairs were being done. Nothing major anyway. Damaged parts of the ship always feel... out of place, maybe even debilitating. Having the debilitation made right actually feels good. I never would have known before."

"I never would have guessed that either."

"Oh, have you met Randall's helper? He hired a guy to help him with repairs. Sounds like he has hired him before."

Sonja seemed awfully chatty to Roger this morning. Getting back to sleep was obviously not going to happen. "Nope, I haven't met him yet. Guess I will now." He got up and got ready for the day. As he got ready, he shared with her what he had picked up on the last couple of days. "Have you talked with others stuck in pearls yet?"

"Yes. Some of them are a mental wreck. A few like myself are just holding it together, even if by a thread. The only thing that seems to help the situation is shutting down the entire ship and only running bare essentials. Like right down to just life support systems and pearl system, if possible. They say it's possible to almost achieve sleep at that point. Recovery is faster anyway. I've been trying it given we are docked in a secured bay and it does help."

"That's good to know."

Roger left his quarters and nearly tripped over a sphere robot that was walking in the hallway. The Robot had four legs. At the moment it walked on the back larger ones. In its three digit hand was some sort of tools. The robot had stopped to look up at Roger with its single optical sensor in the front center of its sphere body. It waved the empty hand at Roger as if to say hello.

"Sparky! I need that fastener! I can't hold this all day!" Randall hollered from a room down the hall.

The robot acted startled and quickly moved down the hall and around the corner to the cargo area where it disappeared.

Roger heard a torch pop followed by more banging happening outside the ship. It must have been the other guy working.

Roger went and found Randall. He had a compartment that accessed the trashed thruster torn apart to get at some of the internal components. Roger was amazed the man could get any work done in such a tight space, given how big he was.

"More to the left," Randall said. Something inside clinked. "Yeah, just like that." Randall pulled on something with his mechanical arm that was buried deep into the thruster's parts. Roger heard parts lock onto each other. "Yeah! Good job, Sparky! Now put the tool away and bring back some of that hi temp manifold sealer. Put a good bead of sealer around that sucker."

"Me do it, me do it," Sparky said. The legged sphere came out of the compartment like some contortionist escaping a box. It dropped to the floor and quickly walked past Roger down the access ramp to outside.

"Oh, hey there!" Randall said. "Met your lady... in a manner of speaking. She's cool. I like her."

Roger smiled and laughed softly. "She has her moments though."

Randall laughed, "I've been married before. They all do man."

"You men are no different!" Sonja warned.

Roger looked to change the subject quickly. "If you have a moment, I would like to get your opinion on some of the purchases I've made."

"Not a problem, boss. Whatcha got?"

"I tried to get some ship packages and components yesterday to put aside for a new ship. Everything seems to be sold out. Next best thing I could get is a builder's copy of the blueprints, which cost me a king's ransom." Roger told him where he could access the files he had bought on the ship's computer. "From an experienced engineer's perspective, would any of these help this ship, or should I just save them for the real cargo ship I hope to get? Or did I just waste a load of cash?"

Randall looked through the list of blueprints and dived into a few of them. "You are one seriously lucky dog sir."

"Oh?"

"One... these are high quality prints of some really good tech. I could only wish to have such items for a project I've kicked around for a long time. Might be time to get into that project again sometime soon. Two... As of this morn'n all blueprints have been pulled from the market and are reserved for actual ship builders and select engineers with the proper certifications. Somethin about price controls which don't make no sense to me.

"As for help'n this ship... maybe the mining setup. It'd cost you the defense turret. Not a wise choice I think, given the types of jobs you seem to take." Randall looked through the rest of the prints before looking back up to Roger. "These prints are easily worth a hundred times what you paid for them yesterday. If I were in your shoes, I wouldn't sell them. Wouldn't even tell anyone I had them, if you know what I mean."

Roger did all too well.

"You got the tooling to build all these?"

"No, that was an issue I couldn't resolve yesterday. Until I can find help for Sonja to get out of that pearl, my plans to acquire another ship seem pointless at the moment. Not that I could get a ship now, anyway. The price for them are skyrocketing."

"That makes sense," Sonja chimed in, "With mist travel slowing, more ships would be needed locally to gather resources that would normally be brought in."

A slender man walked in, wiping his hands on a rag. "Got the framing rebuilt for the thruster exhaust."

"Good man," Randall said as he stood up. "Captain, this is John Wilder. Hired him to help with repairs. I've hired him before and he does good work. He's one of them ministry types, but he's harmless. Aside from chatting your ear off."

John laughed and offered to shake Roger's hand. Roger accepted. John's grip was firm and confident, a good sign in Roger's book. Roger picked up on the man's hair. It was mostly gray. He didn't seem to be frail though, as some people he had seen. "Pleasure to meet you, sir. And interesting too."

"Interesting in what way?"

"I see a slight glow around you. I'm curious. Have you been in the presence of I AM?"

Randall leaned his back against the wall and crossed his arms as he rolled his eyes. "Oh, brother! Here he goes..."

Roger just looked at the man carefully for a long moment. "I have actually."

"Really? What was it like? What did he say to you?"

Roger told him about the parts that were not personal to him.

"He gave you a part of His Spirit?! Can you do to me as He did for you?"

Roger was very taken back by the request. He had never considered such a thing. He certainly wasn't a religious man by any stretch of the imagination. He wasn't sure he liked where this seemed to be going.

"Please just try. It would have great meaning to me even if it just seems weird and nothing to you."

Roger gave in. He placed his right hand on the man's forehead. Nothing really happened. Maybe the words were important. Roger couldn't remember what was said exactly, so he just spoke the first thing that came to his mind, "To those who accept I AM as their God, He receives them back as his children. As a sign of His promise He gives..." Roger was shocked as he watched a mist of light flow out to his arm and swirl at the end of his forearm and hand that rested on John's forehead. "... His Spirit."

The light flowed gracefully from Roger's hand into John's eyes, ears, nose, and mouth. After the light had completed transferring the man slowly dropped to his knees with his arms out stretched. Roger could still see the light swirl in the man's eyes and open mouth. John's hair changed color from gray to a natural brown. His body filled out and looked more healthy. His skin transformed to look rejuvenated and had more color to it.

The light eventually faded and John stood back up. He had the biggest smile on his face. Roger just stood there stunned. John stepped up to him and put his hands on Roger's shoulders. "You have no idea what just transpired, do you?"

Roger just shook his head.

"The Event, we all lost our connection to the source of life. We lost our connection to I AM. What you experienced, what you just shared with me, is a reconnection to I AM. He made a way for restoration."

Roger looked at the floor for a long moment.

"Dude... that was the most trippy thing I think I've ever seen yet," Randall said.

"I keep telling you, your missing out," John said to Randall.

Roger broke free from John's hands and ran to another section of the ship. John looked at Randall, who just shrugged. John jogged to catch up with Roger. Randall followed out of curiosity.

Roger was at the pearl. He laid a hand on it and tried to speak the same words he had just spoken over John. They didn't come out right and he couldn't remember exactly what he had just said, as if something was preventing him from doing so. Nothing happened.

Randall looked at John, then back to Roger. It dawned on him. He closed his eyes and bowed his head.

Roger tried rephrasing the words. Still nothing happened. Roger's jaw clenched, and he growled in frustration. He beat a fist against the pearl's surface. His head sagged in defeat.

Randall poked at John and motioned him to leave with him.

"That's unfortunate it didn't work for the pilot. It must need to be a touch in person for it to happen," John said softly.

"She's not just a pilot to him," Randall said as quietly as his gruff voice could.

"Oh!" John suddenly felt bad for the both of them. "Surely there must be a way. I will have to seek I AM about it. I can't wait to share this with the other believers."

The Unknown

Chief Aarons carefully sat at his station and set his fresh cup of coffee on a section of his console that was made for refreshments while working. His station was on a raised platform to overlook all the other stations around him. He pulled up his typical screens that showed all ship traffic around the station. He started going through reports of ongoing security issues for both ship traffic and within the station itself that needed to be dealt with. As he read he partially listened to the half dozen traffic controllers and station security just below him as they gave directions and made assignments. Aarons expected a smooth day as no dignitaries or military convoys were scheduled.

His ears perked up an hour later, when one of the controllers repeatedly called out to a ship to identify itself. Apparently someone thought his day was too calm. "What have you got, Sgt Higgs?"

"Unidentified class four ship, on a direct course for the station. ETA 45 minutes. No response on any frequencies. Ship doesn't match anything in our catalogs. No identifiable markings either."

"Not in our catalogs?" Aarons went through protocols in his head. "Dispatch law enforcement to investigate. Ready tugs to divert if necessary. Class four... probably better let the military know just as a courtesy. Doubt it's a pirate, but a class four could make quite a mess if it were. Better safe than sorry."

Radio traffic picked up as ships were diverted from possible harm of the newcomer.

Roger held one of the last metal plate covers to the thruster in place while John Wilder secured it. John was teaching him repair tips and tricks as the two of them worked together.

"Don't tell him everything!" Randall roared with laughter from another section of the ship, "You'll put us out of a job."

Roger laughed, "Hardly."

"Roger, can you come to the bridge please," Sonja asked.

It seemed an odd request.

"I've got it from here," John said.

Roger walked to the bridge area and took a seat in his typical chair. "What's up?" he asked quietly.

"That ship is coming!"

Like a switch being tripped, Roger sat up with a changed composure to deal with a threat.

"Radio traffic is flooding the comms. Ships are being diverted towards the planet side of the station in a holding pattern."

Roger's heart began to race. "Surely it wouldn't attack the station just to get at us."

"I don't know. From what I've picked up on the comms, it's coming in fast."

"Keep me posted. I would think there is enough firepower out there to keep that ship at bay. Possibly even take it down. Go through a systems check in prep for flight if we have too. I'll talk to the other two."

"Five law enforcement interceptors responding. ETA 5 minutes to intercept."

Chief Aarons pulled up the incoming ship on his screen. An unexplainable sense of foreboding crept over him. "I don't like this," he whispered.

"Class four ship has fired upon the law enforcement ships! All five interceptors are off scope!"

Chief Aarons cussed as he watched each law enforcement ship exploded in flames before drifting as debris. "Sound general alarm! Notify the military, the class four ship is hostile! Get the ships around the station out of here now!"

Aarons activated an emergency broadcast for the first time in his life. "This is Dakkas station on the emergency broadcast channel. Dakkas station is under attack by an unidentified class four vessel. All non combat ships are to turn away from Dakkas station and stay away until further notice. I repeat Dakkas station is under attack by an unidentified class four vessel. All non combat ships are to turn away until the hostile has been dealt with. This is not a test." He set the message to repeat itself for the next hour.

Roger came to the cargo area of the ship, "Randall, John, we may have a problem!"

As if on cue, sirens blared loud in the docking bay. The PA system made an announcement, "All personal are to seek shelter immediately. This is not a drill. All personal are to seek shelter immediately. I repeat, this is not a drill. Dakkas station is under attack!"

Randall came out of the service access. "Attack?! Who in their right mind would attack this station with military types around?"

"Someone with a large enough ship that might be able to take them on," Roger said. "I want to get all the parts outside on this ship just in case."

Randall nodded. "Best load up the rest of my tools too. It'll be a tight fit getting all that in here."

John ran out of the ship and disappeared among a mass of people fleeing in different directions. Roger, Randall, and Sparky exited the ship and moved as quickly as they could to load up all the parts and equipment outside onto the cargo bay lift and any usable space in the cargo area.

Aarons monitored the movement of ships in response to the emergency calls. The chatter on the floor was loud but controlled. He watched as law enforcement ships gathered up and did their maneuvers to engage the hostile ship.

The officers for the station security were barking orders into their comms. An air of panic was threatening to grip the room. A couple of the other station Chiefs in recent months had been complaining that there really should be more emergency drills to cover such events like today. Aaron had been among those that been a little too willing to put them off. He hoped they didn't all pay for that today.

The screen lit up in front of him with weapons fire from all sides. The class four ship didn't even bother to change course in the face of the engagement. It just absorbed the hits with its shields and a few impacts to its hull. Its own weapons, however decimated everything it came up against. The blips on the screen that were law enforcement ships disappeared at a frightening rate. The unknown ship plowed through them all without flinching.

"This isn't going to end well," Aarons whispered to himself.

It felt like time was slipping away too quickly. Both men were loading the items as fast as they could. Progress was feeling too slow. The panic in the air was so thick and palatable Roger felt like he could cut it with a knife. The docking bay was beginning to thunder with the roar of engines as ships got clearance to leave the station.

Chief Aarons hollered, "Sgt Marshall, activate station defense weapons and peg that class four ship as an enemy. Let military ships know this hostile has engaged with military grade weapons."

"Activating weapons systems. Class Four ship is tagged as foe."

"Chief, Corvus military ships are already en route at max speed. ETA 10 minutes."

Aarons heart sank. Having served on a destroyer in the Corvus navy several centuries before, during a long since forgotten war, he knew they didn't have that kind of time. "Higgs, tell those military ships these exact words: Echo one. Bring the fire or bring the bags."

"Aye, sir."

Aarons heard the change in the security officers first. One of them must have been former navy as well. He explained the coded message to the other security officers around him. The head of security made a decision to change focus from locking down the station to evacuations. Chief Aarons didn't correct him or say anything to reverse that decision.

"Attention everyone," the PA announced, "Dakkas station is now under evacuation order. I repeat, Dakkas station is now under evacuation order. Make your way to the nearest life pods and leave immediately." The message repeated itself over and over to the backdrop of sirens.

Roger looked up at Randall. Both were sweating and breathing hard. There were still parts and tool cabinets that needed to be saved.

"We can do this!" Randall said.

Roger knew they seriously needed the parts and probably the tools too. He understood it was Randall's lively hood at stake if he were to lose the equipment. It wouldn't be much different if Roger lost his ship. They moved as fast as they could.

Time seemed to race by. Aarons watched as the Class Four came within range. It fired first. The ship turned broadside and unleashed a volley of projectiles and laser blasts. The projectiles all hit the station hard, exploding on impact. The laser seared holes in random places around the station. The holes exploded outward as atmosphere ripped the walls open to the vacuum of space. The station was designed to seal up small breaches from accidents or asteroids. Nothing of this magnitude.

The shock waves from the explosions rippled through the metal frames of the station like a stone thrown in a still pond. Sparks showered as electrical lines were pinched and shorted between moving metal. Lights flickered as the sirens continued to blare with occasional static interruption. Toxic smells of a mixture of fluids permeated the air and singed the nostrils.

The invader ship's smaller weapons were targeting civilian ships all around it with impunity. Each and every ship burst into brief fireballs under the military grade weapons. Aaron had thought his days of seeing blood baths in space were over. He never suspected such a thing would ever happen here. Hundreds of lives were being snuffed outside. He could only imagine the casualties inside the station itself. Past experience had taught him the death toll would do nothing but climb fast. This fight was just getting started.

Once the ship got within max range of the station's weapons they open up on the target. Chief Aarons held out a small hope that the capital ship sized weapons would prove effective enough to buy them time. Large red bolts of energy filled the view from the station's few laser cannons. The bolts that hit the invader ship pounded on the vessel's shields and eventually started to chew into the ship's hull.

The ship seemed undeterred by the pounding it was beginning to take.

People were scrambling to ships still in the docking bay. Others like Roger and Randall were still frantically loading up cargo or getting people aboard for transport. Some were yelling and screaming about what could be brought and what had to be left behind for lack of room. A few fights had broken out as well.

The whole bay shook and the sound of metal groaning under intense strain filled the area. More sparks showered from fixtures all over the bay. A few fires broke out from the electrical fixtures and panels. Black smoke drifted to the ceiling and the smell of burned plastics, rubbers, and other materials filled the air.

A shaking knocked everyone to the floor like a massive earthquake.

Roger noticed John Wilder get back up and start running from the bay entrance in their direction. Roger and Randall were both back on their feet and they finished securing the parts and tools to the cargo lift.

An explosion erupted as a solid object came crashing up through the floor of the bay entrance and ended into a docked ship. Roger heard the secondary explosion from within the ship. Metal fragments scattered across the bay, impaling or hammering themselves against whatever they hit.

Roger felt something blunt strike him in the left shoulder and knocked him down to the floor again. Small metal fragments ricocheted everywhere all around him. Roger couldn't move his left arm. Adrenaline dumped into his system. He saw Randall was also on the ground and bleeding. Three metal shards grouped together the size of a small knife protruded from his back.

He looked for John. John was also on the floor, crawling on his belly towards the ship ever so slowly. The bodies of others littered the floor of the bay. There was more screaming and yelling, this time of people in pain.

"SPARKY!" Roger yelled.

The droid came running down the ramp.

"Help me get Randall into the ship!" The two of them got a hold on Randall's massive form and dragged him up the ramp into the cargo area. Roger heard the ramp pistons activate as well as the cargo lift. "WAIT! Don't lift the ramp up yet. I need to get John!"

The ramp stopped and lowered again as Roger ran down it. He ran to John and, using his only functional arm, he wrapped one of John's arms around his neck and dragged him to the ship. Blood was soaking John's front from his right side. A woman grabbed John's other arm and put it around her neck.

Roger looked at who the woman was that just showed up out of nowhere. Roger couldn't believe it. She might just kill him yet. "Move!"

The two of them dragged Roger into the Pedlar's Omen.

As soon as they got John up the ramp, they laid his body next to Randall's. John noticed that Randall was still breathing.

The ramp pistons sounded off again as the ramp raised. "Getting clearance for take off," Sonja said.

"Forget the clearance! Get us out of here!"

Roger went to the terminal in the cargo area. He activated the sectional energy barriers that were designed to keep any hull breaches contained. It would eat up the power supply with prolonged use. They would have to deal with that later. He wasn't sure what might still be opened up to the outside uncompleted repairs. The pain in his shoulder was starting to hit harder as the shock started to wear off.

He felt the engines fire up. There was another explosion, and he heard the atmosphere outside the ship vent into vacuum, taking debris with it. The ship moved as thrusters hammered at max speed, causing Roger to nearly fall backwards.

The invader ship turned and made another aggressive pass with the other side. This time it stayed just outside of max range of the station's weapons. Another rapid fire of volleys were shot at the station. Explosions were scattered all over the space station in more strategic places this time.

"SIR! They're wiping out our guns!"

Aarons thought about it. He realized they charged at them hard on purpose. "The station is lost! Everyone needs to get out now!"

"Station defense weapons are ALL offline!"

Another round of volleys. The bottom section of the station broke loose and drifted downward. Smaller ships left the hanger bays like bees after their nest had been struck. The station guns, having fallen silent with destruction, practically gave an invitation.

The invader ship moved in closer. Its weapon systems rapidly switched from one ship to another as they tried to flee. A red bolt of energy pierced the command center. Chief Aarons and all the staff were killed instantly.

Roger got back up off the floor and staggered to Sonja's quarters. He wasn't sure where the woman had disappeared to. He could tell the ship was taking wild evasive maneuvers. It didn't feel the same. He wondered if they had taken more damage or if flight controls were partially disconnected.

"ROGER! Some woman is on the ship! She just took over piloting!"

Roger growled with irritation. That would explain the difference. "How is she doing at it?"

"I... well... As much as I hate to admit it, she might be a better pilot than I am. At least for this kind of thing."

"Then let her for now. No point fighting back and forth for controls and getting us killed."

He got into Sonja's closet that had the bag with the medical devices, then staggered his way back to the cargo area.

John had rolled himself to his back and was struggling with breathing. Randall was still face down and passed out. His chest still showed that he was breathing as well. Roger pulled John's shirt up to expose the hole in his side. Whatever had hit him hadn't passed through the other side. With exposed skin, Roger fumbled around with the medical device, that would repair the damage for John.

The device was powered on and stuck to John's skin. John

groaned initially as the device examined him. He quieted down after it gave him something to numb the area.

Roger pulled his shirt half off to expose his left shoulder. He got out the only other device he knew, the one for broken bones. He was guessing that was his problem having had them before. If not he was going to be in real trouble. Roger had slid down to his butt on the floor. His head was pounding from the pain at this point. He activated the device and managed to get it to his shoulder.

The pain intensified dramatically with the analysis. Roger passed out.

A bit later he woke up to a plinking of metal falling to the floor. He opened his eyes and saw that the nanites had pulled a metal object from John and had ejected it to the floor. John was nearly patched up at that point. Roger's device indicated it was only about half done.

He could feel what felt like bugs crawling inside of him, pulling, pushing, fusing, whatever it was the nanites were doing. He knew they were tiny, it still felt like bugs.

John was awake and looked at Roger. "What happened?"

"Explosion in the bay. We all got hit. An unknown ship is attacking the station. We managed to get out of the bay just before it was ripped apart."

The device on John gave an audio signal that the damage was repaired. Roger walked John through the process to clean it and prepare it again to use on Randall. Once the device was ready, John pulled the three shards out of Randall's back and put the device over the wounds.

With Roger's instructions, John moved his sore body to clean up the blood that was all over the floor at this point.

Two Corvus destroyers along with a small missile ship rushed onto the scene of a station being blown apart. The missile ship went high above the chaos and locked onto the invader ship. The hatches protecting its payload snapped open and guided missiles poured out of the hull.

The two destroyers split up, going low in opposition of their missile ship, one to either side of the target. They dodged other ships and debris as weapons locked on to the alien vessel.

Missiles rained down against the ship at various places from fore to aft. The invader ship's weapon systems had switched from shooting civilian ships to the incoming missiles. There were too many. Impacts erupted in flames all along the black vessel.

The invading ship turned toward deep space with surprising agility and speed. The destroyers unleashed their weapons at a now fleeing target. The invader ship's thrusters put out an impressive glow the likes of which men had never seen. The destroyers slowed as it became obvious they could not even attempt to keep pace with the enemy.

They circled back to the station.

Sections of the station drifted in different directions, now derelict. The destroyers circled, giving intelligence to local authorities for rescues. They kept their weapons at the ready, diligently watching for the invader ship, should it return. The call for help had gone out. More military ships would arrive in the next few days. Until then, it would be up to the three of them to defend against this never seen before enemy ship.

Escape

Roger dragged himself up to the cargo area terminal and activated it. Using what he had learned from cargo captains on Dakkas station, Roger picked a system between where they were and Lestat station. It was a more out of the way place where they could get materials if they needed for additional repairs that might be needed already.

"You got that, Sonja?" Roger asked. His head was still throbbing.

"Yes. I'm topping off the capacitors now. I should be able to get us there in about a day."

"Take it easy on yourself and don't push too hard. You never know when we might have to be on the run again."

"I'm painfully aware."

Roger turned again and put his back to the wall and let himself slide down to the floor again. The phantom drive thrummed, and the stillness settled on the ship as it transitioned to the mists.

The repair device on Roger was still going. John looked through the bag that still had medical devices in it. He picked out some round cylinder thing and took it to Randall. The device on Randall had just finished a few minutes before. Gently, John removed the device from Randall's back and set it aside. He twisted the cylinder and put it near Randall's nose.

Randall stirred back into consciousness.

"Welcome back to reality, my friend," John said. He helped

Randall sit up.

Roger watched with curiosity. John twisted the cylinder and put it back in the bag. He got out one of the other devices and set it up on Randall's chest. He attached a cord to it and hooked it up to another device that had been in the bag. It displayed some virtual screen of what looked like bio-diagnostic information.

"You seem to know what your doing. How?" Roger asked.

John kept looking for something. "A very long time ago I served in the Antaris Territories military. I was trained as a field medic. I'm a bit rusty, but it seems to be coming back to me."

"You're a convenient man to have around. Engineer's assistant, and medicine, what other tricks do you have up your sleeve?"

John chuckled. "I've mostly been a minister of I AM. When I was a field medic, I got a closeup look at just how frail life can be. That's when I came to know I AM. After I left the military life, I went into ministry. I didn't particularly want to see war anymore. So I came to the Corvus Commonwealth. I got to know a few engineers that I ministered to. They taught me how to do ship repairs to help me pay my bills. It's all I really know."

Roger just nodded. Randall was quiet as he sat there. John finished whatever he was doing and removed the device from Randall's chest.

"Well doc, what did you find?"

"I'm not a doctor. I can patch holes and deal with simple ailments is all. Just enough to get someone back on their feet and into the fight, or stabilized enough for a real doctor," He moved the equipment over to Roger. "Your spinal device says processors three and eight are not functioning. Other than that, your physical body is repaired enough to function. You're short, about one point two liters of blood. That will have to come back with time. Under ideal circumstances, I would recommend bed rest for the next three days."

John hooked up the device to Roger's chest. It stung a bit when John activated it. John apologized when Roger groaned in pain. The device pulled information from the one attached to his shoulder. "Looks like some serious damage was done to the joint. That's why it's taking so long. There is also a lot of soft tissue damage that will need to be repaired."

He looked at the remaining devices in the bag and pulled one out. "Lucky for you, the device needed for that is here." As if realizing something, "You don't have a medical bay on this ship or medical officer. Where did you get these?"

"They actually belong to Sonja. A good friend of her's gave them to her as a gift."

John's eyebrows raised, "Military forces keep a tight control of these kinds of devices so they don't fall into enemy hands. They don't just give these things out. So unless this friend was on a death bed on some battlefield…"

Roger looked at John sternly, "That may very well have been the case. She doesn't talk about her past much. It seems to cause her pain, and she wants to make sure it stays buried as much as she can. Understood?"

John just nodded in agreement. He went back to work looking through different screens, looking for other problems. He didn't find anything else. He left Roger hooked up and went over to help Randall up. The two of them got Randall situated in the room he had already been staying in during the repair process.

Roger noticed that John was also still slow at getting around. After the bone device had finished, John was going to help Roger to his room. Rather than exert that much effort at the moment, he had John just setup to do the soft tissue repair right there in the cargo area. He tried to relax as much as he could.

He practically had to give John a direct order to go to one of the rooms that would now be his for as long as he would be on board. John finally relented and left to go rest. It would be hours later when the soft tissue device finished that Roger finally got up. The use of his arm had been restored, even though it felt like he had been beat on by a dozen batons. He left the medical device with the others. He desperately wanted to go to bed. There was one other issue he had to deal with before he head to his quarters to sleep.

He went to his storage closet that had his combat supplies. He got his sidearm setup and strapped it to himself. He knew he was suppose to accept her. However, she had tried to kill him once already, so he wanted to have some insurance for survival.

He locked the closet and made his way to the small bridge of the ship. As he suspected, she was still there, sitting in the pilot's seat. Her head turned slightly in his direction as he entered. She seemed to be just sitting there relaxing for the moment. She never looked directly at him and looked down in front of her. "I wouldn't blame you for shooting me and dumping me into space. You would have every right to," she said solemnly.

"A few weeks ago, I probably would have done just that. A lot has changed for me the last few weeks."

"You asked my forgiveness for what you had done. I wanted you to know... I do forgive you."

Roger watched the side of her face from his typical seat. She looked like a sense of relief came on her as her features relaxed.

"I also ask your forgiveness for..." she seemed to hesitate, then gave in, "all the grief I've had part in causing you."

Roger couldn't believe he was having such a conversation. She seemed to be very sincere about this, from what he could tell. He got the impression she was holding something back. Details she apparently felt guilty for and wasn't ready to share. His mind flashed back to the station where he first encountered I AM and all the things he felt guilty for doing. "Whatever it is you've done... I forgive you. Not a single one of us is without fault."

He saw a tear fall from her cheek.

The subject was becoming uncomfortable for him. "So it seems you know how to fly as a ship. Or was that beginner's luck?"

She sniffed and looked up at the mists outside the window, still unwilling to look at Roger. "I used to fly Stigg-79s and Reaper IVs."

Roger was silent. He gathered from that she knew how to fly, but had no clue what those things were she mentioned.

She finally looked at him, and he shrugged his shoulders. She rolled her eyes, "I was a fighter pilot for the Corvus Commonwealth Navy."

"Ah," Roger said. She had turned back to face the window.

"You obviously know who I am. Who are you exactly?"

She started to say something, then hesitated. She seemed like she might be having an internal argument with herself. She closed her eyes and let her head tip backward, hitting the headrest in apparent defeat. "My name is Faith Jerin. As for who I worked for and that name," she finally looked at him, "it needs to be left dead and buried with that station."

Roger considered it. "Understood." The two of them just sat there a moment in silence. Roger had a sense to offer her a job as a pilot. Roger struggled with it. Eventually he gave in. He took a deep breath, not believing he was about to do this. "Given you are currently unemployed, I could use a pilot. My mist pilot is having to pull double duty for both jobs. Now that she can't get out of the pearl, it makes it even more difficult for her." It felt like a very stupid idea to him.

Faith laugh with disbelief, "Are you serious?" She looked back at him like he was out of his mind. She saw that he was serious. She turned back around and let her back slam against the back of the pilot's seat. The look on her face was something that seemed just dumbfounded. "I..." she eventually threw up her arms and let them fall to her lap, "What the..." she seemed to be having another internal struggle. "Okay, sure." She put her face in her hands and muttered something about not believing she was doing this.

Roger turned to the terminal and set her up as the pilot and gave her access to the pilot's quarters. "Come on, I'll show you to your quarters." The two of them got up Roger showed her where things were at in the ship then left to get some rest.

He took his sidearm off and put it where he could easily get to it from the bed before climbing into it. "Sonja, let me know if you run into any trouble or as soon as we get to the system, please."

"So what kind of grief did this woman do to you?"

"I'll tell you later when I'm not hurting so bad. Keep an eye on her and let me know if she does anything suspicious."

"I will. Sleep well, my friend."

Roger had taken something for the pain. When it kicked in enough, Roger became dead to the world as the Pedlar's Omen was in a state of stillness as it moved through the mists.

Sonja woke him as the Pedlar's Omen began its descent back into the physical realm. It was another system barren of life. There were a handful of other ships in the area either hiding out or picking through the asteroids and planet surfaces for the small deposits of minerals. The mining operations had long since passed up this system after taking the larger deposits for profit.

Roger got up. His arm was still somewhat sore, better than it was earlier though. He got up to find John had already been up and about. He had picked up the medical devices already and cleaned them up and reset them for the next go around, when and if they were needed.

Randall had unpacked a few things that he could manage into what space there was in the cargo area. His shirt was removed, and he was down on his knees with his massive hands resting on his thighs. Sparky was doing some work on his spinal device.

"Hey man, how's the arm?"

"Better. How are you doing?"

"A little sore. Made up some replacement processors for my spine," Randall looked away, "I, uh, cannibalized one of your replacement parts to do that. I promise to repay you for that."

"Repairing prosthetics should have a higher priority. If you need anything more, then take it. We'll figure out ship parts later. Safety and wellness of the crew comes first."

"Told you," Sonja said.

"Thank you captain," there was relief in his voice.

"Speaking of the ship and keeping the crew safe, what do we need to work on to seal up the ship properly again?"

"John's already been working on that. Start'n to wonder if that man ever sleeps. He told me about an hour ago he only had two panels left to put in place."

Roger looked at the ad hoc pile of parts and tool chests. There wasn't much of any space left to work with in the cargo area. "I think it might be safe to say that Dakkas station is not going to be back in operation anytime soon. So where do I need to take you? And how do we go about finishing the repairs?"

Randall just looked at the floor for a long moment. "I've

been considering that the last day and a half."

Roger just realized he must have been out longer than he thought. He got immediately concerned that it took Sonja longer to get here than she anticipated. He would have to follow up on that with Sonja later.

"My ex-wife's lawyers have been hounding me like dogs. They practically strip me of every credit I earn, leaving me with nothing but scraps to live from. Been think'n it's time to live on the move again. Lot harder for the legal types to track me down that way."

Randall looked up at Roger. "I gotta project I've been working on. No way I could get what I need to finish her up."

Sparky finished what he was doing. Tiny lights lit up on the spinal device and Randall stretched as if testing how well it moved. He stood to his feet and thanked Sparky. He turned his attention back to Roger. "You saved my life when you could have easily left me behind to die. John, too. No one would have known or blamed you if you had. But you risked your own neck to save ours. I owe you my life. And you save all my tools, which is pretty much all I have left.

"So, as I see it, you and your lady friend could use a ship more suitable for the kind of jobs you do. Your lady friend has been telling me of all the help you do for good people in difficult places. I have a ship, most of one anyway, that I'm going to give to you. It lacks a phantom drive and pearl is all. The rest of it is rebuilt and waiting to be finished up. I also ask to have a place aboard the ship and serve as it's engineer."

Roger didn't know what to say at first. "Your offer is generous. I don't have the money to get a phantom drive and pearl. Even if I could, it still wouldn't help Sonja."

"Nah, man. Sonja needs more protection around her. I would put the Pedlar's Omen in the place where it once had an old phantom drive in the heart of the ship. I'd hook up the Pedlar's Omen to the rebuilt ship so the two would be one. Sonja would be safe. The ship I've worked on would finally have a phantom drive and pearl.

"This ship has been a work of love for me. Even if I could get her completed, them lawyers would have it seized and sold. I'd rather see her in your hands. You actually seem to care. So I'm ask'n, please accept my offer."

Roger took a deep breath. Accepting the offer also meant looking after another crew member he didn't know that well. He was having a hard time believing Randall would offer such a thing. He suddenly remembered the time in the mist with I AM. I AM mentioned He had provided a ship and that it wouldn't be what he expected, but he would need it. Sonja and others would need it.

Roger looked back up at Randall. "I accept your offer." He hoped that this was what I AM had mentioned and not something else. Nothing right now was going in a direction Roger ever thought it would.

Randall got a big smile on his face. "This makes me a happy man. You have no idea." He told Roger where the ship was stashed. It was in another remote system that wasn't too far from where they were.

Sonja said she was still feeling strong, so they moved back into the mists.

John emerged from the service hall. "Where are we going?"

Randall told him.

Roger asked John, "Where do we need to drop you off at?"

"I've been asking I AM about that. My impression is that I'm to stay and help you for the time being. That is, if you'll have me as a crew member for now."

Roger couldn't believe this was happening. This wasn't how the other captains had told him you gained crew members. He couldn't think of any good reason not to for now. Maybe if pay became scarce, they would flee at some station or planet. "Sure, why not?"

Turning back to Randall, "So what exactly is this ship that you've been working on?"

"She's an older one, but a good one! I'll wait to tell you about her until you get a chance to actually see her. You'll appreciate her more that way I think."

The Relic

The Pedlar's Omen dropped back into the physical realm. Faith was already in the pilot's seat and took control the moment Sonja released it. Before them was a red star with several dead planets and a couple of asteroid belts. Randall assured Roger there would be little if any ships out here as the system had been picked clean by mining companies already.

Randall gave Faith the coordinates for his stash in the system. Sonja was as eager as the rest of the crew to see this new 'host' of a ship that she would become. They approached one of the larger asteroids, of which there were many, in the outer asteroid belt. Out of caution, Roger had Faith approach slowly to ensure there wasn't someone that had decided to move in during Randall's years' long absence.

They got close enough for Randall to access the dormant computer systems of the ship. It responded and restarted several of the ship's systems. He went through the ship's security logs and found the ship hadn't detected anyone's approach.

He had a special anchoring system he had built to keep the ship docked inside of the asteroid and out of sight. The only way someone could have found it is if they came and saw a ship hidden in the hole, or scanned the asteroid itself for ore.

Randall activated the controls for the anchor system to extend the ship out into the open so that it could be fully viewed and worked on.

The front half of the ship was somewhat wide. A large cargo area made up a bulk of the starboard side. On the port side, mashed in between everything, was a tubed corridor with a smaller cargo area outside of that.

As the ship continued to come out, the joined cargo areas attached to a sphere shaped area that was split open top down at the front of it and extended out with pistons. The sphere section was embedded into a boxy looking section that was raised at a forty five degree angle upward. Towards the top of this boxy end were four large thrusters.

It took Roger a few minutes to figure out where the bridge was. He found it just below the edge of the boxy part on the sphere.

"My god," Sonja said.

"You like it?" Randall asked.

"I've never seen a ship so badly beaten with an ugly stick before!"

"Sonja, be nice," Roger said.

"She ain't totally wrong. It'll grow on ya though. She wasn't made for a beauty contest for sure."

"So what exactly are we looking at? And why is it split open at the front of that section?" Roger pointed at the pistons extending the front of the sphere.

"She's split open because she needs a phantom drive and pearl installed in her. Those are not built on a ship. They are built in specially designed factories and sent to shipping yards already completed. Most of the time ships are built around the phantom drive and pearl. Most larger ships have the piston system like you see in the event the drive needs changed out. You just cut off the outer plating and open her up. Small ships like the Pedlar's Omen, they just peal her open at the top and pull it out.

"As for what she is... A Triton Federation military blockade runner. Triton Federation used these specialized cargo ships to get supplies past enemy lines to systems that were under siege. She can haul a good bit of cargo, she's armed to the teeth, and can take a good hit. One of the few ships that is considered truly balanced."

"So why don't ships like this still get produced?" Roger asked.

"Change in tech and tactics. Triton's enemies developed a missile system specifically for the ship, and they built gunships made for the sole purpose of hunting these ships down. Triton Federation lost their advantage. Once these cargo ships were getting blown out of the sky on a regular basis, the ship design was dumped for something else."

"How long ago was this?"

"About seven centuries ago."

"So where do you plan to attach the Pedlar's Omen?"

Randall pointed inside the sphere, "Where the old phantom drive used to be. They used to be monster sized back then. Now day's they're smaller and more powerful. This ship's phantom drive could easily be four times more powerful than what she was originally built with. I've made a number of upgrades too."

"This ship have a registered name?" Roger asked.

"Yeah, registration is already taken care of. Just need to transfer ownership. Named her after my daughter. Bethany's Hope is the name I gave her."

Sonja let out a small whimper of a sound.

Randall got kinda quiet. "She was a real fighter, that child, right up to the end."

"What happened?" John asked from somewhere in the back.

"Bethany and I were on a city transport on our way to our new place from a major spaceport. Wife got a new job, and we were moving up in the world. She was already there. The transport suffered a thruster failure. Found out later the city was skimping on repairs and maintenance. Transport went down at the city's edge. I lost my arm and had spinal damage. Bethany suffered worse. She fought to live for nearly a standard year after that. Eventually she got tired of fighting. I don't blame her. Kid always had a lot of hope that things would get better.

"Her mother got angry with me. Nothing I ever did was right after the accident. I think my wife's anger at me upset Bethany and broke what was left of her heart. Nothin was the same after she died. Wife left me soon after. I moved on to become a ship engineer, initially with the hopes of ending such accidents. Bit naïve to begin with, but here I am."

Randall had Faith slowly fly the Pedlar's Omen into the opened sphere and orient the ship in the position needed to begin attaching it. Roger could see the value of the ship despite its appearance. He would have to fully go over the ship's system and learn it like he had to do with the Pedlar's Omen. He figured it should go faster this time, given he knew way more than when he got started in this business.

He realized he hadn't heard a peep out of Sonja after he told her to be nice. He went to his quarters and closed the door. "Well, aside from the fact if lacks a little in the beauty department. What do you think?"

"I can't believe how ugly you are going to make me."

"It's not you! You are a beautiful woman. You are not the ship, you fly it."

"But I am the ship now. I'm stuck in this damn pearl for who knows how long. Maybe even the rest of my life! Have you considered that possibility?"

Roger had wondered about that. He considered her statement. "If you are a ship, than you're the Pedlar's Omen. This new ship will be nothing more than a less than attractive, dress. One that one day you can ditch for another. If Randall can hook you up to this ship, he can disconnect you and hook you up to something different later."

She was quiet for a long time. "I suppose your right. It still makes me feel ugly though."

"For now, it will keep you safer. That's important to me."

"Okay," she said softly. "I do like the name of the ship. Though not because of why it got its name."

"The name reminds you of someone special?"

"Bethany is the name I was born with."

"Oh?" Roger had other questions, but he let them go for now. He would wait and let her divulge more if she wanted to.

"I need to rest as best I can."

"You might as well. We are probably going to be here for a long while. I can only imagine how much has to be done to make this work. I still expect repairs to be done on the Pedlar's Omen as well."

"Thank you."

"You're welcome. Sleep well, my friend, as best you can."

Randall and John went to work diligently. Randall seemed

to be enjoying every minute of work as he fabricated all the parts and pieces that he needed. He had set up a very elaborate engineering workshop. Roger wouldn't have been able to tell aside from the fact he recognized a few expensive equipment pieces and this new ship had a very spacious room for him to work in.

All the tooling had been unloaded from the Pedlar's Omen now that Randall had fully setup shop in the new ship. Roger explored and got to know it from the inside. He helped with the modifications as much as he could. Most of the time he felt like he was more in the way than a help.

Sonja was quiet as she tried to rest. She could feel when Randall hooked up a new set of systems to the Pedlar's Omen. Day by day she was feeling like she was expanding well beyond the small cargo ship and becoming the larger one.

"Randall!" Sonja called out.

He stopped wiring for a second, "Yes ma'am?"

"What is this 'thing' in the compartment near the living quarters?"

"Uh..." Randall was trying to figure out what she was talking about.

"Whatever it is, it's attached to an ungodly amount of computer processors!"

"OH..." Randall's face got a little red. "That's um... it's a personal companion droid. Her name is Abbi."

"A what?"

"Personal Companion droid. You know, like the rich folk have to go on dates with and... such."

"Ewww, are you kidding me! You have a boy toy stashed in a closet, is what your telling me?"

"You make it sound so juvenile. I used her to keep an eye on me while I worked out here in the past on my own. Saved my life a couple of times from accidents."

"So you didn't use it for anything else?"

"Well... after my wife left me... needs, a man has needs."

"Disgusting."

"Yeah, well, they make them very real anymore. All the biomechanical stuff is amazing. She looks, acts, and feels very close to a real person. Not like a typical droid like Sparky. No room in the body for processing computers. That's why they are linked to all the processors hosted by the ship. It takes that much to mimic a real human's body movements and personality." Randall took a deep breath and stared at the floor. "In the end, though, it's not the same as a real woman. Kinda nice when you feel alone and she's sleeping next to you though. Almost feels real at times. It really does help when a guy feels alone."

"She sleeps in a bed?"

"Yeah, they eat, sleep, produce body heat, just about mimic all facets of a normal human."

Sonja was quiet for a moment. "Like she actually sleeps?"

"Yeah, like I said. Why... Oh, I get what you are thinking." Randall seemed to consider something. He put up the back of his prosthetic hand and established a terminal. He looked though several specs and data sheets. "Smart girl. It might just work. Do you have a current body scan of yourself?"

"They're required for all pearl pilots. Why?"

"Personal companions can have their appearance altered to match a body scan of anyone the owner would like. If you have the morph tank, which I do. The companion is tied to the ship because of the processors. I know how ugly the ship is. I'd be willing to give up the personal companion to you, and morph its appearance to match you, if you would like to try it. Maybe your on to something and you can shift to being the ship to just being in the droid and be a little more yourself."

"I... I..." Randall could practically hear the tears in her voice, "I would like that very much."

Randall got up from what he was doing and headed to the living quarters. "I'll warn you now, there are a few lines in the skin on the sides of the face and along different places of the body."

"That's okay."

Randall entered the locked compartment. He setup the morphing tank with the body scan that Sonja sent him. He backed up the AI of his Abbi to another section of the ship and setup the processors to be controlled by Sonja through the pearl's systems. He accessed the controls to open up what looked like a glass tubed shaped casket that contained the droid.

He gently picked her up and out of the storage place and carried her over to the morphing tank. He carefully placed the droid body inside the tube, then activated the controls to seal it. The computer system registered Sonja's body scan and started the process of altering.

Sonja gave him access to her quarters to get her typical clothes she liked to pilot the ship in. He left them for her in the compartment. It would take a few days for the process to complete. Sonja would study how to take over the body once it was finished. Randall just returned to working on putting things together. He left it to Sonja to share with Roger what had been done. Assuming it even worked.

A few days later Roger was on the Pedlar's Omen checking on the supplies for the pearl. He had just refilled the feeding containers and was checking that there were no problems. He had the sense that someone had stepped into the room with him. He glanced over to see if it was John, Randall, or maybe Faith before turning back to the diagnostic screen.

He did a double take. It couldn't be. He slowly stood up and approached her. "I must be seeing things," he whispered.

Tears were forming in her eyes. "Sort of. Technically, I'm still in the pearl."

Roger saw the faint lines on the sides of her face. He gently brushed one with a finger. Her skin felt warm. The pupils of her eyes barely betrayed something mechanical happening behind the black.

She couldn't hold back anymore. She hugged him tightly and cried. Roger held her tight as well.

Her crying eventually faded. "I haven't tried it yet, but Randall says this droid can sleep. I think it might be true. I'm still connected to the ship but, I'm mostly in just this body. It feels like the pearl in reverse. I'm going to try and sleep." She pulled away from him just far enough to look at his eyes. "I had to see you first."

His eyes weren't dry either. They spent some time with each other before she went to her quarters to sleep.

He realized he hadn't finished checking the pearl. Seeing that everything was fine, he went to find Randall.

Randall was installing new conduit from a very large piece of equipment that was nearly half the size of the Pedlar's Omen. It was situated not far from the rear of the Pedlar's Omen.

Roger hollered out Randall's name.

"I'm in here!" Randall yelled back.

Roger came walking in. "I want to thank you for what you did for Sonja! I owe you big time for that."

"Ah, man. You don't owe me nothin. She finally getting some sleep?"

"Time will tell. I hope it works."

"Me too," Randall said as he fiddled with a wire bundle to get it ready to shove into the conduit he was working on. "It tears at the heart to see good people forced apart, not to mention knowing she suffers to boot. It brings me peace and happiness to help like this. It's why I learned to be a ship engineer."

Roger looked at what Randall was working on and realized he hadn't seen this particular piece of equipment before. He wasn't sure how he had missed it. "What is that?" Roger pointed to the equipment.

Randall took a second to remember there was a lot Roger didn't know still. "Take it you've never seen one before? This being a military ship, she had privileges. Now days they don't put them on the smaller ships and keep them only on the large flag ships." Randall had finished with the wire bundle and dropped it. He put a hand on the equipment. "This is a very small Fold Space Generator." He looked at Roger to see if he realized the gravity of what he just told him.

"You're kidding me!"

"Do you know how they work?"

"All I know is that I have to have access to one to access data streams. Oh, and they can be dangerous."

Randall rolled his eyes. "Okay, man. Here is what you need to know about this thing. One, the ship has to be absolutely still while it's in use. If the ship moves, it can destabilize the space fold and cause it to go boom on our end. Two, regulation dictates these devices are only activated far outside edges of a populated star system. Reason is, if it does go boom, it will unleash enough energy to wipe out half of most star systems."

Roger's eyes got wide. He wasn't sure if he ever wanted to activate it.

"Three, all primary capacitors have to be fully charged to get the Fold Generator up and running. That's why this ship has so many of them. Once the generator is running it doesn't take too much power to keep it stable. Here's the thing though, those same capacitors needed to power it up, have to be empty to shut the thing down again. The power that was used to create it comes flooding back when it closes down. Overload the capacitors before it's closed, and things go boom."

"I could see how that might get used as a weapon. It would be extreme but effective."

"Yeah, it was once. It's also why only military ships, and now exclusively flag ships that are too costly to throw away, are used for that." Randall smiled. "Been nearly a week since we got a comms update. Want to fire her up? Kinda curious on what the outcome was with Dakkas station."

"I thought you just said we had to be on the outskirts of a system to turn it on!"

"Outskirts of a populated system. This system is barren. Still frowned upon. But you can do it. I've done it before when I've been out here for months."

Roger had to admit he was curious as well. "Okay, but just long enough for a refresh on queries and news. Then we shut it down again."

Randall agreed. He took Roger through the process. It took nearly an hour for it to get up and running. The data refresh and queries only took five minutes once they were hooked into the data streams. It took another hour to shut it down again.

Roger finally understood why remote systems only did this periodically through the standard weeks. As they waited, Roger pulled up some of the query information he had requested. The station was considered a near total loss.

Thousands of people had died that day, and many more later. Hundreds of ships had been destroyed. It had taken time to compile the list as some ships had to be declared destroyed based on station logs, given many couldn't be determined from the debris that was left.

Roger flipped through the ship logs, looking over all the names. Randall was going through names of people listed as casualties. Randall burst into laughter. "I'm a dead man." Randall just kept laughing for a long while before he went back to looking through the names list. "Suck that ya lawyers." More laughter.

Roger found what he was looking for. "Pedlar's Omen is listed as destroyed on the station as well." Roger considered the implications of that.

"Ya... You, Sonja, and John are also listed among the dead. Won't that surprise people when you three show back up! I plan to stay dead, pickup a reforged ID. Fresh start would do me good."

"What about Faith Jerin?"

"Oh, is that her name? Was wonder'n. She seems to keep to herself." Randall looked it up. "Yup, she's dead too." More laughter.

"I can't speak for John. Sonja and I could use a fresh start. Faith has already mentioned to me about needing her life to be dead and buried on that station. Next problem is, I have no idea where to get reforged IDs."

Randall looked at Roger and smiled big. "I do."

Incognito

Roger was hesitant as he sat before the blank messaging screen. "Okay... I'll do it," he whispered. He addressed a message to any ship crew that might receive it.

To anyone with a trapped mist pilot:

My crew has made a discovery that may be of help to you. They have found out that having a companion droid that is tied to the ship can serve as a reprieve to a mist pilot. The companion droid we happen to have is one capable of sleeping.

The pilot can inhabit the droid while vaguely aware of still being a part of the ship. It works like the pilot being in the pearl, only in reverse. Our mist pilot has been able to sleep and recover at a near normal rate. It's not a perfect solution, but it has greatly helped our mist pilot cope. This might be of help to you too.

Captain of the Bethany's Hope

"Who do I send this too?"

An address code that he didn't recognize came to mind. He entered in the code. The computer system checked with all currently known addresses and flagged it as unknown. He hit send anyway. The message was cued up for the next time a data stream became available.

"Well, I suppose if it fails to go out, no harm will be done."

He left his quarters to go find Randall. It wasn't hard to find him.

"THAT'S IT. HIT IT!" came a muffled yell from within the

Pedlar's Omen.

The sound of a heavy hammer on steel rang throughout the section where the Pedlar's Omen was suspended. He looked at the ship in the large cavity of a room. Supports from the ceiling, floor and walls had been welded at both ends, locking the two ships together.

Power and data cables protruded from access panels all over the Pedlar's Omen. Some dangled to the floor, others went into the wall or ceiling loosely tied to the supports. It reminded him of a spider's random webbing going off to the different areas of the Bethany's Hope, linking both together as one.

John was on top of the back of the Pedlar's Omen. The large two handed hammer he wielded was hoisted up and then forcibly brought back down again with another crash against metal.

"THAT'S GOOD! STOP!" Randall yelled.

Roger could hear the faint fizzling sound of a welder melting steel together. John took notice of Roger and waved. Roger waved back before climbing the scaffolding like staircase to the lowered ramp of the cargo area. He followed the sound of the welder.

He waited for a pause. "How are we looking for being able to get underway?"

"Bethany's Hope is ready. I need about two more hours to button up the flight controls on the Pedlar's Omen so we don't have an accident in here, then we will be ready to go."

"I need to plan out what we are doing. I think the next person we need to go see is your contact for reforged IDs. Are you at a stopping point to get that done?"

Roger made the announcement to all the crew that they were firing up the space fold generator. He then locked the piloting controls as a precaution. He rejoined Randall away from the noise of machinery.

"Been a while since I talked to her last. Hope her ID is still valid."

Roger leaned against the wall, out of sight of the terminal camera. He looked at Randall sitting at the desk. It looked almost comical.

The man was so big he looked like he was trying to squeeze

into a setup made for some kid. Hunched over so his face would be in the view of the screen instead of his barrel chest. His knees were nearly to the floor with his feet almost tucked back behind the seat.

"Rosalie? Is that you?"

There was static mixed in with the audio. There was more than just the static that was out of place. Roger thought he heard sparks and a generator that was making awful sounds. He moved to get a better view of the screen.

The visual image had static in it as well. There was a woman there with matted hair and dirty face. She seemed to be working on something. She was frantic. The room behind her looked trashed. Broken knocked over chairs, dead consoles, and was that... Roger leaned in closer over Randall's shoulder. Yeah, it was blood on the floor. "What kind of friend is this?"

It looked like Rosalie called out to someone behind her while she fiddled with something above the terminal.

"She's a contractor for the government department that handles witness protection. Always been in a proper office. Nothin like this."

The audio popped really loud. "Can you hear me?" Rosalie asked.

"Can now. Was just givin you a call about getting some reforged IDs. Whatcha got going on there?"

"Oh god... Are you a part of a rescue operation? Is anyone coming to help us?"

"We don't know nothin about a rescue. You get hit by an asteroid or somethin?"

"Aliens! They were here. Whole fleet of ships. They broke into the station here. Took nearly everyone. Please, you have to help us!"

"Ma'am, where are you at?" Roger asked.

"The Koba system. Please come quickly! We don't know when they might be back."

Roger pulled out his datapad and started doing calculations.

"Can you get local help? Do we need to try and call someone there for you?" Randall asked.

"As best we can tell the aliens hit nearly everything here. In system communications are sketchy at best. Everyone seems to be in bad shape. We're stranded on the lunar station at

Eatos. Me and Cesar seem to be the only ones the aliens didn't find. We haven't been able to get a hold of anyone else for help."

"Rosalie," Roger said as he moved so she could see him in the camera, "It's going to take us three days to get to you. How are you two doing for food, water, power, and air?"

"There's plenty of food and water to last us a month. We're not sure about power. The generator seems to be failing. We only have four days' worth of air. We've been trying to find all the leaks. There's so many."

Roger dropped his head briefly. "Okay, we'll get underway as soon as possible. Just hang in there."

"Thank you!" the woman had tears running down her dirty face.

The link abruptly ended. Roger wasn't sure if that was a bad omen or not. He rubbed his forehead, trying to think.

"Guess I need to hurry up and get those controls finished up."

"Yes," Roger said without bothering to look from behind his hand that was covering his eyes. Randall struggled to get out of the seat and left. Roger got on the terminal and looked for current information about the Koba system. The system was marked as a dangerous disaster site, and everyone was being warned to stay away.

The military had all resources it could muster in pursuit of an unknown threat. An alien fleet had attacked two other systems since the attack on Dakkas station. The level of destruction this fleet was doing was still unknown. One rescue operation had been attempted only for the alien fleet to return. All contact was lost with the rescue operation.

System rescue ships for Koba were being prepared and waiting for combat ships to become available for escort. Official estimate was five days out for them to get to Koba.

Roger was leery about going there now. The one ship was bad enough. An entire fleet of such ships? If they didn't go, Rosalie and the other person would certainly die. Besides, he already told her they were coming to help them.

As soon as Randall was finished, Roger summoned all of them for a briefing. There was actually a place on the ship for just such a thing. It had capacity to seat nearly twenty in what might still pass as a briefing room.

"I'm not sure who knows what at this point, so I'm going to summarize. Koba system is the third system to be hit by an alien fleet. It's considered off limits and rescue ships are waiting for a military escort and don't expect to get there for another five days. Rosalie Spence, and some guy named Cesar, are on a lunar station around the fifth planet. They have four days of air left. We can be there in three days.

"So, we are going to go in there. If the aliens are not around, we will do a snatch and run. We'll then make a run for the Aldis system. Aldis has a pretty good commerce hub. We drop off the passengers and sell off some of the extra parts Randall and John should have made up by then. Hopefully I can pick up some corporate cargo runs to start getting some income coming our way. Any questions?"

"What if the Corvus military is already there?" Faith asked.

"Then we get out of there before they blow us out of the sky and make a run for it to Aldis."

"So now that we have an actual pilot for physical space, what do you want me to do while we are in Koba?"

Roger shrugged his shoulders. "Rest, I guess. What do mist pilots normally do between jumps?"

"Not much," Sonja said. "This is going to be weird."

No one else had any comments, so they all dispersed. Sonja put the droid body back into the living area where the droid storage compartment was to charge.

Roger and Faith went to the bridge of the Bethany's Hope. Roger got into the actual captain's seat in the middle of the bridge. It still felt strange to him, having only been used to being in some crew seat on the Pedlar's Omen. He double checked the space fold generator was fully shutdown before unlocking piloting controls. The thought of accidentally wiping out half a star system with that thing sent a shiver up his spine.

Faith acknowledged flight controls and moved the ship out of the asteroids. Roger saw on his status displays that that ship's phantom drive had begun to engage and drew on the power reserves of the Bethany's Hope to transition the ship. He didn't feel the thrumming of the deck plates when it started to make the transition. It felt wrong to him.

The darkness of space gave way to the mists. Even with the Bethany's Hope there was a stillness that came over the ship. At least that's the same, Roger thought to himself.

Faith got up from the pilot's seat. It was almost a half pit she sat down in. She walked up to him. "Captain Vance, with your permission, if we encounter the military I want to speak with them. I have some vital information that needs to be in their hands."

"So why not just transmit it to them next time we link up to the data stream?"

"I," she took a deep breath and looked up at the ceiling for a moment, "I have to be very careful who I give this information to. If I give it to the wrong person, we could all end up dead."

Roger raised his eyebrows. "Just what exactly have you got?"

Faith looked to Roger's waist before looking back up to his face. "You seem to be a man of your word. If I tell you, I want your promise you won't kill me, or in any way have me killed."

Roger suddenly felt tired. "This have something to do with why you tried to kill me back at Dakkas?"

"Sort of."

Roger just looked at her. She was harder to read then most people he knew. "I give you my word not to kill you, or have you killed."

She just gave a slight nod. "I was working with a group of leaders that was... preparing for the government of Corvus Commonwealth to implode on itself. Arrangements were made for many things, things I now regret having participated in, to bring that fall about in a controlled way. At the time, it sounded like the right thing to help with. After all that has happened in the last few weeks, I found myself on the wrong side."

She took a deep breath. "I have evidence I have collected for the last several months of this covert government engaging in activities to overthrow the current system and replace it. I'm still missing some key pieces, but I believe I have enough to bring what remains of this covert government down."

Roger just looked at her with a smile on his face. "Your turn to make a promise. If I were to give you encrypted data that belonged to someone I suspect was also involved with what your talking about, you need to promise me to share with me what those files have in them. Double cross me and I get to arrange your funeral."

"What possible data files could you possibly have that would help me?"

"Director Dewey Maddox had a data storage device that had a large cache of files on it."

She noticeably perked up. Then she seemed to suspicious, "Are you joking with me?"

"Take it you knew him? I also take it he might have something you needed?"

She folded her arms and smiled back at him. "You snagged his files? Here and I pegged you for a dumb knuckle dragging prison officer."

"Deal?"

She just kept staring at him as if trying to figure something out. "Alright, you have a deal."

Roger pulled a data storage device from one of his pockets and tossed it to her. "Think you can crack the encryption?"

Her smile faded as she looked at the device, "I don't have to crack it."

"I'm probably already on Maddox's hit list. He gave me and Sonja IDs that gave us permission to enter the Nedra system. Those IDs burned up not to long after we came out. It wouldn't surprise me if Sonja and I were setup and are now being hunted by Maddox."

"You don't have anything to worry about as far as Maddox. He's dead. That's unfortunate about the IDs. That would have been good to have copies of."

"I have documented images of them. I'll give you copies of that too."

She laughed for a second, then looked at him seriously. "I think I may have seriously underestimated you, captain. That's not a bad thing."

Roger wasn't sure if that was a good thing or not. "What exactly was your most recent job? I've dealt with assassins before, you don't fit that bill."

She looked to the floor. Roger thought he recognized her as having one of those internal arguments. Once again she seemed to lose. She looked back up at him. "I was a director for the Interior Intelligence Division of Corvus."

Roger felt like his heart froze for a split second. He had heard stories. He had even seen inmates panic when they got a visit from someone from the Intelligence Division. Sometimes the inmates went straight to the morgue after a visit. Suddenly nothing on the ship felt safe from her. If this was the caliber of people that comprised this rogue government she was a part of... I AM have mercy on him and his crew. The aliens might just be easier to deal with.

Snatch & Run

Roger took his seat in the captain's chair. Faith came to the bridge a few minutes later and settled down in the half pit of one of the pilot's seats.

"Just checking," Sonja said, "there's a quarantine buoy near the system here. We are still ignoring that, right?"

"Yes. Go ahead and get us in there."

A few quiet minutes passed.

"Dropping out of the mists."

"Acknowledged," Faith said. She cracked her knuckles and let out a long, slow exhale.

"Nervous?" Roger asked without looking up from his countdown display.

"Nah," Faith smiled, "To be honest, I really miss doing this. I'm realizing now that, just because you are really good at something you don't particularly enjoy, doesn't mean you should leave something you really enjoy doing."

Roger considered what she said. He considered his long service as an officer. He was good at it. It had become something he hated though and couldn't wait to get away from. As hard as it was to be a captain of a cargo ship, he did enjoy it more. Leaving it to do something like, going back to law enforcement felt like a death sentence. "I would agree with you."

The endless white of the mists dissipated from view, giving way to the faint sparkle filled darkness of space.

Faith's hands moved quickly from one set of controls to another as she got her bearings and locked in where they needed to get to. The computer plotted the course and found no obstacles in getting there. She was slightly disappointed. "Destination locked. In route." She hit the thrusters for max speed. Both occupants on the bridge sank slightly into their seats.

Roger saw the side of her face get that slight happy thrill look, like a drug addict getting a long awaited fix. He just shook his head. He risked an active scan of the system. Information came trickling in at first. Scanners were already flagging areas of unusual amounts of debris. Information started to come flooding back to him.

The military had external communications locked down and rerouted to only them. It didn't surprise him. Nearly all local communications systems were showing errors or offline. There were thousands of distress calls and emergency beacons throughout the entire system.

"Faith, do you know how much damage a typical naval fleet can inflict on a system?"

"Not without using a lot of analysis tools. Why?"

"Give it a shot in the dark. Assume a large fleet, the largest Corvus would ever deploy."

Faith looked back at him as if to say, really? She turned back facing forward in her seat and thought about the request. She rolled her eyes as she considered the multitude of variables that would factor into it. She shook her head and decided to just make a guess based off what she knew from the top of her head. "Guessing something like an invasion fleet that was used to quell the uprising at Yari... That was a large enough fleet to take on a populated system."

"How long would it take a fleet like that to completely wreck a system?"

"Maybe a month... if locals could put up a bit of a fight. That's just a educated guess. Why are you asking this?"

Roger was still pooling information. "Based on what I've seen from escape pods and distress calls..." He kept looking to see if he could find anything newer or older. He gave up. "The alien fleet managed to wreck this system in just three days."

She laughed. "There is no way any one fleet could wipe out

a system in just three days! There is too much space to cover!"

"Prove me wrong. Do an intelligence analysis when you get a chance."

"Okay... I'll look for what you obviously missed someplace. I'll piece the intel together and prove you don't know what your talking about." She rolled her eyes and muttered to herself, "Three days. There is no way."

Roger tried to contact Rosalie and Cesar. There was no response. Bethany's Hope sped on to the target moon, anyway. He went to his new quarters on the Bethany's Hope and put on his armor.

Sonja had occupied her droid and was now sitting in one of the pilot half pits. Faith had gone to suit up and grab her pistol. Randall, and his pet droid Sparky, were also getting ready to join the party. The lack of body armor for everyone and personal weapons wasn't helpful.

Course he wasn't sure if he could fully trust them all with a weapon at the moment either. He had no idea if Randall even knew how to use a weapon. Faith could potentially shoot him in the back when no one was looking. The only real hope in this scenario was that Sonja hadn't felt anything dark just before dropping into this system.

Roger returned to the bridge to monitor their progress. Faith was back in one of the pilot's spots beside Sonja. When they were within thirty minutes of the lunar outpost, Roger's scanners detected movement in one of the debris fields. Roger had already switched sensors to only pickup passively and avoid tipping anyone off that they were there. He kept a close eye on the movement.

The ships were not broadcasting IDs, which didn't make Roger feel any better about it. They were too far away to pick up enough information passively to even determine the ship types. Whatever it was that was moving, it was still hanging close to the debris.

When they got within ten minutes of the lunar outpost, the movement in the debris field changed directions and began heading their direction. Roger hoped they weren't military ships running silent.

Roger made a ship wide announcement, "Looks like we have company heading our way. No contact with Rosalie or

Cesar. We need to make this fast."

Faith came up on the lunar outpost hard and fast. Roger tensed up, feeling as though she might just plow right into the structure. He noticed that it looked like the station had taken several shots from what only could have been ship weapons.

Faith feathered up the movements at the last moment and gently touched down on what used to be a landing pad. Normally an energy field would encompass enough of the ship to do cargo and personnel transfers. Roger took notice that no field engaged, no lights could be seen from anywhere that they could see.

Roger and Faith didn't waste time getting out of their seats and running down the corridors and stairs to where Randall and Sparky were waiting. Randall and Faith both hit their switch to their small backpacks. An energy bubble formed around them, sealing in the air and recycling it through the filtration ports in the backpack.

Faith pulled out her pistol. Roger pulled his as well. "I'll take lead. Open the ramp."

Randall accessed the controls for the ramp. A bluish energy shield covered what would be the opening. Seals hissed as the locks disengaged and the pistons lowered the other end of the ramp down to the ground.

Roger slowly came down the ramp. His eyes scanned the surrounding area as he made his way from the ramp to the airlock of the outpost. Roger glanced over his shoulder. Randall was close behind with Sparky. Faith was bringing up the rear, being just as watchful as he was. It was a little reassuring that she seemed to know what she was doing.

Roger accessed the control panel. Lights were out.

"I'll get it," Randall said. The man didn't have any weapon, he did however have his working outfit that Roger was sure had several dozen pockets. Randall walked up close to the control panel so that his personal bubble sealed against the wall all around it.

It was a dangerous move, Roger realized. If there was a leak on the other side of the panel, Randall could lose a fair amount of air before he could back off. He searched the edges of the plates around the switch until he found what he was looking for. He bumped one of the steel plates with his gloved fists and it popped open. He looked back at Roger. "Manual door control for emergencies. Ready?"

Roger and Faith stepped to either side of the door, just in case. Roger nodded to Randall.

With his gloved hand, he reached in and pumped a plunger. Once it had enough pressure, he twisted it. The door split apart as it snapped open. There was no gush of air. More of a drifting puff was all that was in the airlock.

The other three followed Roger in after giving him a few seconds. Randall sealed the outside door. Sparky popped out a light from his spherical body.

Randall opened up the next door. Roger stayed at the lead and moved in. Roger had his armor analyze the air. "Carbon dioxide is really high. Best keep your barriers on."

Roger went in first. The light on his helmet revealed his surroundings. The whole place was dark as a tomb. They could hear something rumbling and squealing in the distance. There were burn marks from weapon's fire all up and down the hallway. Blue fluid was occasionally found in splotches as they moved forward.

"Sounds like the generator is suffering a horrible, slow death. If it's putting out any power at all, it ain't gunna last long."

They kept moving forward. Here on the other end of the hallway he was seeing red splotches that were turning brown. He was familiar with these. "The smell in here has got to be rancid," Roger said.

"I'm starting to thing those blue ones back there might be alien." Faith said.

"That's my guess."

"Roger! Passive scans showing a dozen small ships and three larger ones incoming fast!" Sonja said.

"Great."

A man jumped out of a nearby doorway and started to charge at Roger. Roger raised his pistol. "DROP THE WEAPON NOW!"

The man had a pipe with what looked like three kitchen knives attached to the end of it. He didn't get very far in his charge. His eyes got wide as he started gasping for enough oxygen that wasn't there. He dropped the spear and collapsed to the floor.

"Was that Cesar?" Faith asked.

"No clue. We didn't actually get a look at him on the video," Roger said.

"Rosalie!?" Randall yelled.

"Randall?" a feminine voice answered softly. A weary and dirty woman stumbled out of the same doorway the man had come from. "I thought we were going to die for sure." She started crying.

"No time! Is there anyone else here? We need to leave right now!" Roger said.

"It's just us."

"Take it you don't have space packs?"

"We used them already."

Randall reached down and picked up the man that had collapsed, bringing him into Randall's bubble. The man gasped for air as he woke up with Randall's air supply. "I got you, man. Just hang tight."

Faith moved and brought the other woman into her bubble. She put the woman's arm around her neck and held her close so she didn't fall out once they were outside. "Let's move before the smell kills me," Faith said.

"Sorry," the woman said.

Roger had them go first so he could secure the door behind them. They emerged from the dead outpost and ran to the ramp.

"Roger," Sonja said, "Their too close. They look like they have raider markings."

"Raiders here to pillage the dying," Roger said, "Why am I not surprised." They reached the top of the ramp where John was waiting to help. "Sonja, get ready for a jump. Faith, leave her with John. Randall, help John get these two to medical so he can help them."

Everyone acknowledged and dispersed. Roger and Faith were on the run again, back to the bridge this time. "How do you feel about engaging in ship to ship combat?"

"Don't tease me like that unless you mean it."

She almost sounded giddy to him. "It wasn't a tease. The Pedlar's Omen has a fail safe that prevents it from mist jumping if weapons are engaged."

"Are they really that close?"

Sonja chimed in over the speakers. "Yes!"

Roger got into the captain's seat and Faith plopped down into the pilot half pit. Both of them were executing computer commands as fast as they could.

Within seconds the Bethany's Hope was secured and off the lunar surface. "Incoming transmission," Faith said as she put it on the intercom.

Roger was going to tell her to ignore it, but he was too slow.

"Cargo vessel. You are in raider space. Power down your thrusters and prepare to be boarded. Failure to comply will result in your deaths."

Roger looked at all the ships which were now identified by the ship's computer. A dozen fighters, two Invader cargo ships, and a gunship. "This might be rough." He cut off the transmission from the raiders.

He activated all the ship's weapons and prioritized the targets for the computer. He was really grateful he got that upgrade now. "Fight's on. Targets locked. Try to keep us from getting hit too much."

"Fight to the last man, or until we can run?"

"They're raiders. We take them all down."

"You surprise me again," Faith whispered.

For a bulky ship the Bethany's Hope was surprisingly agile. Roger could sense the movement of the ship. Visually it was almost enough to turn a person's stomach just looking out the bridge windows. Roger remembered something about the ship. He activated the battle bridge mode.

Heavy shutters slammed together as they sealed off the windows from outside.

"HEY," Faith yelled out, "Hard to fly-"

A visual projection appeared all around the bridge, as if the bridge itself became near transparent. All the ships could be seen and were outlined in red, having been targeted.

"YESSS!"

The visual of movement wasn't quite as bad for Roger now that he could see everything happening around him. He watched as fighters burst into flames and disappeared from tracking. He watched as the shields took several hits from a multitude of directions. The shields had only dropped to eighty-three percent though.

The Bethany's Hope was pouring out way more firepower than Roger would have dreamed. The Invader ships shields collapsed within minutes of the barrage. The cannons punched hole after hole into both of the large cargo ships. Even the gunship was struggling at not getting pounded.

Faith was doing flight maneuvers that he could hardly keep up with. It looked like the raiders were trying to escape. Faith just kept cutting them off.

The gunship exploded. Within the next few minutes, the two cargo ships were also adrift. Roger looked to see how many escape pods had been launched. Roger took a deep breath. The targeting computer had picked up every one and gunned them down. There were no survivors. Roger wasn't sure how he felt about that. He knew it was considered wrong to shoot down people that were stranded in pods. Yet, how many raiders had he killed, and then finished off in person? How was this any different?

He went into the settings for the targeting system and found the option to target escape pods. He switched it off for now.

There were no more targets for the computer to find. Roger retracted the weapons. With it, the shutter doors to the windows opened and the battle bridge mode disabled automatically.

"Ah," Faith said, "we should fly around like that all the time."

"Doesn't work without weapons being deployed."

"Sonja, jump when your ready."

"There's so much power still on this ship I don't even have to wait."

Bethany's Hope ascended to the mists.

Roger thought about the inability to jump in the midst of a fight. He wasn't sure if Randall could fix that or not. It was a phantom drive issue programmed in there for the Pedlar's Omen. One thing was for sure. The Bethany's Hope might be ugly, but she turned into an absolute monster to be reckoned with when her teeth were bared.

Everything Lost

With the flight controls transferred to Sonja, Faith turned to the pilot logs. She noted everything she could think of that happened and issues that had come up during this last flight session for Randall to adjust as soon as he got a chance.

Next, she pulled up her data collection programs and shut them down. She felt more alive than she had in years. There was nothing more for her to do here for the next several days. She climbed out of the half pit. Roger looked to be fully engrossed in whatever he was looking through. She started to walk out.

"Good job, by the way," Roger said without looking up.

"Thank you."

At first she headed to her quarters. She stopped when she realized it wouldn't work for what she needed to do. As much as she wanted the privacy, she was going to have to go without. She turned and went to the small briefing room. The layout wasn't very good, but it would at least have the equipment she needed.

She reconfigured the displays as best she could to fit her workflow. "Probably should have asked first." She stood at the front of the room surrounded by open holographic displays waiting to be filled. She loaded up some of her special analysis programs and started loading in all the information she was able to capture when sensors went active in Koba.

Locations and times started to appear on virtual maps of

the system, bringing together a picture of what might have happened and when.

Roger looked though the cargo run postings by nearly a dozen large-scale corporations in the Aldis system. There were a handful that his ship was just barely large enough to handle. Nearly all of them were to move tools and equipment to more remote places and then bring back minerals from those same places. Roger would have to be careful about the minerals. Some were so heavy that he was sure the ship couldn't get off the ground, let alone back into space.

Before he could even take any jobs, he was going to have to sort out the ID situation. Something that might be in doubt now that Rosalie probably didn't have what she needed to do it with. There was only one way to find out.

Roger closed down his terminals and headed to the medical area.

Rosalie was there laying on one of the beds while John ran a test through the computer. He must have let her shower and had her clothes cleaned. Her pants, shirt, and vest were all a little worse for wear. At least they were clean now. He could only imagine what they might have smelled like at the lunar outpost. Her red wavy hair seemed to spill out everywhere on the pillow.

"Captain," John said.

"How is she?"

"Remember, I'm not a doctor. So as far as I can tell, she's fine. I was about to medically release her."

"And Cesar?"

Cesar was sleeping two beds away.

"The computer analysis doesn't think there is going to be any long term damage. He just needs a day or so to rest and recover and he should be good to go as well."

Roger turned his attention to Rosalie. "I'm sorry we couldn't get there sooner."

"It's not your fault. We had a few more air leaks develop after you contacted us. We got just enough power back online to try and contact my home planet side. No one answered. We started to find out about all the distress beacons all over the system." She looked away from Roger to the ceiling. Tears rolled down the sides of her face. "We think everyone might be dead."

"We're heading to Aldis system. Do you have family someplace you can get to from there?"

"All my family is on Kabo. I've lost everything I've ever known." She hid her face in her hands as she sobbed.

Roger didn't know what to say that could help. Roger left to go find something he could actually fix.

Randall was in his elaborate workshop attaching some part to a mining laser setup. He spotted Roger walking in. "Hey boss! Is she a good ship or what?!"

"She is very impressive in a fight. Question though," Roger wasn't sure he wanted the answer, "are the weapons she has... legal?"

"Ehhh... they fall in a gray area. They're military grade, so some will say no. But... they are old tech and are technically grandfathered as far as legality for a salvaged ship for private use is concerned." Randall smiled big and shrugged his shoulders. "I know of a lot of ships that flirt on the edge. With this ship being in the hands of a former law enforcement officer. My guess is they will let you slide. Especially considering you probably will only use them on raiders."

Randall grabbed another part and started to mate it up to the setup. "If they ever get a whiff of you engaging in piracy, though... might as well kiss the ship goodbye."

"That shouldn't be a problem. Speaking of problems. I don't know if the reforged IDs can still happen or not."

"Got mine!"

"She did one up for you?"

"She already had one. She already had my information and did it up one day as an example for a trainee a while back. Fortunately she still had it where she could get to it. It'll activate the next time we get access to a data stream.

"Unfortunately, she doesn't know if she will be able to make anyone else one. All of her access was through that lunar office."

"So what do we do about the ship registration then?"

"Needs to be in your name. Otherwise, the legal issue with the weapons gets a bit more dicey."

Roger looked frustrated.

"Sorry, man. I don't know of anyone else that can do reforged IDs either."

"Not your fault. I'll talk to Faith and see if she has any tricks up her sleeve. If not, I'll have you transfer the ship to my name." Roger rubbed his forehead. "What do you think will be ready to sell by the time we get to Aldis?"

Randall listed off what was completed and what should be completed by the time they arrived. He also told him approximately how much they were worth. It was a good chunk of credits.

"Thank you for this ship and all of your hard work. It's beyond amazing."

"Welcome, man!" He laughed and went back to building the device.

Faith caught a glimpse of Roger slowly entering into the briefing room. She wasn't exactly looking forward to this. She kept working. The analysis that she had been working on for hours on end was near completion with the information she was able to capture.

She looked over at him. He had sat himself down in one of the chairs and was quietly watching her without a sound.

"I owe you an apology it would seem." She stopped and leaned against the podium near the center of all the displays.

"I didn't come here to gloat. I just made a snap observation in the heat of the moment. An observation that could have been wrong, hence I asked you to look. So... What did you find out?"

Her respect for him went up a notch. She had met so many under her that would gloat on the very rare occasion she was wrong. "Your snap observation was correct. I still have no idea what kind of ships the aliens had, but they hit hard and fast. Based on what I'm seeing here, I don't know that the Corvus navy can really counter it."

Roger looked stunned. "That's a pretty dire analysis."

"The Koba system is a pretty dire mess. If the other systems that have been hit by a full fleet look anything like this... then yeah, it's looking a little hopeless at the moment."

Faith just stood there looking at Roger. Roger seemed to be

looking at the data screens. Particularly the map that showed the path the fleet took through the system.

"Well," Roger said finally, "I was going to ask you if you had any ideas on how the rest of us could get reforged IDs. After what you just told me, it's probably a moot point."

Faith laughed. "I figured she wouldn't be able to reforge any IDs. She'll be lucky if she even has a job still. The contractor was based in Koba, so that's likely gone."

"Guess all of her family was on the main planet too. Born and raised there. So she's homeless now too."

"Yes, she was. So long as there isn't some surprise gap in the information gathered, it's very likely her family perished in the bombardments. She is very much a refugee in every sense of the word, with nowhere to go. Cesar on the other hand isn't quite so helpless."

"You pulled up information on the both of them?"

"Surprised you didn't."

"I've been a little busy and haven't gotten that far."

Faith crossed her arms. "Fair enough. Cesar Ramsey is a newcomer to the reforged ID scene. He's only been at it less than a year. There was a bit of a time gap in his work history. Before that he was a marine for about five hundred years before he was kicked out."

"Kicked out?"

"Seems he enjoyed his job a little too much towards the end. The military cut him loose before he became a liability. If he held a job in between the two, it was something off the records. He may have been in a warrior recovery program too. Those don't always show up in a history."

"So he might be fine, or he could be a killing machine? I will make sure we drop him off at Aldis for sure."

"He didn't have any episodes at his current job, and he didn't kill Rosalie when stress got high. I would place bets on he's not broken at the moment."

Roger thought about it. "For now, he's crashed out in the medical room. I guess we'll see how he is when he's up." Roger sighed. "Can you make reforged IDs or know someone who can?"

"My skill set is in analysis. I had people under me that could make IDs or reforge them. I'm trying to stay retired by means of death. So no, I don't know anyone anymore."

"Looks like I am out of luck then. I can't hold off without an ID by the time we reach Aldis. We need work and the ship has to be registered as soon as we enter."

Roger got up and left the room.

The ID issue was now a real concern for her as well. She legitimately didn't have the resources or full knowledge how to reforge an ID. She opted to go talk to this Rosalie lady. Perhaps she could do enough to create a temporary solution. Faith closed down all the visuals and put the setup back to the way it was as best she could remember. She then headed out to find Rosalie.

The remaining days pass quietly. Roger talked some more with Rosalie and accepted her request to remain on as a crew member for now. Having a background working station traffic control, she opted to help with communications and cargo management.

Cesar seemed to be fine. He even apologized to Roger for charging at him, thinking he was a raider. Roger was very understanding knowing how raiders treated prisoners. His plans were to depart wherever Roger landed and find a new job to move on to. It didn't break Roger's heart to hear that.

Everyone had gathered together on the bridge for the reentry. Rosalie was already checking things to make contact as soon as they could access the data stream. Randall rarely ever got to see the transition. Everything was running well, so he came to witness it first hand.

John and Cesar had no other place they needed to be, and there was plenty of space on the bridge. They sat in passenger seats at the back.

"Coming up on Aldis. Feels like it's quite the hub of activity."

"It is a commerce port," Roger said.

"Yeah, I know. I've been to those before. This feels busier than those that I've been to."

Roger immediately frowned. He started to wonder if he should be concerned. "There isn't anything dark mixed in with that, is there?"

She didn't respond immediately. "Not that I can tell."

"I would think a very large fleet wiping out a system she

would notice. Just a thought," Faith said.

"Point taken."

"Are we ready to drop then? I've found a safe spot."

"Do it."

Bethany's Hope surged forward and began its decent between realms of existence. The familiar transition from white to a star speckled darkness played out before them. Roger thought he would never tire of the surreal feeling it invoked.

"Holy crap!" Rosalie said.

Roger's traffic display lit up. Dots representing ships kept being added by the computer. "That's too many ships clustered in one system. Something isn't right here. Maybe we need to go someplace else."

"Captain," Rosalie looked at Roger, "The military is contacting us."

"Wonder if we came at a bad time. Put it through."

"This is Commander Elkins. You are hear by notified that the Bethany's Hope and all members aboard the ship are now drafted into service of the Corvus Navy. Your ship ID has been recorded and entered into service already.

"Any persons aboard your ship are now considered crew and will remain with you for the duration of your service. Any crew positions you have not fulfilled may be assigned by the Navy. Failure to comply will result in a military court marshal or being shot out of the sky.

"Report to the coordinates I'm sending you now for the planet surface. Go straight there and receive your assigned payload. Once you are fully loaded and crewed, return to space for your group assignment. This is not a drill, and this is not optional. Commander Elkins out."

Roger was irritated. "The last government job I was strong armed into didn't go so well. Not a good omen," Roger muttered.

Drafted

Bethany's Hope made its way to the planet as instructed.

"Cesar, we need someone to be the cargo manager. Are you willing to fill that? Or do you have a skill set we don't know about that you might be more suited for?"

"I can do that," Cesar started to say something else, but then stopped.

"The job is yours then. John, congratulations, your officially our medical guy."

"Can they really dictate we do this?" Rosalie asked.

Cesar laughed. "Oh yeah. We all just became government property. In circumstances of extreme emergency it's a little scary what they have authority to do."

Rosalie was on the comms with planetary traffic control. She fed the information to Roger and Faith as they were given instructions to follow.

Bethany's Hope descended into the atmosphere of the reddish planet. The sun was high as they flew over the top of a red and orange forest that seemed to stretch to the horizon. Scattered among the trees were occasional clearings. When Roger looked as they got closer to the clearings, he saw the structures were a long way below the tree canopy. Roger guessed the trees must have been nearly two hundred meters tall.

The Bethany's Hope circled around one of the clearings as instructed before coming in for a landing. It touched down on something like a hardened concrete surface. Roger noticed this ship was a bit more stiff when it leveled off than the Pedlar's Omen.

"Now what?" Roger asked.

"If this is like a typical military operation," Cesar said, "it's hurry up and wait. I always hated logistics missions."

"Confirmed," Rosalie said, "we just got told to hold our position and remain on the ship until they get to us."

"So I'm a prisoner on my own ship?"

"Welcome to military life," Cesar said as he got up. "I guess I'm off to my new post. So excited."

Roger hated this new loss of freedom already. Working for the prison was bad enough. Being told when to be on shift and when he could go home. His life was nearly owned by them. His jaw clenched. This was already worse.

He pulled up the jobs board that he had looked at before. It was wiped clean. He did a query for local news and found Corvus as a whole, had declared a state of emergency. Resources were pouring in to shore up defenses around the systems that had already been lost. Rumors were flying that the navy had already suffered substantial losses.

Roger questioned his sanity at getting into this business. This isn't how he imagined his life would go. The same went with his current crew. He had imagined doing interviews and hiring people that had the skills for what was needed and wanted to do this kind of work. Sonja had been taken on as a favor, Faith had tried to kill him then ended up being his pilot, Randall was probably tied to the ship for life if nothing more than for sentimental reasons, and so on. Roger wrestled with the ideal, as apposed to how it was playing out.

Speaking of thing not turning out. He realized the military could acquisition the mining package and other parts that Roger had Randall make up. He got up and quickly went to rectify that and make sure those things got stashed away as spare parts for the Bethany's Hope.

"About bloody time!" Roger could hear Faith say in the distance. "Captain! Officer is finally here and wants to speak to you outside," she yelled.

Roger dumped his eating utensil onto the plate of half eaten food and took one last drink to wash everything down. Two days of just sitting around. Roger was in no hurry to meet the guy. He gradually made his way to the ramp and accessed the controls to drop it. The fresh air carried the smell of woods. It made him wish he had things opened up sooner.

The yellow sun was just starting to go down. No sooner had he stepped onto the ramp and started to walk down it he heard a voice that rubbed him the wrong way. "Come on! I don't have all day!"

Roger's teeth clenched. He really wanted to accuse the man of wasting two days of his. He held his tongue and glared at the man as he folded his arms across his chest. The officer was accompanied by a marine in full battle armor and weapon at the ready. He seemed to be put a little on edge by Roger's stance. Roger could imagine there may have been altercations with other captains that hadn't kept their anger in check.

"Are you the captain of this relic piece of junk?" the scrawny officer asked.

"I am."

"Give me your name and ID number."

Roger really didn't want to. He thought about giving a false name for a split second. Something warned him not to do it and to be honest. "Roger Vance." He rattled off the ID number. So much for any chance at staying dead.

"Cargo capacity?"

Roger gave him the specs of what the ship could carry. The man got frustrated with something. He banged on the side of his data pad. "Come on!" the scrawny officer looked up at Roger, "Looks like my device doesn't like your ship either." He looked back down at it, "Guess I just needed to pass on my equipment's displeasure and it's back to working."

The man went back to tapping and swiping at his very large datapad. He stopped at one point and looked at Roger. Disdain was all over his face. It made Roger just want to reach out and deck the man square in the face. He knew the type. Full of pride in their position, thought they were so important no matter how insignificant the job. When a real fight came, they were among the first to turn and run to save their own skin.

The man sighed and looked up at his ship before looking back down at the data pad. "Based on your bad attitude and your pathetic relic you have the gall to call a real ship, I'm going to have to diversify your cargo to cut our losses if your ship rattles apart before you get to the destination."

More tapping and sliding. The marine risked a glance at what was being assigned. At one point he started chuckling. The scrawny man smirked when he realized the marine knew. Roger took that as a bad omen.

He finished. "Cargo will arrive first thing in the morning. Get it stowed and get this scrap heap off my landing pad. Control will direct you where you need to take it next."

"What time?"

"Just be ready very early and don't keep the crew waiting like you made me wait."

Roger just stood there, jaw set. The scrawny man turned and walked off to the next ship. The marine wasn't so quick to turn his back to Roger.

"Come on, Franklin!"

The marine turned and jogged to catch up with the officer.

Roger waited until the man was far away. He was trying to cool his jets before returning to the crew. At least now they would be doing something. He wasn't sure if it would be a good thing or not. He walked up the ramp. He considered leaving it open for the fresh air. He decided against it just in case some critter decided to take the invitation.

The crew had gathered around the ramp area. All except Faith. That made Roger curious.

"What a jack wagon," Cesar said as Roger secured the ramp.

"Cargo will be here sometime tomorrow morning. He wouldn't say when."

Faith came walking down the corridor. "They won't be here until almost noon."

"How did you manage to find that out?" Roger asked.

Faith just smiled. "Would you like to know more?"

Roger just looked at her and chuckled. He thought back to the officer banging on his data pad. He smiled, "I would."

"What he said about a diverse cargo load out was true enough. We'll be hauling food, basic medical supplies, tools, and a wide range of equipment parts. We are also transporting a platoon of marines that have been flagged for Reaper Duty."

"Ah, man!" Cesar said. He groaned.

Roger guess this must have been what the marine earlier chuckled about. "What's special about Reaper Duty?"

Cesar answered. "It's a basically a take out the trash unit. They are soldiers who have behavior issues so bad the military would like to get rid of them. So they get assigned to a Reaper Duty unit. It's pumped up as a special elite thing that you have to be hand picked for, but unofficially it's a death sentence. They send those units constantly out to the front lines where survival isn't expected to be very good. The only good thing about them is, the ones that have survived long enough to be around a while, are so battle hardened they tend to get business taken care of."

"Great." Roger rubbed his forehead. "Anything else?"

Faith smiled at Roger, "Our impatient and annoying little logistics officer is about to find out later tonight that he has been reassigned effective immediately. He will be shipping out first thing in the morning on another ship for front line combat duty. He just happens to be tagging along with us to whatever system we are going to."

Roger wanted to laugh, but the gravity of what she just said was unnerving. "You're scary."

"They really need to work on their security protocols." Faith said as she crossed her arms. "At any rate, we have been assigned to the flagship Victor VII. Destination and time of departure is still classified."

Roger gave everyone directions to get prepared for the next day. He talked with Faith in private to see if it was possible to get a few items assigned to the Bethany's Hope, now that they were technically a part of the military.

Crossfire

Fully loaded, complete with a pack of warriors that sounded more like a rowdy group of bar hoppers, Bethany's Hope waited for instructions on where to go next. Roger normally left the door to the bridge open for everyone to easily get to where they needed to go. He couldn't take the noise anymore. The bridge door slid shut.

"Thank you!" Faith said. "They're like a bunch of juveniles."

Rosalie answered the call from the control tower and passed on the information received. Everything matched up with what Faith had pulled from the military information system. Roger gave the command and the Bethany's Hope lifted off and went into space.

As they got to space, Roger was surprised to see so many ships scattered all over the place. It looked like remotely organized chaos to him. Roger worried about having a collision. He looked over at Faith. She didn't look a bit concerned, as if this was just another day.

The Victor VII flagship came into view. The ship was so massive the Bethany's Hope was mere gnat flying up to a human in comparison. Other large warships were stationed in a bubble pattern all around the flagship. What must have been hundreds of cargo ships, ranging from very large to smaller ships like his, were sandwiched in between the warships and the flagship.

"We're among the last to join the formation," Rosalie said.

Faith pulled the ship up into a spot near five other cargo ships that were clustered together.

Roger was getting nervous. "Sonja, do you even know how to stay in a formation like this in the mists? This is awfully close."

Faith laughed. "That's not how this works captain."

"Enlighten me. Because at this point it looks like a wreck waiting to happen!"

"We won't be using our phantom drive. That will all be handled by the Victor VII. The Victor VII will create a travel bubble that encompasses every last one of these ships around it. That way we all stay together and end up together in the same place."

"Sonja still needs to use the thrusters to keep up though, doesn't she?"

"No, we have to submit to a tether just like a tug would use to rescue a stranded ship. They will use our thrusters to keep everyone in position."

"So we have to give them flight control of our ship too?"

"Parts of it, yeah."

Roger shook his head. "What could possibly go wrong with that."

"I can give you a list if you would like."

"No thanks. I'm already paranoid right now thinking about them using my ship and crew as a meat shield to save their own skins."

Faith brought the ship to a complete stop and gave tether control over to the flagship. She looked back at Roger. "A meat shield! I've never heard of someone using a tactic like that. That would be very devious. Not to mention a quick way to make enemies of your own people."

"If the chances of survival were slim against an enemy that was powerful enough to wipe out a system in just three days, things change. When your fighting for your very life, sometimes what is considered unethical goes right out the window."

Faith and Roger just looked at each other for a long moment. "That's a very dark place to go."

Roger leaned forward. "What was once trapped in the Nedra system has gotten loose, and they have a powerful weapons stash. It's very much like inmates are ransacking the prison, killing everyone in their way. When the bloodshed, the screaming, intense fighting, ambushing all gets going... it gets really dark rather quickly."

Faith turned back around. She held the palms of her hands in front of her and looked at them. She clenched them into fists and let them rest on her lap as she looked down.

Roger wasn't sure what she might be thinking. Perhaps his thoughts did go too far down the dark path. He had been there many times before. He realized those around him might not. He thought about officers over the years that couldn't handle it and ended up quitting. Some mentally cracked under the stress of fighting. He didn't wish that on his crew.

He looked over at Rosalie. She just stared at the screen. Roger thought she might even be shaking a little.

"I'm sorry. I didn't mean to make everyone believe that we are all going to be killed in some horrible way." He wasn't sure if that even helped. "It just that I've been through a few things and I don't wish anything like it on any of you."

Roger heard Rosalie try to hide a sniff as she wiped her eyes. Faith was stoic, deep in her own thoughts.

The ship's intercom sounded off making Rosalie jump in her seat. "Attention all ships. Tethering of all vessels is complete. Mist pilots, you will not be engaging your drives for this flight. I repeat, do not engage your phantom drives for this flight. We will depart in about twenty minutes."

Roger rolled his eyes. He would keep his mouth shut and not say anything he didn't dare to have widely known. If they had access to some of the flight controls and now intercoms, what else did they have access to? Would they be listening in too? He would have to ask either Faith or Randall about that and how to rectify it if that was the case. The ship was all he had at the moment to call home.

Over the next several days, in the stillness of the mists, Faith and Sonja traded out manning the pilot's seats, just in case there was a mishap. The last thing he wanted was to be 'dropped' by the flagship and come face to face with an asteroid or something and no one ready to dodge it.

The Marines mostly kept to themselves in a loud, boisterous way. Somehow they had managed to sneak some booze aboard and were having a roaring good time. Roger didn't care so long as they didn't get into anything they weren't supposed to.

It only happened once towards the beginning of the trip. One of the strongest of their members got to poking around Sonja's companion droid closet door and was making an effort to get inside. Roger ended up in an altercation with him and ended up ruthlessly tasing him. Some of his comrades had run to find out what was happening. Roger gave them fair warning if they didn't stay put, he would interpret their actions as a threat to his crew and ship. Being tasered would be the least of their problems next time.

They surprised him by willingly yielding and respecting his wishes.

Roger looked in on the other crew. They kept themselves busy working on the ship. Randall had built the security closet that Roger had asked for. During one of the night periods when most of the marines were sleeping, Roger, Faith, and Randall unloaded the special crates that an unsuspecting scrawny officer had procured for them. Roger took some time and trained Randall on how to use one of the laser shotguns.

"Dropping out of the mists in about 10 minutes," the intercom announced.

Roger made his way to the bridge. Faith was already in the pilot's seat. Rosalie walked in and took up her station for communications. Sonja had put her companion droid body into its charging and maintenance dock in her closet.

It was somewhat early in the morning. The marines were getting restless and wanted some action. Even if it was a dull patrol. Anything besides being cooped up in a ship. Roger was ready to be rid of them too.

The mists began to fade and all the ships reappeared in the same formation and seemingly locked in place as they descended back into the physical realm. The moment she could, Faith kicked off the tether. Roger pulled information from the data stream as soon as the tether was disengaged, fearing the military might cut it off as soon as they were settled.

Rosalie was very busy coordinating directives from the military and making arrangements with their first stop in the system.

"Captain, we've been instructed to drop off the cargo at Toraloo station first, then take the marines planet side." Rosalie passed on approach and docking information to Faith.

"Understood. Looks like we are in the Dela system, folks. Let's get this done," Roger said.

The Bethany's Hope spun and shot forward out of the formation and on to the space station. Faith had got there so fast they were near the head of the line for docking. The entire fleet of ships began to disperse. The smaller ships took off in groups to avoid collisions. The warships assembled in new formations and began to move about. Faith had learned from one of the marines that this was the second of three groups that would be coming here to take up defensive positions.

Toraloo station was in a far orbit around the planet of Dela. The flagship had dropped them just behind and between the planet and the station. As soon as Bethany's Hope was docked the marines helped Cesar with getting the cargo off the ship. It was more to speed up the process of getting them to the planet's surface than a real desire to help. Regardless of their motivation, Cesar didn't mind. Cargo Master wasn't exactly a job he wanted, anyway.

Station bay personal received all the containers they were expecting and cleared Bethany's Hope for departure. Faith was right on it, pulling the ship away from station and speeding their way to the planet.

"You realize they're going to make us cue up once we get to the planet's orbit?" Rosalie asked Faith. "Not sure what your screaming hurry is."

"We drop off the marines, then convince whoever is running logistics to let us go and get another run. A lot can happen between here and wherever they send us."

"Does your plan include telling me what your thinking of doing?" Roger asked, "Or where you just going to commandeer my ship?"

"I was planning on telling you as soon as we got a minute. Preferably after we dropped off the additional ears."

Roger nodded. Her paranoia was understandable.

"We're being ordered to slow it down and be more careful," Rosalie said.

"Roger, something is coming! I can feel them!"

Roger made sure all sensors were activated and recording. A small ship, black and thin with three sphere orbs evenly spaced apart, dropped into physical space between the flagship and the planet. "There!" Roger said, "I see it!"

The alien ship shot forward at incredible speed. Once it was well ahead of the main flagship, the three spheres put out a green glow.

Roger started to breathe a little heavier.

Very large ships started to drop into physical space all around them. Weapons fire from what could only be alien battleships scattered through the Corvus fleet targeting the larger ships.

"GET TO THE PLANET! GET TO THE PLANET!" Roger yelled. He activated the battle mode. All the internal doors of the ship closed. The heavy shutters slammed closed and the virtual scene appeared.

Small ships like fighters poured out of an alien carrier in the hundreds. The cargo ships scattered in obvious panic. The Corvus flagship weapons were returning fire in a target rich environment.

Roger set the targeting computer to only shoot at fighter sized ships that were pursuing or in the way. Bethany's Hope was getting sprayed with weapons from shots intended for it and shots that had missed their target. The fighters seemed to pair up in groups of six. They were very small, very fast, and fortunately they didn't hit too hard. Though with six at a time shooting, the damage added up quickly.

Cargo vessels were exploding left and right. Corvus fighters had launched and were now in the mix. The larger ships were maneuvered to get the best shots they could and still not get pounded themselves.

Faith struggled to make a lot of progress towards the planet while keeping them from getting bombarded with hits.

"She's a blockade runner. Not a fighter. She'll take the hits. Run for it!" Roger said.

Faith conceded and refocused on getting to the planet and avoiding debris on the way there. The shields were now taking much more of a beating. The aft weapons of the ship strongly discouraged followers and made them earn their hits.

The ship's back jolted violently downward as a battleship

shot hit them. The lights flickered, and the sound was so loud it took him a few seconds for his ears to stop ringing.

Faith fought with the controls and had them heading back toward the planet again. "Lost number two thruster. Number one is 60% power."

Roger had a moment of dread, "Sonja? You still with us?"

"Yes! It didn't get me."

Roger looked at the list of systems and sensors that had stopped responding at the rear of the ship. "Randall?"

"Yes sir."

"We're heading for the planet for cover! Be ready to work on thrusters so we can get the hell out of here again."

"I saw that. Will do."

Roger watched as three larger Corvus warships fell to the gravity of the planet. They were completely torn to shreds. Their lights, thrusters, and weapons had gone dark. The other warships didn't seem to be fairing too well either. The flagship was putting up a good fight.

Roger glanced over at Rosalie. She seemed to be frozen. He could only imagine all the screaming and desperate calls for help that were flooding the comms.

There were just too many enemy ships. The Aliens seem to had suffered only one large ship loss. Some mid sized alien ships were moving in on Toraloo station. One of the alien battleships that had finished off a Corvus warship was taking up orbit around the planet and bombarding the surface. A few more mid sized ships joined.

"Faith put us on trajectory with one of those Corvus warships that are about to crash to the planet's surface. We'll use it for cover and maybe pickup any survivors."

"Yes, sir."

The closer they got to the planet, the fewer fighters seemed to be interested in them. Roger could only guess why they lost interest in shooting them out of the sky. Maybe the aliens figure they had essentially been shot down, or they would just bombard them from orbit after they landed.

"Try to make it look like we are crash landing on the surface if you can."

"That won't be hard."

Faith managed to trail one of the downed battleships.

As they got to the atmosphere, the battleship turned into a fireball leaving a trail of debris. Faith had hung back a way to give the dead ship enough time to fully impact the surface and settle before attempting to 'crash' next to it. Several pieces of debris hit the ship despite Faith's efforts to dodge.

The battleship plowed into the side of a large hill overlooking a valley of jungle. The explosive force of all that mass was impressive to see and feel as it rattled the ship like a surface bomb went off. Dirt and stone flew through the air, and the dust slowly began to settle.

Faith barreled her way right in nearby, just up the hill. She wasn't able to feather the landing as nicely as she had before and hit the ground rather hard. She seemed to hang her head in shame.

"Your landing was very convincing. Well done." It probably wouldn't help a pilot's pride in soft landings, but maybe his words would take a little of the sting away.

Death Toll

Roger left the weapons systems on and changed the targeting to only shoot at any alien ships that came too close. The laser cannons would be less effective in atmosphere, anyway. No point in putting on a light show if the enemy wasn't close enough.

"Faith, keep us ready to launch just in case something comes to investigate."

"Will do."

"Rosalie, for now, maintain radio silence. I don't imagine anyone is coming to help and I don't want to give away our position as a survivor."

"Okay."

There was a thundering boom as debris from space crashed down nearby. The ship slightly shook from the impact to the ground.

Roger got up to go address the marines. He wasn't really sure what would happen with them at this point. All of them were sorting through their gear in what looked like getting ready for a fight. One of them noticed Roger as soon as he entered the main cargo area. "Were we shot down, captain? Guessing from the massive explosion, we didn't make it to Aldra Base."

"My guess is any city or base has been, or will be shortly, hit by orbital bombardment. We're shot up pretty bad but, still flyable. We've put down next to one of the Corvus battleships that went down. That's the explosion you heard. So what are your orders to do from here?"

The man laughed and looked over to one of the other men. "Brogan, you know what that means don't ya!"

The man called Brogan rolled his eyes. "Yeah, lucky me."

The rest of the marines laughed.

Brogan looked at Roger and squinted his eyes. He pointed a finger at him. "I might be field promoted to sergeant of this motley band, but he," Brogan shook his finger at Roger, "is a drafted captain of the ship we are currently assigned to. So according to regs, he's in charge."

There were some groans of disapproval. One of them piped up, "Do you even have any military experience captain?"

Roger seized the opportunity, "No, none at all."

"That might be," another one said, "That chick said he was a prison cop. Supposedly has a high body count and keeps his skills up capping raiders. Is that true captain?"

Roger really didn't want to answer. "I'm not qualified to lead a bunch of marines."

"That's too bad," Brogan said, "Just like I don't have a choice in field promotion, regs is regs. You're our commanding officer now."

Roger had colorful and inappropriate words storm through his mind. Most of the marines seem to watch him, making judgments.

"So what are your orders... sir," Sgt Brogan asked.

Roger couldn't think of a way out of being saddled with this. How do you argue with a bunch of armed marines? There wasn't time for a bunch of arguing anyway, so he gave up.

He leaned on his experiences as an officer and came up with a plan to keep them busy with something useful. "We need time to repair the ship. Secure the immediate area. Once that's complete, start a search for survivors on the battleship next to us. Secondary priority is to secure any weapons, medical supplies, or anything of critical value that might keep us alive. Food would be a good find if you want to keep eating. Don't go anywhere you might not be able to get yourselves back out of and be ready for immediate evac in case trouble comes our way."

There were some nods of approval.

"You heard the man. Let's get cracking," Brogan said.

Roger went to go find Randall. He found him and John in the workshop putting parts on a hover cart.

"Hey," Randall said, "Just got back from lookin at the thrusters. Number two is a gonner for now. I need at least ten hours to patch up number one. There is no way we are going to be able to buy the parts to rebuild number two. We'll need raw resources for it."

"I'm going to venture a guess that the aliens won't hang around for more than a few days. If we don't get caught, there should be enough debris for us to pull from. If we can stay put here, you could get what you need from the downed battleship."

"Will cost me more time, but yeah."

"I'll see about putting Cesar on that task. You work on getting thruster one back up."

"You got it, boss."

Roger found Cesar and put him to work pulling salvage from the battleship. Roger switched between helping Cesar to get started, then transitioned to helping Randall by breaking down the scrap in the small refinery. The day seemed to pass by for all of them quickly. Debris was still raining down in spurts as far as the eye could see. Sometimes it impacted near them. No survivors were found aboard the battleship. Some supply crates were being recovered.

"Captain! We have incoming!" Faith announced over the intercom.

Roger started to run to the bridge. He came to the cargo area on his way. "Get everyone back here now! We have incoming!"

The marine got on his secured radio and let the sergeant know.

Roger got to the bridge and plopped himself down in his chair. "What can you tell me?" He was pulling up information screens as quickly as he could.

"It's a smaller ship. About our size. Doesn't look like it's a warship, more like a sort of cargo or dropship, maybe. It's not moving that fast."

Roger finally had it pulled up. "Looks like it's not going to pass over us either."

Sergeant Brogan ran to the bridge. "Marines are all close to the ship. Any orders, sir?"

"Not sure what this alien ship is doing yet. It may just pass close by and not see us."

The closer the ship got, the more information became tied to it on the projected battle display of the bridge. Roger pulled up a large 3D topographical hologram in front of him that plotted the ship as a red dot slowly descending to the surface of the landscape.

"Looks like they are coming in for a drop. Probably there," Brogan pointed to spot on the 3D map. Roger pulled up new virtual screen and a camera and focused it down in the valley where Brogan had pointed. For a jungle that was probably as best as could be expected for a natural clearing.

The alien ship slowed even more and approached the site. Two long wriggly things ejected from the back of the ship and disappeared below the tree level into the clearing. The alien ship pulled up and circled away from the downed battleship.

"Requesting permission to send a squad to that spot and get recon on alien activity."

"Is that something you would normally be sent to do?"

"This is what we do. Normally against our own kind. The alien thing should make things exciting."

"I'm not sure I share your sentiment about exciting. Permission granted."

Brogan laughed and walked off the bridge and started hollering at the other marines.

"The alien ship is off scope." Faith announced.

Roger took a guess that it might take the marines about twenty minutes or so to get there on foot, depending on how much gear they packed with them. He heard a bit of commotion coming from the cargo bay. Roger rolled his eyes. "Guess I'm going to go find out what's going on in there."

He got to the cargo bay and found men rushing equipment to the other side of the ship to the storage areas. Roger followed in their direction, crossing the midsection of the ship into one of the storage rooms.

"Here it is!" one of the marines yelled.

"What are you guys doing?" Roger asked.

The marine that had hollered hit a switch that was hidden

behind a panel. A large section of the wall slid open revealing old style monitors and a bunch of embedded equipment he wasn't sure what it was. "I told you this thing was an old military ship. The room is missing a bunch of terminal desks that normally go with it. But we can use the monitoring and relay equipment we brought!"

"How long?" Brogan asked.

"Give me five minutes and I'll have her up and running."

"What up and running?" Roger asked.

Brogan came over to him. "Looks like you have a command ops relay setup. Most of one, anyway. You holding out on us, sir?"

"I had no idea this was even here. I haven't had the ship that long. I thought this was just another storage room. So what exactly is all this equipment I'm seeing?"

"It's a military command setup. Small one for sure, but it'll work just fine for what we need. It uses the ship's communications equipment to interface with the body cameras and encrypted radios on each soldier. They become the eyes and ears for those running the operation here on the ship. Everything they say, see, and do is recorded. I'm also sending out a couple field cameras for them to hang on a couple trees. If that drop ship comes back after the guys come back, we'll still be able to see what is happening."

"That I understand. They have a similar setup for prisons. I was normally the guy on the ground though."

The marine hooked up all the portable equipment the marines had brought with them to the equipment on the wall. Within just a few minutes, everything was powered up and running. Holographic monitors and virtual terminals were up and running. Roger caught the marine's name was Davis.

"Jefferson, light yourself up, man!"

"Hey hey hey," a voice said. A helmet cam started panning around to the other marines. "You got me?"

"Loud and clear," Davis said. "Tilly, your up!"

Tilly responded, then Blyth, and finally Ratliff.

"Alright, it's party time," Sgt Brogan said. "Cpl Tilly, get your team moving. Not much daylight left."

"Sir, yes sir," Came the reply.

Roger watched as the four men departed and headed over to

the clearing area. The jungle was fairly thick with vegetation, which impeded their progress. Despite that, the men were in very good shape and got near to the site just before the sun started to get low. As they got closer, they moved more slowly. One of them reached a place where he could see the edge of the clearing.

They had split up into pairs. Each pair had a field camera. They crept up on the opening.

Roger looked carefully. "I'm not seeing either one of whatever that was that dropped out of the ship in that clearing."

"Me either," Sgt Brogan said, "Men, get the cameras hung. Search the perimeter. Watch your backs."

The men acknowledged with hand signals. Two more visual and audio feeds were added to the display setup. "Got them both," Davis relayed to the men.

Again they acknowledged with hand signals before beginning to look for the two items dropped by the alien ship. Their movement was slow, measured, and cautious.

"Alien ship is returning!" Faith said over the intercom.

"Does it look like it's coming back to the same spot or another one?" Roger asked.

"Same trajectory and speed. I'd say it's coming back to the same spot."

Roger looked to Brogan. "Men, you got that same incoming ship. Looks like it's coming for seconds. Duck and cover." Brogan hollered to the other two squads, "Suit up. Recon might need rescuin!"

Roger could hear them scramble, reattaching equipment and checking weapons.

There was commotion on the screens. Roger caught a glimpse of something slithering out of view. The men saw it too and brought their weapons to ready. The thing popped up out of the foliage like a pole with arms.

The men fired their laser rifles at it. The alien fired the weapon in its hands at the two men. The skinny alien slithered out of the way before it could be hit. Five metal rods stuck into the upper body armor of Jefferson. A sixth one also stuck through his neck. He dropped to his knees, unable to breathe.

Ratliff kept up his firing into the brush where the thing had gone. His energy clip was spent. He dropped it and was about to slam another one in. The serpent like creature leaped up into the air and spread wings. It was up above Ratliff when it shot off several more metal spikes. Two of them found gaps in the armor. Ratliff fell.

"Those damn things fly!" Roger whispered.

"Tilly, Blyth, fall back if you can. They're like serpents. They can fly and have weapons. Ratliff and Jefferson are down."

Green laser shots erupted all around Tilly and Blyth. They returned fire as they tried to hot foot it out of there. Blyth got seared in the right arm and right leg by the enemy weapon. He fell to the ground screaming in pain. Tilly kneeled down beside him and fired off a barrage of laser bolts. He did a combat reload and kept up the fire. The green bolts stopped firing.

Tilly hoisted Blyth up and the two of them made a hobbling run for it. Metal rods pierced the flesh of one of Tilly's legs. The two marines fell to the ground, both of them were screaming in pain.

The alien dropship roared as it lowered into the clearing. Roger watched the field cameras as the ship slowed to a stop and the back opened up. Out of the back of the vessel stepped out what looked like red-haired men. Only these beastly looking men were easily six meters tall. Their hands looked unusual for a typical human hand and their heads were a bit more oblong at the back.

Roger glanced at the other monitors of the fallen men. The cameras that were still functional showed the men being dragged along the ground. Tilly and Blyth were still yelling out in pain.

The giants shouted in a language that just sounded violent in nature. Their clothing seemed to be like a primitive leather type coverings. They pulled out of the ship five large crates that looked so large and heavy, Roger wasn't sure humans could move them. So far there were six of the giants. After the last crate was pulled from the ship, the back door sealed up and the thrusters fired to start gaining altitude.

The serpent creatures dragged the four men into the clearing and dropped them off near the crates. They seemed to communicate with the giants briefly before taking off into the air after the ship. The serpent creatures were able to catch up to the ship and disappeared into it. The giants gathered around the four men. Roger, Brogan, and Davis watched with their eyes glued to the screen to see what would be the fate of the fallen warriors. What they watched was horrifying.

Davis lost it and turned his head to puke on the floor.

Roger left, "Randall!"

"Ya boss?"

"How much time before that thruster is fixed?"

"Bout an hour."

"We may not have an hour. Button it up unless you want to be eaten alive by aliens."

"Think I'll pass on that."

Brogan wasn't far behind. "Pack yer bags!" he yelled at the other teams, "Looks like we ain't stayin! Get them sentry guns up and loaded. These aliens ain't no joke."

"What about Tilly's team? We just going to leave them behind?" one of the marines asked.

"There's nothin left to save of them."

Snared

Roger got to the bridge and pulled up his screens. It took him a few minutes to figure out, but he managed to find the camera feeds from the clearing and he pulled those up as well. He watched.

The giant beings were in some sort of discussion. They could barely be heard speaking above the noise of the jungle. Even their language had a harsh and violent tone. The group looked in the direction of the cameras up the hill to the crashed battleship. There was a bit of hand waving and maybe arguing. One of them pointed to the large hillside on the opposite side of the valley from the battleship.

They seemed to be in agreement. Five of them each picked up a container and slung them over their backs. They made their way through the trees like it was tall brush. They disappeared from the camera's view.

"Looks like we might be good for the night," Sgt Brogan said.

Roger practically jumped in his seat. He took a second to get his wits back together. "I'd guess your right. Although I wouldn't be surprised if they start getting to know the surroundings soon. I wouldn't put it past them to investigate the battleship tomorrow either. Some of them seemed interested in it before they left."

"Setup base camp. Sweep the area. Investigate the ship. If they act similar to humans, that's a good bet."

Roger pulled up the intercom, "Randall?"

"Ya boss?"

"Looks like you may have a few hours to spare. We're going to try and hold out until morning."

"Only need little more than a half hour and she'll be done." Roger acknowledged.

The remaining marines kept watch while the crew tried to rest for whatever the next day would bring. Aside from the occasional curious critter, the night was quiet. Roger's mind had a hard time letting go of questions. Why had the aliens dropped off these giants? Would the serpent things be back for them before they left the system? Were they left here to infiltrate or claim the planet? The serpent things were vicious fighters. How hard would it be to take down one of these giant things? Did the aliens leave giants behind on other habitable planets of the other attacked systems?

As morning began to take hold of the landscape, Roger finally turned his thoughts to something he could work out answers to. Reflecting on the devastation of yesterday, he remembered telling Faith to quit trying to fly the ship like a fighter and fly it like a blockade runner that it was designed to be. It was something that stood out to him and made him consider his own way of thinking about the ship.

Another thought came to the surface of his mind. I AM told him He had a ship for him and it wouldn't be what he expected. It would be what he, Sonja, and others would need. The thought came that he should not consider or utilize the vessel as just a simple cargo ship, but as it's designed purpose of a blockade runner.

Roger was starting to wonder if these thoughts were really his or not. They made sense to him, so he took them to heart. Roger took a deep breath. It meant not hiding out until the alien fleet left. They should make a run for it. Two days or more was likely too much of a risk to hang around.

Roger activated the comms for his quarters. "Sonja, are you there?"

"Yeah, I'm awake and ready."

"We need to make a run for it. It's too dangerous to hang out in this system. Are you rested up enough for that?"

"Yes. Even if we have to pop in and out several times. I'm in great shape. It's a huge help to have another pilot around and actually be able to sleep again."

Roger notified everyone on the ship to prepare to leave. Within minutes the Bethany's Hope was prepped. Faith fired off the thrusters and started the launch into space. Off in the distance, massive fires burned what remained of human settlements, ports, and bases. Black smoke billowed and overshadowed large swaths of area around them.

Occasional debris was still streaking fire across the sky. The jagged metal ripped through the jungle as they struck.

Bethany's Hope breached the atmosphere. Passive sensors picked up on several scattered debris fields near them. They headed into deeper space to get away from the planet's gravity field. Three groups of six red dots lit up and closed in on them.

"Keep running. Don't worry about them," Roger said to Faith.

"Yes, sir."

Roger changed the targeting computer to engage them if they managed to catch up. The ships were the small fighters. Laser fire showered against the Bethany's Hope, lighting up her shields. Her cannons responded in kind with disproportional heavy hits.

"Out of the gravity field," Sonja said.

Roger considered letting the canons finish. No, he thought, they were not there to engage in combat as a warship. Roger shut down and retracted the weapons. The shutters to the windows opened, and the projected display all around them shutoff. "Jump."

They made the transition to the whiteness of the mists. Sonja got away from the system as fast as she could in the hopes an alien ship wouldn't follow her.

"I know we have to have the weapons down for a jump to happen, but can Randall change the window shutters and bridge wide HUD to be on a separate system?"

Roger agreed.

"Looks like we weren't followed," Sonja said, "Back to Aldis?"

"Yes."

Several days later, Bethany's Hope dropped back into the

physical realm in the Aldis system. Roger noted that there were not near as many ships in the system as there had been when they left. There was still a strong military presence. They received orders as soon as they came into the system to land at a planet side port.

The ship made its way back to the tall forests and gracefully descended to the landing pad they were instructed to. Three large hover trucks sped to the landing pad. Roger could only image what cargo they were going to be forced to carry next. He got up and went to the ramp to find out.

The ramp lowered, letting in the fresh forest air. Roger walked down the ramp and was greeted by soldiers that were jumping out of the back of the hover trucks. They raised their laser rifles and shouted for him to get down on the ground. Roger complied, making sure to not do any sudden moves that might justify them shooting him on the spot. They cuffed his hands behind his back and kept him face down on the ground. His head was turned to the side so he could see the ship's ramp. His mind was racing, trying to figure out what they might have done wrong.

The rest of the soldiers ran up the ramp and shouted at all the others to get down on the ground as well. There was a bit of yelling and a quick brawl where the marines were in the cargo area. Roger heard a medic vehicle sound off in the distance and race it's way to the ship.

Everyone of his crew was marched out in cuffs and loaded up into the trucks. One of the marines came out with a bloody lip and a smile on his face. Sonja was the only one they couldn't and wouldn't remove. They came for Roger last. They hauled him up and shoved him roughly into one of the other trucks. He caught sight of two of the soldiers being helped down the ramp that had been hurt. The leg on one was dangling at a very wrong angle. The other had blood running down his face past his hand as he screamed about his eye.

The trucks moved out and took them into an underground facility. They were roughly pulled out and shoved down a series of hallways to place where there were solitary confinement cells. Roger was the first to be shoved into one and the door sealed shut behind him. They opened a cuff port on the door and demanded he put his hands through it.

Roger complied without saying a word. They took the cuffs off him and sealed up the door again. The room had a combination metal toilet and sink setup. For sleeping, he was only afforded a large steel platform bolted to the wall. At least the cell was clean, he thought to himself. He'd seen much worse.

For three days he sat around in that cell, choking down something that could barely pass as edible food.

A sound chimed in his cell. "Hey, you awake in there?"

"Close enough."

"Good. Make sure your appropriately dressed. You have a visitor," the officer said.

Roger sat his aching body up on the steel platform and leaned against the wall. He wasn't sure how visits worked in this place yet. A holographic image of a man appeared standing in the middle of his cell. Roger tried not to stare but struggled. The man's hair and short trimmed beard were completely gray and perhaps transitioning to white. His skin was wrinkled in different parts of his face and somewhat baggy under the eyes. His body looked like it was deteriorating.

The image looked at him. "Captain Roger Vance?"

"That's me."

"I'm Captain Dex Remy. Take it you haven't caught up with the news much given how your looking at me."

"I've been a bit busy."

The man smiled. "Scientist have been trying to figure out what has been happening to people like me since The Event. Turns out the entire human race, as far as they can figure out, is dying. Our bodies are breaking down over time. Has something to do with how old each person is. Those who were hundreds of millennial standard years old were the first to suffer the worst of it. Most of them are already dead of organ failures. It seems the older you are the faster you died of what they are now classifying as Old Age."

Roger was shocked. As if humanity didn't have enough problems to deal with at the moment.

"Enough about me. I'm here to let you know I've been appointed as your legal defender for your military court martial."

"For what?"

"Abandoning your assigned post, destruction of military property, theft of supplies, and abandoning soldiers to die on the battlefield."

"You've got to be kidding me?!"

"Unfortunately not. Oh... and I almost forgot. There is also conspiracy to overthrow the government, thanks in no small part to your pilot, Faith Jerin. Your whole crew is on trial as a single unit, which is not normal, but there is a war time provision for. Do you know of Ms. Jerin's actions?"

"Not really."

"Hmmm. I'm not sure I can use that in your favor, but I can try. Unfortunately, this is likely to be a very fast trial. Much of the evidence has already been reviewed by the court. I will continue to do as best I can."

"How many years am I looking at? I feel like someone is out to get me here."

"It's not exactly a secret that First Admiral Haman has been trying to find one of the many drafted captains and crews to make an example of to the rest. You're the first one he could find good enough dirt on to put his plan to effect. He has brought up charges serious enough to have you and your crew executed. It's believed by him that by doing this, it will instill in all the other draftees a, shall we say... more willingness to comply with orders given."

Roger rubbed his face with his hands. He wanted a shower so desperately. "And just how bad is the deck stacked against me?"

"It's not good. Your day in court is scheduled for tomorrow afternoon. Two more sessions are scheduled before then. Like I said, I will do what I can. That said, Admiral Haman has... adjusted things in a way that he is very likely to get his way. I wish I could bring you better news."

Roger let his head tip back against the wall and stared at the ceiling. The holographic image of the man disappeared. "So, this is how it's going to end then?" he whispered. His thoughts went to Sonja and what they might do to her. Dark thoughts assaulted his mind the rest of the night.

An Example

Roger was seated in the courtroom. His hands cuffed in front of him. To his left sat Randall practically taking up two seats, then Rosalie and John. On his right Faith, and Cesar. They were all cuffed, just as he was. In a row behind him were the marines he had brought back, all in cuffs as well. Half of them looked like they were ready to go ballistic the first chance they got. Roger was surprised they weren't shouting obscenities at the panel of five judges sitting at the bench facing them.

The actual lawyer that had spoken visited Roger yesterday stood at a podium in front of him. Some uniformed officer stood at another podium off to the left side, facing the middle of the room. To the right were the doors to the place. On either side of the doors were two soldiers in full combat battle armor, rifles raised towards the ceiling, ready to be brought down and shoot anyone that got out of order. Off in the corner of the room sat an officer that looked to be of pretty high rank.

Roger took a glancing look at his crew. They must have all gotten the same message he had yesterday. Faith was the only one that looked pissed off. Everyone else looked a combination of depressed and scared. Something he understood well in that moment.

Roger's lawyer turned and came close to him. He whispered. "I looked into your records. An honorable man like you doesn't deserve this. I've called in a favor. I can't promise how it will go, but it may help." The lawyer returned to the podium.

The middle officer among the five judges looked at a clock. "It's time," he said. Formalities of starting a court session commenced. The names of the judges were announced as Commanders, Wooten, Komm, Harding, Morgan, and Vulan. Eventually the charges were read off to those present.

Commander Harding looked directly at Roger. "The convening of this court has been very unusual, and as of this morning, it continues to be so. Now that we are on the record, I've been instructed to ask a few questions directly to Captain Vance."

Cpt Remy stepped aside from the podium and invited Roger to come to it. Roger stood up and stepped forward and stood there without saying a word.

"Captain Roger Vance, you are the official captain of the Bethany's Hope, correct?"

"Yes."

"Are you the captain that sent out a message on the Corvus Emergency Communications channel with regard to using a companion droid to help mist pilots with their current condition?"

Roger swallowed hard. "Yes."

"That channel is reserved for use by the Magistrate and top military officials. Where did you get access to that message channel?"

Roger didn't want to say. How would they ever believe him?

"Please answer the question, captain."

Roger was unsure how they would react. "I AM gave me the address."

Cdr Harding did as best he could to suppress a smile and laughed softly to himself.

Cdr Komm looked at Harding with a sharp look. "That's not a damn bit funny! So now this guy is some religious fanatic too!? Your devotion to that stupid religion is influencing your decision!"

Harding's smile faded. "Your anti-god devotion influences yours!"

The man sitting in the corner stood up. "ENOUGH! I don't

know who gave you those questions, but no more. Get on with it."

"Yes sir, Admiral Haman," Cdr Komm said.

The admiral sat back down. Roger thought the admiral gave off a sense that was pissed off with the world and wanted to see it all burn before him in judgment. To Roger, the five judges looked like they were getting nervous.

Cdr Harding took a deep breath. "In light of the evidence presented to us, including the new evidence from this morning, it's the decision of this court to dismiss all charges with exception to the charges that apply solely to Faith Jerin. For serious acts of treason against the Corvus Commonwealth, Faith Jerin is sentenced to death."

"WHAT!?" the admiral yelled. "What new evidence?"

Cdr Morgan answered. "New evidence was routed to us this morning that was missing from the initial submission at the beginning of this trial. All of it is valid."

"All the PERTINENT evidence was already submitted for this court. It is THAT evidence you are to base your decision," Adm Haman said. "This entire crew is guilty of treason and is to be executed!"

Cdr Wooten was trying to stay calm. "With all due respect, admiral. The evidence that was collected and submitted to this court was legal."

The admirals jaw was clenched tight. The tension in the room was palatable. "So be it." He looked at Roger with a look that said, I will get you yet.

Roger couldn't believe what he was about to say. He looked back at Faith. She looked like she was struggling to hold a lot of emotions back. He looked back at the judge in the middle. "With due respect to the court." The room suddenly got still and dead silent. "I will not leave here without ALL of my crew."

"Captain Vance," Cdr Morgan said, "You are in no position to make any sort of bargain on this matter."

"Please hear me. I'm not the one bargaining. I AM gave the Bethany's Hope to me. I AM has sent each and everyone of these crew members to serve under my command. I AM gave the solution for mist pilots. I AM gave me the message address and code to send that message out to help others. I AM has saved me, and Faith. So I'm here asking you... I AM put this ship and crew together for a purpose. Are you going to take a stand against Him in tearing it apart?"

Admiral Haman pointed a finger at Roger. "He has just threatened this court. He has said he won't leave without that traitor. What more evidence do you need for execution?"

Men could be heard running down the hallway. Four soldiers in battle armor burst into the room, much to everyone's surprise.

A holographic image of a stately man appeared in the room. Everyone in uniform jumped to their feet and held a salute. Even the marines behind Roger at least stood and bowed their heads.

The holographic image looked around the room, then walked over to the admiral. "Admiral Haman, effective immediately you are relieved of your command." He motioned to the four soldiers that had just come in the room. "Take him to his new home please."

The soldiers cuffed the admiral and escorted him out of the room. The doors closed behind him.

"Are we done recording what we need?" the holographic man asked.

"Yes sir!" Cdr Harding said. He entered in the commands to end the court session and shutoff the recording systems. "It's done, sir."

Roger's eyes got wide when he realized it was the Magistrate of the Corvus Commonwealth himself.

"Good. Now that we are off the record, I need everyone in this room to know that everything surrounding this court case is now deemed classified." He walked over to Roger. "Captain, I want to personally thank you for sending out that message about the mist pilots. We are applying that fix to all of our ships as fast as we can. Because of you, we are reestablishing our otherwise crippled navy. I also wish to commend you and the marines here for bringing back vital footage and information surrounding the aliens. We need all the help we can get, and the kind of information you brought back has been scarce at best."

The Magistrate looked down at Roger's cuffed hands. "You don't need those." He looked over to one of the soldiers,

"Come get these things off these people."

The soldiers ran to Roger and removed the cuffs. He went down the line going to Randall next.

"I've also had crews scanning your ship. I think we could really use ships like yours right now," he smiled, "with a few upgrades to make them a bit more modern. However, they are going to take some time to get built and we have a job that desperately needs done. I think you're probably the only one available at the moment that could do it right now. Before I get to that, I need to address this lady here."

The Magistrate stepped over to Faith and looked at her very carefully. Faith took a deep breath and looked up at him. "Ms. Jerin... I suspect some of my advisers may be correct in thinking you willingly put yourself in harm's way to infiltrate a very dangerous organization. I've seen some of the materials you acquired. Have you been actively trying to take down this organization?"

Roger notice a change in her, something like relief. As if maybe the Magistrate did something to give her a way out of whatever she had been doing.

"Yes, sir."

The Magistrate smiled and nodded his head. He still looked at her as if looking for something. He leaned in. "The admiral that was just here was number five."

Faith looked happy to hear that. "What about three and four?"

"We got four last week. Three is still at large."

Faith nodded that she understood. Roger took in the information to ask Faith about it later.

"My team will make sure the records are straight, that you were working on behalf of the Corvus Commonwealth in your actions. Your data helped us more than you know. Please don't take offense at this, but I really don't want you in the intelligence group right now. The captain here is the best bet to keep you on the move."

"It's good sir. I actually miss doing the piloting."

"It's settled then. Your special assignment from my office is now with him," the Magistrate pointed his thumb at Roger. He moved back to Roger. "Captain, I officially discharge you, your crew, and your ship from drafted military service. I have a favor to ask of you though.

"We're losing thousands of service men and women. It's estimated nearly a billion people have been killed by these aliens already between the five systems we've lost so far. The people that are responsible for setting you up to go to the Nedra system received a lot of critical information and alien technology before the aliens got loose. We need someone to retrieve that and bring it back to us."

"Where is it?" Roger hoped it wouldn't be in the Nedra system.

"It's in the Halmea system, one system away from Nedra. There is a research station this corrupt faction had that has everything they got from the aliens in it. We need as much as can be retrieved out of there. We've already lost two fleets trying to get it. They went in and never came back out."

Roger considered it. At least it wasn't the Nedra system itself.

"We desperately need whatever it was they got from the aliens. I will make it worth your while, even if I have to pay for it out of my own pocket. A large fleet obviously isn't the answer. Considering you managed to escape an alien occupied system, a blockade runner is likely the key we need. You... are the key we desperately need right now."

Roger looked at his crew. None of them seem to outright object. Not that they would. The decision would fall on him ultimately. He looked back to the Magistrate. "Alright, we'll do it."

"I'm very glad to hear it. Your crew is kind of small and you will likely need troops to keep you safe on the ground. So I'm going to send troops and equipment with you to help you get stuff loaded as quickly as possible and keep it safe."

Roger nodded.

Raid Run

Randall was getting help from the military base to get the Bethany's Hope fully repaired and few upgrades installed before they made the trip to Halmea system. Roger had been sent for and was escorted to a command center on the base. The moment he stepped foot in the room he understood why Brogan had said his setup on the Bethany's Hope was tiny. There were nearly two dozen officers in here processing information scattered about the room.

In the center of the room was a large holographic table that honestly made Roger a little jealous. Two women and a couple of men stood around the table in the center.

"Captain Vance," Cdr Morgan said, "You may remember me from the trial. I'm Commander Morgan. This," he used his hand to indicate the woman to his right, "is Major Meadows. She is in charge of resource and troop deployment for combat missions."

Roger looked at her and nodded.

She smiled and nodded back. "Pleasure to meet you captain."

Morgan motioned to the man at his left, "This is Major Preston. He's our intelligence coordinator."

Preston simply nodded and Roger nodded in return.

"And this is Colonel Shaw. She's the commanding officer of this base."

Roger nodded again.

"I've been told you volunteered for this mission despite the fact we have lost two fleets attempting it already. At first I wasn't sure if you were brave or just stupid. Rumors have been flying around this place and after checking, they seem to match up with your personal record. You have my respect, captain. Now let's get too it. Preston, show him what we have."

Preston pulled up information he has set aside. The table top changed to a different location. It appeared to be at the base of a steep mountain on an arid and rocky planet surface. Roger looked at the readout. Cold, little to no moisture, and it had an atmosphere that was not breathable for humans.

Preston hit a couple more commands that caused the mountain to become transparent. The entrance at the base of the mountain expanded without much detail into the mountain and downward. "As you can tell, we don't have a lot of information on the structure itself. Intelligence officers were in process of getting that when the aliens arrived and took over the system. All we can really tell you at this point is that it's initial design was to stockpile everything they could get their hands on for distribution to labs in other remote places. Something happened and they must have reconsidered because they started to build labs into the structure there."

"That's concerning to us," the colonel said, "as we don't know if there is a biological part of what they retrieved or if it was just the likelihood of being caught that was the issue. I'm sending with you cryo containers and pods to bring that back if necessary. That said, I hand it off to Major Meadows."

"Given you are essentially going behind enemy lines and the critical nature of this mission I've put together a platoon comprised of heavy fighters, four mech units, and a squad of logistics personnel that could put a professional kleptomaniac to shame. Given two entire fleets were lost attempting this already, I began with asking for volunteers," She looked over at Shaw, "So that might be my fault for the rumors about the captain. People started looking him up before committing." She turned back to Roger, "Once word got around... I have a very long list of soldiers on the sidelines ready and waiting to step up if one of the picked ones can't go with you at the last minute."

Roger didn't know what to say. Surely if they really knew

him, they wouldn't be so eager. Perhaps, he thought to himself, he should have them talk to Sgt Brogan first about how four men faced a grizzly death. He looked at the map and had a thought strike him. He remembered their descent to the planet at Aldis. An idea quickly formed.

"I have an idea that might help keep us alive on the planet's surface. You'll have to tell me if you have the equipment I need for my ship to pull it off." Roger described what he needed and what it would be used for. "Is that possible to get that?"

The blond haired, no nonsense, practically chiseled in stone demeanor of the colonel, actually cracked a half smile. "I've never heard of such a tactic being used before. Very clever captain! Very clever." She looked to Cdr Morgan. "Make it happen."

"Yes, ma'am."

"Captain," Col Shaw asked, "is there anything else you need from us?"

Roger considered it. "I don't believe so."

"If you think of something, don't hesitate to ask. Now that I've met you, I trust the lives of those I send with you are in good hands. For the sake of us all... I pray for your quick and safe return."

Cdr Morgan ushered Roger out of the command room and walked with him to get a few more details about his plan. Morgan made calls and authorized additional equipment for the ship.

When they arrived at the Bethany's Hope, Roger called for Randall and the three of them discussed the modifications.

Roger stood outside with his arms crossed against his chest in the warm afternoon as watching the progress of loading. The ship had been fully equipped and was near ready to go. The cryo containers had arrived and were being loaded onto the cargo lift. The four mechs Roger had been told about were here as well. It would be a tight fit getting them into the lift and up to the cargo hold. With everything they were taking, it was starting to make him wonder how much space they would have for whatever it was they would be bringing back.

The soldiers were starting to show up. This latest hover truck had a group of familiar faces. It caused Roger to raise an eyebrow.

"Captain Vance! Good to see you, sir!" Brogan saluted.

"I'm not official military anymore. Just a private ship captain."

"A private captain running a military operation. They call them mercenaries, sir." Brogan laughed. "Just means your better paid than we are."

Roger rolled his eyes and saluted the man to make him stop. "Load up then."

"You heard'em boys!" Brogan yelled.

The rest of the marines that had been with him the last go around, save one that wasn't there, grabbed their gear and went to the ship's ramp. Roger saw another man shake his head and roll his eyes. He turned to the other marines that were still standing near the trucks. He gave them a hand signal to load up. The man came to Roger. "I'm sorry about that sergeant's behavior captain. I'm Lieutenant Olson, platoon leader for this group. I'll be sure to deal with Sgt Brogan."

"Not a big deal to me, Lt Olson. I'm just glad you know what your doing, and that your in charge of this operation."

"Actually sir, I know your technically not military anymore. However... Col Shaw personally informed me, in front of all the soldiers coming on this trip this morning, that I was to follow your instructions, however crazy it might sound... to the letter. She told us all our very lives might very well depend on it."

Roger wasn't sure about this. The weight of the responsibility he really didn't want tried to settle on him. "Surely that's against the law somehow."

Olsen laughed as he nodded. "I can think of half a dozen regs that order flies in the face of off the top of my head. Despite that, she's earned our respect enough that we trust her. Whatever you've said or done, she seems to have full confidence in you to pull this off. So we will all do our part... under your command. Sir."

Roger thought back to when it was just him and Sonja doing hell hole jobs. It seemed so long ago already, and so much simpler. Olsen seemed to be waiting, Roger realized. Roger motioned his head for Olsen to get on the ship. Olsen just smiled and grabbed his gear before heading up the ramp.

Roger slid a hand down his face. He just wanted things to go back to the way they were. Back to normal. He wasn't even sure if that was possible anymore.

The Bethany's Hope dashed and darted through the mists, trying to avoid being noticed as she made her way to the Halmea system. She cautiously approached the system and Sonja felt her way around inside of it, searching for a place to safely drop in near where their target should be. She dropped from the mists back into the physical realm.

She stayed put as her crew got their bearings and looked at what was around them. There was a stillness in the system. The five planets here were devoid of natural life. Only the second planet had an atmosphere. A space station drifted as a dark hulk in orbit around the second planet. Sonja had dropped the ship between that and a drifting mass of what once was a fleet of Corvus naval warships.

Bethany's Hope fired her thrusters finally and quickly made her way to the debris. Her crew did short scans and confirmed the identity of the fleet. Several smaller ships seemed to be missing or simply couldn't be identified in the drifting mess. Bethany's Hope gently flew into the field of debris. Smaller chucks of the ships began to stick to her hull.

There was movement in the distance. The Bethany's Hope let her thrusters go cold and just drifted in the midst of the debris. Six alien fighters approached the debris and circled around it. After a long period of time they moved on to the dead space station. Bethany's Hope continued to wait.

The fighters moved on, circling the planet. After the fighters could no longer be seen, she fired up her thrusters and dropped out of the debris. Her pilot had located the goal landing spot on the planet's surface. She made a run for it. Fighters that had been adrift that she couldn't have seen came after her. Two groups of six. Their lasers repeatedly struck her shields.

The Bethany's Hope unleashed her own cannons. Four of the fighters burned up in the silence of space. The fighters kept up their attack. A fire streamed out of one of the newly installed components and left a trail of black smoke. The fighters kept up their barrage of weapons fire.

More fires started from more of the surface of the ship. Her weapons fell silent. Massive fires that gave way to smoke was pouring out of the back, top and sides of the ship. She seemed to fall to the planet's gravity. The fighters broke off and remained above the atmosphere. They tracked along with the Bethany's Hope as she went down.

More fires started from up front of the ship. She looked like a slow falling fireball heading to the ground. The ship came to the ground at the base of a mountain. Debris went flying outwards, and the fireball ballooned into a small mushroom cloud. Black smoke filled the air, covering the wreckage site. Small fires on her surface could still be seen by the fighters still in orbit. Bits of her debris smoked all around her.

The fighters stopped tracking with the fallen ship and moved on.

Under Fire

Roger got on the intercom. "We're down! You better get those smoke barrels out there, ASAP. We only have 20 minutes worth left of chemicals on top of the ship!"

He heard the shouting of orders. The ramp dropped, and the lift dropped with its first load. The mini geo-satellite they had launched while in the debris field was feeding them information to give them a heads up visually.

"Excellent work, Faith! They didn't even seem to hesitate when they left."

"Never would have guessed I would get compliments on faking crash landings."

"I never would have thought I would be doing anything like this either. I started with a ship, thinking to have a simple life of cargo runs. I missed that mark somehow."

Faith laughed. "You missed it by a lot!" Faith squirmed in her chair. "It's going to take a bit getting used to wearing this armor while flying."

Roger looked at his own military recon armor he was wearing. "Yeah, better safe than sorry though."

"I'm not complaining. Not after you showed us the video clip of what happened to the marines."

Roger noticed Rosalie put a hand up to her mouth. She had puked the same as the marine had when he saw it happen. Of all of them, she struggled with it the most. She was given the option to leave when they got back to Aldis, yet she chose to stay. Roger knew people like her back in the prison system. Most like her quit. The ones that didn't, eventually hardened up and were able to endure it easier with time.

"I'm going to go check on the progress of things," Roger said. He headed through the hustling activities in the cargo bay. All the barrels were outside already, along with one of the mechs. The second mech was still in a balled up position and was scooting towards the lift.

The other two mech pilots stood by their mechs getting ready. Their shirts were removed, revealing all the implanted ports along their spine and head. From what had been explained to Roger, it was a more raw and invasive form of the pearl. The warriors would become the machines they wielded.

Roger moved on to the ops room. Lt Olsen greeted him as he entered. "Logistics team is already working on the door. The security system seems to be a pretty good one. If they can't get it open in the next ten minutes, I'll have them burn it open. Half of the barrels are opened up. The rest are being positioned now. There's no wind at the moment, so we should be good for at least four hours."

Roger looked at the wall where the old monitors and other equipment had been. All of it had been replaced with the modern equivalent to do this mission. A much smaller and less elaborate version of holographic table was positioned in the center of the room. It wasn't as nice as the one at the base they had come from. It would work for what they needed. There were two information control desks in here now too. A marine occupied one of them.

Roger had the sneaking suspicion that he was going to end up doing a lot of military jobs for a little while. It was a motivating factor in him agreeing to do this particular request. If they found what they needed to nip this war in the bud in the early outset, the sooner things could get back to normal.

He watched the armored suits of men and women move equipment around, create and take cover behind defensive positions, and break in to what was beginning to feel like a small fortress gate.

"Vault Buster One to LT, We've cracked it, sir!" the leader at the door said.

The lieutenant responded. "Copy Vault Buster One, proceed... phase two."

Two teams of four logistics marines in recon battle armor drew their sidearms and proceeded into the building. Roger watched as they made their way down the hallway. It went for a ways before they started coming to rooms. One by one the rooms were cleared. Nobody seemed to be home.

They made short order of getting into the control room. From there, everything else became accessible.

"Vault Buster One to Vault Buster Two. Pulling data cores is a no go. It would take at least ten hours just to get at them."

"Copy Vault Buster One." Another team grabbed a couple of cases and ran down the ramp and into the building. One of the teams of four was already running back out.

"Vault Buster One to LT... Sir, there's way too much here to take back."

"We knew that would be a possibility. Prioritize the picks, try to sort through it and leave the junk behind."

"Copy."

The team in the control room sent a copy of the cataloged items to the ops room. Olsen pulled it up. Roger looked through it as well. "Looks like they may have found some alien ship debris field, or two. Too bad we don't know what we're even looking at."

"No joke," Olsen said, "Given most of it is labeled 'unidentified' I'm guessing they didn't get very far in their research."

Two teams were shuttling back and forth in the hallway with hover sleds in tow. One team was bringing full crates out while the other returned empty. Roger was impressed with how fast they moved and packed up.

"Heads up, Lt! Satellite shows one of those transport ships incoming," the marine next to them said.

"All radios, we have incoming. Looks like a transport ship, just like the vid we were shown. Get to your positions. Logistics keep loading up."

Roger got on the intercom to the bridge. "Faith, take note of the direction that transport is approaching. When we go to leave, we go the other way."

"Got it."

The transport didn't seem to be in any particular hurry. It landed a good safe distance out of reach of the ship's guns.

"Hold your fire and positions until they get to the smoke perimeter," Olsen commanded.

There were hand signals all around. Roger looked at the progress that was happening in the ship itself. Cesar and another logistics marine were stuffing storage rooms as fast as they could. About a third of the ship's volume capacity had already been reached.

Two serpent creatures departed from the back end of the opened transport. The two of them split up. Six giant humanoid looking men came out as well. They wore some sort of mask over their face, probably for breathing. They split up into threes and each group followed one of the serpents.

Roger focused on one of the ship's cameras closer to one of the serpent creatures. On a planet that lacked moisture in the afternoon sun and no vegetation in the way, it was easy to get a good look at the things.

They were slender, just like a snake. Their upper body stood upright as the lower part slithered and propelled them along the ground. Its face very much resembled a viper with small deep red eyes.

Seeing the eyes made him remember when he was on the station in Nedra. He remembered the eyes of the creature in the shadows behind the tree after he had drank the fluid. There was no question that what he was seeing right now was what he encountered on that station.

Just behind its head was a set of what looked like horns in a flattened crescent moon like shape, large at the base and slowly curled down and outward to a point below the mouth.

It's thin and long muscular looking arms hung from a thick, yet narrow shoulders. Just under the arms, the wings of the creature wrapped tightly around its cylindrical body.

"Good god," Olsen said when he saw what Roger was looking at, "If there ever was an embodiment of pure evil, that's got to be right up there!"

Roger couldn't agree more. He switched the view to one of the giants. They looked very similar to humans. A curious thing stood out to him. They all had red hair. He counted the fingers on the hands of one he could see clearly. Six fingers to each hand.

Aside from the oblong back of the head, six fingers, and giant size, they could easily pass as human. It made Roger wonder where they came from. Was this some sort of experiment the serpent creatures had done with humans? More questions with no way to easily answer.

The two groups of aliens split further apart as if to circle around the smoking 'wreck'. Even moving cautiously, because of their size the covered ground fast. One of the serpents raised its rifle and shot into the smoke. Both groups had stopped their advance.

"Hold your fire!" Olsen yelled.

The alien's wild shot impacted on the ship. The groups continued to get a closer at a slower pace.

One of the Logistics teams dropped a heavy crate on the ramp on their way up. It thudded against the steel. The team scrambled to recover it before it fell off to the ground.

The alien teams halted their advance and all of them raised their weapons at the ship. They were still nearly twenty meters from the edge of the smoke.

"NOW!" Olsen said. "Stay in the smoke for cover. Don't reveal yourselves!"

Laser weapons fire sprayed from dispersed points under the Bethany's Hope. Two thirds of the aliens fell right off. The remaining aliens tried to return fire as they made a run for it.

Roger watched to see if anyone got hit. A couple of the mechs which had the least amount of cover took a few hits that didn't seem to amount too much.

The alien transport closed up its back door and sped off back the way it had come. The retreating aliens fell before they could get very far. Roger looked to see how much time that took. Barely a couple of minutes of the actual fight. It felt like much longer than that.

"They know we're still alive and here," Olsen said over his radio, "Sound off. Check each other and get ready in case they want to go another round."

Roger watched the scene. The Logistics marines never stopped even once the fire fight started. One marine went around and gathered up everyone's spent energy clips to recharge them. He gave them fresh ones in exchange. Roger looked out at the dead bodies. "Lt Olsen, can one of your mechs grab one of the smoking barrels and walk out there and drag a few of those dead aliens back to the ship? If he can get them to the cover of the ship, we can stash them in the cryo pods we brought."

Olsen laughed and handed him the secure radio mic. "Give the order exactly how you want it done."

"Captain Vance to Mech team. I need one of you to grab one of those smoke barrels to give you cover. Go out from the ship and grab both of those serpent things and a couple of the giants and drag them back to the cover of the ship. Use the cryo pods we brought and put them on ice for the trip back."

"You got it, sir! Four cadavers coming right up."

One of the mechs grabbed a barrel that was the least effective in concealing the ship and ran out to the nearest serpent. He was sure to go just slow enough so that the cloud of smoke the barrel put out kept him hidden from site. He grabbed the serpent by one of its horns and dragged the body back to the ship.

The other marines were already prepared with the cryo pod. The mech dropped off the body and went for another one. The serpent creature was loaded up and sealed. The next cryo pod was setup, and the first was sent up the cargo lift to be stored.

The logistics marines were keeping up a steady pace. Once the aliens were in place, Roger estimated they would be about three quarters volume capacity.

"Another two ships incoming. These look different from what we've seen before." The Marine near them said.

Roger and Olsen looked. The ships weren't that much larger than the transport that had just been there. These had a large flat surface to the bottom of them with a large number of bubble looking things embedded in the surface.

Roger handed the mic back to Olsen.

"Lt Olsen to all radios. We have two more ships incoming. These are different than the last one. Get ready."

"Vault Buster Two to Lt Olsen. We have eighty-two percent of the data. Estimate another 20 minutes to completion."

Olsen acknowledged.

Cesar came on the intercom. "Captain, we're nearly full.

They're digging for a couple of special marked pieces. We should be good to go when they get back."

Roger acknowledged.

The ships didn't come to the planet surface. The bubbles under the ships began to burst open, sending tear drop shaped objects raining down in their direction. There were hundreds of them.

"Heads up. They may be doing an orbital bombardment!" Olsen said over the radio.

Roger pulled up another terminal and changed the targeting system to start shooting them down, starting with any that would hit the ship first then working its way out. "Their going to know things aren't as bad for us as it seems here soon." Roger told Faith to get ready to make a run for it.

The ship's guns started to spray the multitude of targets that were incoming. There were too many. The tear drops rained down all around the ground of the ship. The shell of each of the things shattered like glass slamming against stone. What remained looked like a misshaped upside down egg with cavities notched in an array all around it facing the ground.

Mechanical spider looking things shot out, one from each cavity. The spider looking things ran at the ship. Small weapons emerged from their abdomen and small laser bolts started to spray out at a rapid rate. The landscape was quickly covered with a massive swarm of the horrid spider things.

The marines opened fire. One spider blew up after another. They kept coming, sprinting with abandon towards the Bethany's Hope, weapons blazing.

Roger quickly grasped that this was going to be a numbers issue. Roger ordered Randall and Cesar to stop what they were doing, grab their weapons and keep the spiders out of the ship.

By shear number, the spiders breached the smoke and started to attack the marines up close and personal. Roger heard Randall's laser shotgun go off several times near the ramp. Marines were starting to drop dead. The spiders seemed to have some sort of acid weapon that they used up close. They would follow up by stabbing into the softened spot, trying to get penetration through their body armor.

Roger saw a number of the spiders go into the building.

The teams there were pinned down and shooting as many in the corridor as they could.

Two of the mechs had been swarmed. One group of spiders found a way into the pilot and killed him. The other group of spiders seemed to know exactly what to do and repeated it on the other swarmed mech. The other two mechs had piles of dead spiders all around them.

Large groupings of the things diverted to the two remaining mechs. The mechs dealt an impressive amount of damage. The spider body counts racked up quickly, yet they couldn't keep up. The spiders eventually swarmed them and the pilots were quickly killed.

The numbers of the spiders had thinned out considerably. Unfortunately, so had the number of marines that were still alive. The marines in the corridor were about to be overrun. "Olsen, we're done here. Load them up!" Roger ran out of the room.

He pulled his sidearm and checked it as he made his way to the ramp. Randall and Cesar had barely managed to keep the things outside. Only a couple of them managed to get up the ramp before being shot to death.

Roger shot a few that still remained outside the ship. He ran to the doorway and started shooting away. They stopped their advance for a split second, as if trying to decide on target priorities. The remaining marines on the other side took advantage and unloaded fire on them. Roger kept up his fire while trying to stay out of the way from the fire of the marines. The last spider fell in a smoking heap.

He heard the marine down the hall acknowledge a command. Two of them packed up what it was they were bringing and rushed past Roger to load it up. The other two ran back deeper in to get something.

Roger went back to the ship ramp. The dead and wounded were being loaded back onto the ship. Roger caught Cesar on a return trip outside. "Cesar, make sure we get a few of these damn things in cryo containers after all the dead and wounded are on board."

"Yes, sir."

Roger climbed the ramp to the cargo area. Nearly a third of the marines were killed. All the rest of them had injuries ranging from cuts, gashes and burns to near fatal wounds. John was tending to them as fast as he could go right alongside one of their own men that was trained as a medic. The two marines that had run back came with the briefcases they used to get the system information. With them was another dead marine.

"Captain!" It was Olsen on the intercom, "They're sending five more of those spider ships this way!"

"Is everyone accounted for?" Roger asked.

Cesar and Randall brought up the lift with five of the spider things sealed up in containers.

"Everyone is on board," Olsen said.

Roger closed the ramp and made his way to the bridge. Faith didn't wait. The moment the ramp and cargo lift was up, the ship was off the ground. The smoke cloud parted and fell away as Bethany's Hope rose.

"Hover a moment!" Roger told Faith. Roger plopped down in his chair. He set the weapons system to obliterate everything that remained on the ground. He wanted to make sure the aliens didn't get a hold of the mechs to analyze them. He also shot up the entrance to the building and the mountain side all around it. Everything was obliterated and buried. "Now go!"

Roger pulled up a display of information from the mini-satellite. Several groups of fighters and the five spider ships were advancing on their position. Roger was confident they could out run them.

"Sonja, are you ready to jump?"

"As soon as we get out of gravity, yes."

Bethany's Hope escaped the atmosphere of the planet. The fighters were in hot pursuit. There were more of them somehow than what the mini-satellite had picked up on. The spider ships still dropped their payload on the site. They turned and left. The ship's cannons were gradually picking off the fighters.

"Oh crap!" Faith said, "We have another ship incoming. You remember that long skinny ship with the spheres on it you saw when we got ambushed in Dela?"

Roger groaned. "How long before we get out of gravity?"

"Another five minutes at least. That ship will catch us before then!"

Bubble Trouble

The long and slender ship race ahead of the Bethany's Hope just out of range of her guns. The spheres on the ship began to emit their green glowing light. Roger waited for the mass of alien warships to drop out of the mists like happened in Dela.

More fighters had caught up with them from some place and were pelting the ship's shields to death. It wouldn't be too long before some of that laser fire started to penetrate and hit the ship.

Nothing more seemed to happen aside from the fighters attacking them.

"We're out of gravity!" Faith yelled.

Roger triggered the control to stow the weapons. The shutters and projected display remained in place. Roger was grateful Randall had gotten that done. "Weapons stored. Sonja... Jump!"

Nothing happened. "Sonja!?"

"I'm trying, Roger! It's like we are stuck in some sort of invisible bubble I can't get out of! I can't get to the mists!"

Roger fought to keep panic at bay so he could think clearly. He reactivated the weapons system. He looked at the positioning of the ships. "Faith head straight for that ship with the spheres. Push the thrusters as hard as you can."

She changed directions towards the target that was staying ahead of them and off to one side. Faith activated a short power override for the thrusters. It would give them just a quick boost, like an after burner for atmospheric aircraft.

The long ship with glowing spheres didn't take long to respond. It whipped itself away from Bethany's Hope and circled around behind. It positioned itself to keep the fighters between it and the Bethany's Hope. It was too fast and agile for Faith to keep up with.

"I don't think they are having any part of it," Faith said.

"I not so sure that ship isn't what's keeping us here. We may have misunderstood its role in combat," Roger considered the options. The shields were nearly down to thirty percent. "Turn the ship around and keep charging at that ship, through the fighters."

"Are you kidding me?"

"No. Do it!"

Faith complied. The ship banked hard and dived right into the midst of the fighters to get at the evasive troublemaker. Fighters scattered in all directions. Roger had assigned one of the front turrets to only target the ship with spheres. He set the max targeting distance to something ridiculously far beyond the gun's range.

The power generators were working full tilt and sucking down fuel at a scary pace. He rerouted as much power to shields as he dared. The fighters had to take time to come back around on their target. The first volley of shots went out from the ship to the alien troublemaker. A few more fighters exploded before they could get turned around.

The troublemaker darted away. It again maneuvered to keep the fighters as a cover. Faith banked hard again and dived right back into the fighter swarm that had just regathered.

Roger finally smiled a little. The ship wasn't getting pelted near as often with the fighters having to veer out of the way. The shields were starting to gain strength again. It also closed the range for the guns and made for more accurate shots. The fighter numbers were declining quickly.

A few of the fighters broke away and went to the sphered ship. The troublemaker moved once more to use the fighters to shield it from the Bethany's Hope. Faith smiled as she rolled, banked, and dived in to the diminished number of fighters. More fighters went silent, leaving less than a dozen.

The spheres on the troublemaker ship lost their green glow

as the ship turned away and sped off into the distance. What remained of the fighters went after it.

"The bubble is gone, Roger!" Sonja said over the intercom.

"Break off the attack. Let's see if we can get a couple of these fighters to stick to the hull like we did for the debris. Maybe we can take a couple back with us."

Faith found one that was mostly intact and nudged the ship up to it after arming the grippers. The gripper claw shot out and stuck to the fighter. Faith reeled it in until it bumped against the hull. The locks activated and registered the piece as fastened. "Looks like it's a go captain."

"Good. Grab one more, than we get the hell out of this place before something big shows up." Roger stowed the weapons as Faith latched onto another fighter that was mostly intact. Once the second fighter was locked Roger gave Sonja the command to jump.

The darkness of space gave way to white mists. Roger stayed put until Sonja was sure they were clear of the system and nothing was trying to chase and kill them. He had her set course back to Aldis.

Roger got up and left the bridge. He walked into the cargo bay to the small space that was left for the marines. The scene was horrific. Eighteen marines were laid aside on their backs, lifeless. He looked at them. Brogan was easy to pick out. He was pretty sure the rest of the marines he had with him the first trip were also there.

John and the other medic were working on a man with a hole in his chest near the heart. The man was convulsing with one hand, death gripping the arm of one of the medics. John was trying to fix something. Both medics were covered with blood.

Blood ran all over the floor. Other men and women were laying on crates or sitting up against a wall some place trying to avoid the pools of blood and marines still needing attention. Most were trying to keep a mental grip on things. Every last one of them had bandages wrapped or taped down to multiple places. Some of them were obviously given heavy pain meds.

"Damn toxins!" John yelled.

The man he was working on gurgled. His hand fell limp from the medic he had a death grip on. "Not your fault," the other medic told John. He closed the eyes of the marine. Roger saw Olsen holding a rag against another marine's side. Cesar was with another one, holding a rag to his face over an eye. John and the other medic moved over to help him next.

Roger went back to the bridge and got Faith and Rosalie. He wasn't sure how Rosalie would react. He told them both they needed to get the blood cleaned up and let Rosalie know what to expect to try and soften the impact. She was willing to go there, anyway. They returned to the cargo area. The body of the marine that had just died had been moved with the rest.

Normally the bodies would be cremated, and the ashes sent back. Lt Olsen and Roger both agreed the bodies would be wanted for examination in this case. The dead were put into what remained of the cryo pods.

Days later the Bethany's Hope touched down on the same concrete like landing pad. Several medical vehicles were already nearby, waiting to approach. Behind them were lined up several hover trucks. Roger was pretty confident they were not coming to arrest him this time.

The ramp and the cargo lift lowered with the wounded and the dead first. The medical teams moved quickly and had them removed from the scene. The trucks pulled up and loaded up all the alien debris filled crates. Cranes were brought over and removed the fighters that were about to fall off the ship with the weight of gravity. In less than two hours the ship was void of cargo, soldiers, and... stress.

The crew had taken the opportunity to mingle with humanity in a normal setting, away from the ship. He wondered if some of them might not return. Faith would return under a pending threat of violating her deal. Randall would return to the memory of his daughter. Sonja was stuck here no matter what. Cesar, Rosalie, and John were the only ones that might bag it, he realized.

Roger leaned his hands on the railing overlooking the ramp. He closed his eyes and took a deep breath of the nearby forest air.

"Everyone is gone. It feels so... empty. Are you not leaving too?"

Roger opened his eyes and turned around. Sonja leaned

against the wall with her arms folded across her chest.

"Leave and do what? Listen to a bunch of jabbering of people who are scared or go on about nothing? Drink myself into oblivion as many seem to do after what we've just gone through?" He shook his head. "I need the stillness to help keep myself grounded, to process what happened and move forward."

She looked down at the floor while Roger just looked at her. "The fight at the base of the mountain, is that what it was like for you fighting in the prisons?"

"No. It was similar, but different. Men and women falling around you in the fight, the bloody mess and dealing with the deaths afterwards... that part is the same." Roger was starting to wonder if she was having a hard time processing it. "How are you holding up with all that has happened?"

She finally looked up from the floor. "I think I'm alright. I don't process things the same as you."

They just looked at each other for what Roger felt like was an eternity.

"Close the ramp."

"You object to fresh air?"

She smiled and shook her head. "No. I need to talk to you... privately."

"Ahhh," Roger accessed the control panel and secured the ramp. He pulled up a terminal and locked down the ship. He turned back to Sonja. "We are locked in here together. What's on your mind?"

She motioned with her head for him to follow. They went to the dining area, and she got herself a drink and sat down at one of the tables next to him. She seemed to be struggling to talk. It was going to be a patience thing, he could tell.

"My real name is Bethany Murik." Tears were already forming. "I am the only child to Donovan and Aurora Murik."

His mind raced. He had heard the name Murik before, a long time ago. He couldn't place the significance of it.

"My father was elected as Magistrate of the Corvus Commonwealth, probably two hundred and sixty years ago. One day I was playing hide and seek with him. I was only ten years old at the time."

She had to stop to regain composure and wipe away the

tears. "I wasn't supposed to be in there. I was in a hidden closet behind a fake mirror when four men and a woman in military uniform came into his office. I could see them through the glass, even though they couldn't see me.

"My dad gave me a hand signal to keep quiet. They closed the door and then attacked him. They beat him up and killed him. After they killed him they called security and reported that he had killed himself. The medical people arrived, and they went with him to the hospital."

She had to stop and breathe as if she was reliving the moment. "I told my mother and the head of the Magistrate security what really happened. My mother tried to call out to the people that a group was trying to overthrow the government."

She shook her head. "The head of security and my mother sent me into hiding with a new identity as Sonja Brock. I was passed on from place to place, person to person. I found out years later my mother died of cancer a few weeks after my father was killed. People surrounding the investigation died in accidents or from diseases. I, Bethany Murik, was listed as having died from an accident and my body was cremated the same as my mother and father."

"Apparently there got to be suspicion that I was still alive. A dark bounty was placed on my head for any information that would lead to my capture. Over the years, I've paid for information on who the people were that had my parents killed. I even tried once to hire an assassin to kill one of them. That failed badly. I learned they are practically untouchable.

"So I started hiring assassins to kill their loved ones around them. They were much easier to get to. That's when they started to hunt me in earnest." She sniffed and finally looked up at him. "That's why I rarely go out in public and why I came back in bad shape that night on Lestat station."

She looked back at the table. "I hired a body guard that night. I'm pretty sure the assassin killed him. I managed to get away." She rubbed more tears away. "I didn't want to tell you any of this in fear they might come after you. They've come after some of the people I had been with. I'm sure they were killed for information to find me."

"I suspect all those people that were after you probably

have bigger problems at the moment. Now that I know what you were running from I'll come up with some ideas to try to keep you safe." Roger put an arm around her shoulders. She leaned in and rested her head against him.

Now What

Roger stood outside the ship, leaning against a ramp piston. He sipped on a hot stimulant drink as he enjoyed the fresh air. The landing pad area was bustling with activity. People and equipment were being shuttled off to some place in the distance. Roger figured it had something to do with the delivery they had just made.

A military law enforcement hover vehicle made its way against the flow of traffic. As Roger sipped his drink, he realized it was coming in his direction. Thoughts of them coming to arrest him again stabbed at his mind. He tried to reject it with logic. It wasn't going well.

The vehicle came to a stop near his ship. Major Meadows got out of the passenger's side of the vehicle. She looked sharp in her uniform shirt and skirt. Her dark brown eyes seemed to be laser focused on him as she approached. Her long dark brown hair and warm and kind looking facial features took away from her military stiffness. She was unlike Colonel Shaw, who looked like she could destroy a person without giving it a second thought.

She smiled at him when she got close. Any grain of intimidation she might have had was lost in that moment. "Good morning, captain!"

"Major Meadows," Roger nodded respectfully. "Something I can help you with, I'm guessing?"

"Yes, captain. We are needing as much help as we can

to process and learn how to use what you brought back as fast as possible. I've come to request the services of Randall Turner and Faith Jerin. Because this will keep you from going anywhere with your ship, Col Shaw has authorized me to pay you standby fees. In addition, she has asked that we do any upgrades and modifications for your ship from what we learn of the alien tech as a thank you for your service."

"If you need them, by all means. The sooner this war is ended, the better."

"We thought you might say that. We greatly appreciate it. Are Turner and Jerin here?"

"Nope. I think they may have spent the night in the nearby town to get away from it all."

"We'll find them and bring them back to base. Thank you again!"

She turned and got back in the vehicle and was gone. Roger finished his drink and headed up the ramp.

Sonja walked into the cargo area from the living spaces. "Someone here?"

"Maj Meadows stopped by."

"Please tell me we aren't going back to some alien infested system already!"

"We're not. In truth, it looks like we are not going anywhere anytime soon. She stopped by to ask if she could pull Randall and Faith to help with figuring out the alien stuff we brought back. So we are currently getting paid to sit around until they are done with them."

"So... Now what?"

Roger looked around the inside of the cargo bay. "I need to do a bit of research. There's still some things I don't know about this ship. Like I didn't know there was an ops room on this thing. I want to see if I can find records of what these ships used to be so I can better take advantage of it."

"Mind if I help? It's not like I have anything else to do. I can't exactly leave either."

The two of them spent the next several days doing research on that and other things.

Sonja had retired for the night, leaving Roger staring at a terminal looking at targeting tactics. As soon as he knew she was long since gone to bed he swept aside his current research topic. He pulled up information on mist pilots. Particularly what had been found out after The Event. He found a number of text files that described theories of what and how things happened. He was digging more for the actual condition of the pilot themselves.

It took him a while, but he did find what he was looking for. It was a series of pictures of a mist pilot that had been pulled after breaking into a pearl. The pictures were hard to look at. This pilot had been a male. The body looked like someone had been starved for months. Skin was stretched over a warped and deformed skeletal structure. The face looked as though it was in agony.

Roger closed it down and cleared it from his search history. He never wanted to see it again. He imagined Sonja suspended in the pearl in the same condition. The thought tore at his heart. It was his fault this had happened to her. He shut everything down and went to his quarters. Seeing Sonja tomorrow was going to be hard after what he just found out. A small part of him wished he had let it go and not looked it up.

Roger was up early the next morning. He was in the middle of preparing himself a cup of stimulant when someone pinged him outside of the ship. Roger pulled up the camera on his datapad from his pocket. There was a group of military techs standing outside with four hover trucks.

Roger abandoned his cup and went to find out what they wanted. The sun still hadn't come up, it was so early. The ramp lowered and Roger descended.

"Captain Vance?" one of the techs asked.

"Yes."

"Good morning, sir! We're here to start work on your ship, sir." He held out large datapad.

Roger received it. It listed all the changes to be done. Roger raised an eyebrow. The changes were not small ones. He looked back up at the tech. "You're kidding me!"

"Not a joke! We have a lot of work to do and we have been told to get it done yesterday. Some of the equipment is still being fabricated. We still have plenty to get started on. With your permission, of course."

The thought of what they were about to install and upgrade was mind blowing. He wasn't sure how this would work with him being a private ship. The cost of it all was likely more than the ship was worth. The realization of how many ships have likely been lost to the aliens lately came to mind. His ship might be worth more than it ever used to be.

Roger scrolled to the bottom where the cost would be listed and a signature for agreement to pay. No cost was listed except for a note. Roger pulled up the note. It read: A token of appreciation for services rendered to save all humanity. Roger nearly choked. His mind flashed back to the tree on the station. Dark thoughts of all the death and destruction that had happened because of his actions threatened to overwhelm him.

The presence of I AM flooded in him. A thought passed through his mind. 'I've paid the price. You are free. Accept the gift.' Roger took a deep breath and signed to receive the modification. He handed the datapad back to the tech. "Permission granted."

Over the next several hours tech crews and equipment swarmed the Bethany's Hope. Noise of hammering, cutters, techs calling out to other techs, and other equipment sound permeated all around the ship none stop for the next several days.

Roger was grateful to see Randall in the afternoon when he returned.

"I was starting to wonder if I would ever see you again," Roger said.

He just laughed. "I'm glad to be back. We managed to figure out the basics of a good chunk of it. We were all hyped up wonderin if we would be able to figure out anything. Once we were finally allowed to dive into the pieces of what we recovered, we started noticin patterns. Especially in those fighters we brought back. Those ended up being a key to figuring out the rest of it. Turns out, a lot of the stuff we recovered was similar to what we already have. It just looks different."

Roger and Randall walked up the ramp. Sparky trailed behind.

"What got really interestin once we figured out we already had equivalent devices, was how they combined their stuff. They did things in combinations we never thought of before.

When we tried it with our own tech it worked the same, with a few modifications. Wasn't actually hard to reproduce.

"Ship designers were all over that stuff once it was figured out. They cranked out prototypes so fast it could make a person's head spin. Military ships are already being refitted."

"So nothing we brought back was super high game changing tech?"

"There were some pieces I heard that we have no idea what it is yet. Those are going to take longer to figure out. The fighters didn't have anything like them."

"What we did get figured out will make our ships faster, and the weapons will hit harder. They even have a shield add-on to beef them up too."

"Have you seen what they are putting on this ship yet?"

"Heard the big boss here wanted her decked out. Seen she's getting the thruster modifications when I got here. Not sure what else the are working on."

The two of them arrived at Randall's shop. Roger pulled up the document on a terminal for Randall to look through.

Randall ran his left hand over his short mohawk of gray hair. "Whoa!" His eyes got big. He looked at Roger. "They give you a special license to have this?"

Roger shrugged.

Randall went back to looking through the rest of it. "First law enforcement patrol vessel that does a scan of this ship is going to drop a load in his pants when they see what you've got." Randall's jaw dropped open.

"What?"

"You see, the thruster mods they added?!"

"Randall, I'm still not real sure on how those specs translate to reality yet. I'm not a hundred percent sure what some of those add-ons are either. I AM told me to accept it, so I did."

Randall went and plopped himself down in a special chair he made to accommodate his size comfortably. Randall looked at him with a serious face. "Dude... captain... When they get done modifying and adding everything on that's list, you're going to have a very powerful, very MODERN, warship. This thing is going to be what she once was in her prime all those hundreds of years ago. And then some."

Roger felt a real need to look for fine print that he might

have missed. He was starting to wonder if he may have given himself over to servitude of the military without realizing it. Roger put a hand over his eyes and sighed. "Did you happen to see anything in that list that might have notes I might have missed?"

Randall pulled it up over where he was at and looked through it again. "Thrusters, computers, targeting package, anti-infantry pods-"

"What?!"

"Yeah, man. That what the AIP-381s are."

"And just how was I supposed to know that off the top of my head," Roger muttered.

Randall continued. "Flight controllers, five weapon system emplacements, a couple of... MHMS-48s. Those have a note attached." Randall looked at Roger, "Suppose you don't know what those are either."

Roger shook his head.

"Mini Homing Missile System man." He pulled up the note. "Apparently your authorized to have 48 missiles in your possession at any given time." Randall pointed to the next item on the list, "Those are rapid fire anti-ship and aircraft guns. They don't hit quite as hard but, they'll hit faster and more often. They're considerably more dangerous than what we had."

"I'm really questioning a motive in the background here."

"You and me both, man. You're going to need a ship's weapons guy to run all this. No way you're going to be able to do what you were doing."

Roger didn't care for the idea. After learning what was being added, Randall was right. Money wasn't an excuse anymore based on the last time he checked his account.

Randall mentioned several other things that would be added or upgraded. "WOW... they got you slated to try out the new mist gun design!"

"Sonja and I actual got shot at by one of those once, when the aliens first started coming around."

"Other engineers mentioned some ships had been shot out of the mists by them. That was another one of those, we hadn't thought about doing it that way, discoveries."

He got to the end and found a new note. "Well this one's

the kiss of perfection." He looked at Roger. "There a new phantom drive that has been set aside for this ship. A dual pearl drive."

"Dual pearl drive?"

"Yeah. Typically they are only used in military ships, and the occasional ship for rich and powerful folks. Makes it so mist pilots can tag team and go supper long distances in the mists."

"I hope they aren't planning on sending us into the Nedra system."

"Isn't that were the aliens have been popping out of?"

"Yeah."

Randall was now eager to see how things were coming along with the ship he had worked so hard on restoring. Roger went to try and find a quiet place to think about all Randall had just revealed to him. He also took a chance and reached out to Maj Meadows. He asked her where a good place would be to find a ship weapons specialist that wouldn't get him into trouble by being trigger happy.

The days passed and the loud noises day and night gradually decreased. Roger woke up one morning to the chime of an urgent message. He dragged himself out of bed and checked what it was.

He was being summoned to a meeting that afternoon. He was wondering when they would be sent on some suicidal run. Maybe this was it. Maybe not.

He went about his day looking to see how close they were to being done. There seemed to be a long list of little things that needed to be finished. They were getting done though. Last night was the first time in a long time there wasn't some loud noise in the ship to disturb his sleep.

Roger was getting ready to go and was looking for some of his crew that was handy to let them know he would be out for a while. He came to a room where he heard the sound of women crying softly. He came to the open door of the room and saw John saying something softly to Faith as he had a hand on her forehead. Sonja was in the room crying too. Roger moved on, not wanting to get sucked into that.

He came across Rosalie and let her know and to pass it on to the rest of the crew.

Top Brass

Roger took a seat in the large briefing room. The room was nearly half full with what looked like very important military leaders and from what he could tell, captains of actual warships for the Corvus navy. There were a few of either corporate business types or government leaders. He always had a hard time telling based on what he had seen on the news vids. In any respect, he felt totally out of place in the room.

Roger sat in a seat that was distanced from anyone else in there. The people here seemed to know each other and were in small groups amongst the chairs chatting away. Roger didn't seem to be noticed, which suited him fine.

As side door near the front of the room opened and three high-ranking officers walked in. As if the way they dressed wasn't enough of an indication, the fact that the room suddenly got dead silent, everyone found a seat, and all the military uniformed men and women snapped to attention was a dead ringer.

Roger stood up and waited.

"Please be seated," Col Shaw said. She looked around the room. "I wish to thank you all for coming. The last couple of months have not been easy. Much has been lost to this emerging alien threat."

She looked directly at Roger. "Captain Roger Vance, would you please stand."

Roger wasn't so sure about this. He didn't dare disregard

her right at this moment either.

"I want to personally thank you for the sacrifice you have made to willingly go into hostile enemy territory and retrieve vital information and alien technology."

All eyes turned to look at Roger. He wanted to crawl in to a hole right about now.

"Because of your efforts we might actually stand a chance in this fight. I also thank you for loaning us your ship engineer and pilot. Your engineer provided important insight that allowed us to quickly adapt the alien technology to our own. Your pilot has an amazing skill for intelligence analysis and has helped us determine where we are certain the aliens are going to attack next."

There was some applause. Roger just nodded and sat back down as quickly as he felt safe to do so.

"Concerning the imminent attack, I turn this meeting over to Admiral Patrick Dacker." Col Shaw stepped aside and took a seat.

The admiral was even more intimidating. He also looked around the room, and especially at Roger. "I'm not going to sugar coat this. The Corvus Navy has lost nearly sixty-eight percent of our overall fleet to the aliens. We have been heavily out gunned by what seems to be a single alien fleet of ships. I would also like to thank Captain Vance for his efforts, and I pray it's not too late in coming.

"The enemy has slowed down in the last few weeks in the taking of new systems. Based on intelligence we have, we believe it's because they are fortifying their positions before continuing a new push for expansion. Everything we've seen points to the system of Sagan as their next target. Sagan is an important supply of food and rich deposits of metals. It is home to nearly three billion people. We have been pooling up as many warships as we can to defend this system.

"This is essentially a last stand for the Corvus Navy. We have had to call on our neighbors for help. They are sending warships to our aid at full speed. However, we can't wait for them before sending help to Sagan.

"Morale of a people can make the difference between defeat or victory. Despite our trying to contain news and rumors, both have spread like wild fires. Sagan has either learned or figured out they may soon be attacked by the aliens." The admiral looked directly at Roger. "We need something to curb that."

Roger felt a huge weight coming on him again. Here it comes, he thought to himself.

"Captain, I'm willing to bet your not aware of this. You and your ship, the Bethany's Hope, have become well known among the navy personnel in this sector of space. News has spread of your escape from Dela, and bold invasion into hostile territory to grab what we desperately needed. You and your ship have become a symbol of hope against the aliens to our service men and women. Right now that is something that's direly needed in Sagan."

The admiral grabbed the sides of the podium. "Captain, we have critical components that need to get to Sagan as fast as they can get there. But... more importantly, those people need hope. Your arrival in the system would give them that hope. Would you be willing to do that for us?"

Roger wanted nothing more than to not be there in this moment. The weight of being some symbol of hope? It felt heavy enough to crush him. Yet, how could he turn them down? Roger had seen people who lost hope too many times. They quickly died at the hands of whatever they were fighting.

Roger closed his eyes and swallowed hard. He looked up at the admiral and nodded. "I will do as you ask."

The admiral nodded back. "People like you give me hope that we still have a chance to survive this. Our fleet is in final preparations with upgrades. We will send you ahead of us. The fleet will catch up with you soon."

The admiral moved on to issues of making sure combat forces and supplies were ready and in place for departure the moment the fleet was ready. Roger half listened as none of it really applied to him.

After nearly an hour, the meeting was dismissed. Roger slipped out of there as fast as he could. At least they weren't asking him to go to Nedra or back to Halmea.

Roger stood at the base of the ramp with his eyes closed. He took a deep breath. He wished he could bottle up the smell of these woods and take it with him. Perhaps someday he might make this planet a home. The thought of a home seemed almost foreign at the moment. He had one once. A wife and daughters. All taken from him, leaving his heart in pieces so many years ago.

He took another deep breath. This wasn't where he thought his life would lead to. Not that he had a specific plan. He was just after a simple life. The admirals words played back through his head. He definitely didn't want to be some poster child for the military or anyone else. He needed to keep a low profile for Sonja's sake.

How to fix this? How to get back to a simpler life in obscurity? His head began to hurt from the stress of it all.

"You look like a man that has the galaxy pressing on your shoulders," a familiar voice said.

Roger's eyes snapped open. Faith was sitting on the ramp with her arms resting on her knees, just looking at him. "We seem to have a reputation."

"Ahhh... yes. I've heard about that. Top brass was trying to keep our activities under wraps. I think they gave up and just let it fly. Be warned... they might try to use that later."

"Sooner than you think."

Her smile faded. "Oh god... where are they sending us?"

"Sagan."

She cussed and leaned her head back. "They talked about sending someone on another mission to Halmea. I think I managed to talk them out of that one. Not that Sagan is much better. That's just Dela all over again."

"Except we are going ahead of the fleet this time."

"Oh... that makes things all better." She rolled her eyes and got up from the ramp. "Come on. It was Cesar's turn to cook. Maybe that will put you out of your misery and make everything better."

Roger groaned. "Maybe I'll just grab some survival paste and go to bed."

"Ugh. I think I would rather shoot myself than eat the paste. Cesar's cooking isn't that awful." She grabbed his arm and lead him up the ramp. "Come on, Roger. The rest of the crew is waiting. We thought we would eat dinner all together for once."

The last of the modifications were being tested and wrapped up as a logistics crew loaded crates of components into the ship. A number of short haulers were landing and taking off carrying loads of crates into space to load on the military ships in orbit. Another hover truck arrived with more crates for the Bethany's Hope.

This time two men got out of the truck. One of them approached Roger. "Captain Vance?"

"Yes."

"Major Meadows sent me to ask if you had found a ship weapons specialist yet."

"Unfortunately, no."

"In that case sir, my name is Brodie Evans, and I'm your man." The guy was practically beaming from ear to ear as he handed Roger a datapad.

Roger read it. There was a message from Maj Meadows with a letter of recommendation for the man before him, if Roger had been unable to hire someone else. His qualifications were stellar, to put it mildly. Brodie's most recent experience was a gunship for the Corvus navy.

"When did you get out of the navy?"

"It's pending on my being added to your crew roster."

The amount of bending over backwards the military was doing to make things work for him was nothing short of astonishing. In a time of war when help was already short to the point of drafting people for service. Yet, here was an experienced ship weapons specialist practically gift wrapped for him. Roger handed the datapad back to Brodie.

"Permission to come aboard, sir?"

"You realize this isn't exactly the safest ship to be on? A lot of good men and women that have traveled with me have died."

"Understood sir. You and this ship have also pulled off what no other ship has against the aliens. As I see it, my life won't be any longer on a gunship. I'd be honored to serve. My request stands."

"Granted."

The man ran back to the truck and grabbed a large duffel bag. Roger contacted Sonja on his datapad to have her get the new guy situated.

Over the next several hours, the last of the cargo was loaded and signed for. The modifications were complete with a couple of minor exceptions that Randall would deal with on the way to Sagan. The military had sent a few passengers to catch a ride. They were a small group of flight crew replacements for Corvus navy ships that were already in the system.

Bethany's Hope lifted from the landing pad late that night. As they passed by the navy ships, the fleet admiral contacted Roger and let him know they would be less than a day behind. Roger acknowledged and the Bethany's Hope disappeared into the mists.

Arrival

Sonja cautiously brought the Bethany's Hope near to the Sagan system.

"How close are we?" Roger asked.

"Within about twenty minutes. I've stopped for a moment to feel around for what's out here."

"Any sign of the Corvus fleet?"

There was a moment of silence. "I think so. They're still several hours behind us. There seems to be somewhat normal traffic flow in and out of the Sagan system. Mostly ships leaving."

The burning question on many of their minds. "Alien fleet?"

"Ummm... there's a bubble out there in the far distance. It feels similar to the bubble that had us trapped back at Halmea. I can't tell what's in it for sure. It's probably the alien fleet. But I can't sense the normal darkness around them though."

Roger rubbed his head. "So they're here and waiting to pounce like a predator in a hunt." Roger considered waiting until the main fleet arrived before going in. Coming in with warships would at least mean a fighting chance.

Warning the system that the enemy was at their doorstep might save lives. It would give them time to clear out of the cities and fortify positions to last longer against the impending attack. If the people panicked though and started leaving the system in droves, it might cause the aliens to pounce sooner and get even more people killed in the midst of chaos.

He tried to put himself in the shoes of the people there in the system. Every action he could think of had consequences. Eventually he settled on a course of action. "Sonja, take us in."

"Wouldn't it be better to wait for the Corvus Navy and go in with reinforcements?" Faith asked.

"Sagan deserves to have warning the aliens are here. It might give them a fighting chance to dig in or get to safety before they arrive."

Sonja navigated to the system and dropped them into the physical realm near one of the space stations. It was one of three stops they needed to deliver to.

Faith took control of flying the moment they were in real space. The ship handled more like a fighter after all the upgrades and modifications. She was loving every minute of it.

"Rosalie, contact whoever is in charge of the navy fleet here and tell them I need to talk to them ASAP."

Rosalie acknowledged. She could be heard talking with a few people and sending messages. "Captain, I have the fleet commander on a secured channel."

"Send it to me." Roger pulled up a holographic vid screen in front of him. A man that had gray streaks of hair on either side of his head appeared in front of him. The sight of people 'aging' was still hard to believe.

The man smiled. "Captain Vance. It's a pleasure to see you, sir. What can I do for you?"

"You might not think it's a pleasure in a second. Sir, the aliens are not far from here. The system could be under attack within a few short hours, or whenever they decide. They seem to be just sitting in the distance waiting."

The smile faded from the man's face. "I've been sending out scouts to the mists to watch. None of them have seen anything. Are you sure about this?"

"My mist pilot found a bubble that they are probably using to hide themselves in. She believes it's the same kind of bubble that the aliens used to trap us in Halmea."

"Someone reported that bubble anomaly yesterday. I sent a ship to investigate and we haven't heard back from them yet."

"That ship is probably been destroyed, sir."

"Thank you for the heads up, captain. I will be sure to spread the word and prepare for the attack as best we can."

"The naval fleet from Aldis is just a few hours behind us."

"That's reassuring! Thank you again."

The transmission ended.

Bethany's Hope docked with the space station Delacruz. The station orbited between the main planet of this system and its moon. The main naval fleet which only comprised of half a dozen ships was patrolling nearby.

The passengers all departed and caught shuttles to their assigned military ships. The first round of crates began to be unloaded.

Roger remained at the bridge. He was monitoring the local news and ship traffic. It wasn't long before he noticed an unusually high number ships leaving the station. He looked at another monitor that he had set up with a count down timer. It was set for the absolute outset of when the main Corvus fleet would arrive. There was less than an hour at this point. The fleet could drop in at any moment.

The unloading was taking much longer than it should have. Roger couldn't help but wonder if some of the crews had fled the station. He drummed his fingers on his chair arm. He really wanted to get to the planet, which was their next drop. At least on the planet there would be some means of taking cover.

Roger noticed Rosalie starting to shake. "What's wrong Rosalie?"

"I'm picking up a lot of emergency beacons and distress calls all of a sudden. On several channels people are freaking out."

"Where are the beacons at?"

"They're all over the place!"

Roger got on the cargo area intercom, "Cesar! Drop what your doing now! We're leaving!"

Roger watched the monitor outside the ship. Cesar heard the call. He looked at the three cargo handlers that were with him before turning to run to the ship. The weapons activated, snapping out of concealment and into firing position.

The cargo handler's eyes all got wide. They dropped everything they had in hand and ran as fast as they could after

Cesar. The cargo lift registered as closed and sealed. Cargo handlers tried to keep their balance as they ran up the ramp that was raising.

"Faith, get us planet side!"

Cesar helped the three refugees pull down jump seats and strap in. Bethany's Hope shot out of the landing bay at near full thrust, sending crates and equipment flying against the back wall.

A long skinny alien ship with four spheres dropped into real space. This time the ship's sensors were fully active. The ship was tagged immediately as a threat on the projected display of the bridge.

The spheres began their green glow. "Damn it," Roger whispered. Bethany's Hope raced towards the planet at a speed Roger found incredible. They were still too far away.

Alien warships started to drop in ahead of the Corvus naval ships. Right in Roger's way of the planet. The two fleets began to brawl it out.

"Keep going. Get to the planet."

Faith was starting to do a few evasive maneuvers to avoid being hit by weapons fire of the larger ships the closer they got. Roger's timer for the fleet's arrival expired. Except the fleet wasn't here yet. Roger's jaw clenched. What happened to them?

"Rosalie! Are any of the distress calls you picked up earlier Corvus Navy ships?"

"Uh... no. They are all private ships."

At least there was that. A thought struck him. He didn't like it.

"Faith, find that ship with the glowing spheres and do everything you can to stay on it's tail! Brodie, your primary target is that same ship. Do everything you can to take it down."

Both acknowledged.

"I take it I need to get ready for a mist jump?" Sonja asked.

"I think the bubble might work both ways. We can't get out, and no one can get in... except the aliens."

Faith cussed.

The sphere ship stayed to the outskirts of the fighting. Alien fighters were everywhere. Brodie was busy with active targeting. His hand moved quickly as he picked targets and where to hit those ships. Roger realized there was no way he could effectively do that task. Especially not with all the added weapons.

Fighters exploded all around them as they passed through what felt like a stirred up nest. Faith had found the sphere ship and was hot on its trail. Roger kept an eye on the shields that were holding up well so far.

"Target acquired. Missiles away."

The HUD tracked the missiles on the way to the target. One of them was shot down. The other hit. One of the three spheres exploded, and another flickered. The ship ran.

Bethany's Hope gave chase. She still wasn't as agile as the sphered ship, but she was now just as fast. Brodie kept at the fighters that swarmed around the ship at bay. Her rapid fire anti-space craft guns filled the area around her with red bolts like a spectacular light show of fireworks.

Another round of missiles launched. One was shot down and a fighter sacrificed itself to detonate the other. Brodie dedicated one of the forward cannons on the target. It didn't do near as much damage, but it hit more often.

The ship jolted violently. Nearly half the shields burned up.

"We just got the attention of the big boy!" Faith yelled as she pulled on the controls, trying to dodge larger shots.

"One or two hits like that and we're done! Brodie!"

"I'm trying, sir!"

The sphered ship was still zipping around, trying to stay close to its position and still stay out of the fight.

Roger looked to the military ships. One had fallen dark and was drifting. The others were taking a serious beating. They must have had some of the upgrades given they were lasting this long. Roger notice the larger ship hit full thrust and move down and forward against the large alien flagship. The same ship that shifted its focus of fire to the Bethany's Hope.

Roger realized what the Corvus ship was doing. It was a suicidal move!

"Brodie, forget the fighters. Focus all weapons on that ship. The main Corvus ship is moving to shield us from the heavy weapons. Don't let the price they are paying be in vain. Kill that ship if it's the last thing we do."

The heavy fire of the main alien vessel was cut off from the Bethany's Hope. They shifted fire against the Corvus vessel, blocking the way. The alien flagship tried to shift upward to assist their struggling sphered vessel.

The shields stopped lighting up and the laser fire started to impact on the hull of the sphere ship. Fire and smoke began to pour out of its long skinny section. The vessel slowed and got sluggish with turns. Brodie took a chance on launching another round of missiles.

The defense systems must have gone down. Both missiles hit the target. The remaining spheres blew apart and the rest of the ship went into a dark drift.

The Corvus warship that blocked the alien flagship also went into a dark drift towards the planet surface. Bethany's Hope was once again exposed to the alien flagship guns.

Battle's End

Bethany's Hope made a mad dash to get out of range of the alien flagship. The mass of fighters that had closed in on her gradually fell behind as Faith hit the thrusters as hard as they would go.

Alien warships that were dispersed in the system to hit several targets at once turned to regroup with their flagship. Corvus warships dropped into the physical realm all around. A smaller Corvus ship dropped in as a darkened and dead vessel, having already been shot up. Two alien destroyer sized ships also dropped in as dark drifting hulks.

The fight was on. The Alien ships still outnumbered the human ones two to one. Roger ordered the Bethany's Hope to stay out of the main fight and focus on fighters on the outskirts. They shot down nearly a dozen transport ships heading for the planet's surface as well.

Even after all the modifications and upgrades, the Corvus navy was still loosing ships faster than the other side. The aliens were paying a heavy price for their kills. Nearly a third of their ships now drifted in darkness.

"Captain!," Rosalie called out, "mist scouts are reporting two more masses of ships inbound. Unidentified!"

Roger was trying to decide if he should run for the planet or attempt a mist jump. With the ships that fell out of the mists, he wasn't sure they wouldn't get shot down as soon as they got there. He would hold out for a few minutes more. If they planned to flood the planet with those spider bots, the mists might be a better course of action.

Two large fleets of ships dropped into real space. They didn't look like the alien ones.

Rosalie nearly broke down crying, "They're reinforcement fleets from Antaris Territories and the Triton Federation."

Both fleets wasted no time in engaging in the fight. The alien vessels started to jump to the mists to flee. They ended up reappearing not far from where they jumped from. A small ship would detach from them and disappear again. The human fleets continued to pound them with their heavy guns.

Brodie laughed.

"What's so funny?" Roger asked.

"The small ships," he said, "I've heard about those. They call them mist brawlers. They are designed to knock ships out of the mist and back into the physical realm. They're Triton Federation ships to keep the enemy from escaping."

The human warships moved in on the predator fleet of aliens and dispatched them without any mercy. In the next half hour, all enemy ships had been destroyed. The alien fleet that had terrorized the Corvus Commonwealth had finally been put down.

In the hours that followed ships were scattered all over the area rescuing the stranded. The remains of the alien vessels were captured and loaded up by all three navies present. The larger ships would be retrieved by tugs and taken to a join research facility near the borders of the three nations.

There was a huge sense of relief on the Bethany's Hope. They had gone around a picked up a large number of stranded people from space pods. After picking up as many people as they could, Roger ordered the ship to their next delivery point.

They touched down in an area of flat plains as far as the eye could see. Farms of various sizes covered a vast majority of it. The rest looked to be processing plants and warehouses. A military base was plopped down in the middle of it all, looking out of place in an otherwise peaceful scene.

The passengers departed, grateful to see solid ground again and feeling safe.

A logistic officer came to the ship as crates were unloaded. "I'm going to take the rest of the shipment you have. The station for the third leg of your deliveries was destroyed."

"Sorry to hear that."

"Which direction are you headed after this?"

Roger thought about it. "I'm headed back to Aldis."

"I've got a shipment of food that needs to go that direction if your willing to take it."

Roger nodded. "Load it up."

"Thank you! You just saved me from a butt chewing. We're behind in shipments with so many cargo ships running away." The man walked away to make arrangements.

Roger just looked at the ground. Food. Hauling food would be a normal, simple task for once.

After a few hours, Bethany's Hope was once again off the planet. The space above the planet was still a controlled chaos. It wasn't their business anymore, and Roger was glad. Soon they were back in the mists. Roger was looking forward to the smell of the forests again.

There was one other thing he wanted to take care of when they got there. Something he wanted to prepare for.

The crew was in a good mood the whole trip back. Roger even felt an absence of heaviness that seemed to have plagued him a lot lately. He wondered at what he might have to do next. His ship was back to being a heavily armed warship. He thought about how he had been strong armed into doing the bidding of others.

He had no idea what the future would hold. The alien fleet was actually destroyed now. Of course, several systems had still fallen and needed to be recaptured. And who knew what might be happening in the Nedra system.

Bethany's Hope returned to the planet surface in Aldis, landing in the same spot she had been directed to the last two times she visited. The ship touched down on the hardened surface and her thrusters shutdown. Roger got up to get some fresh air.

Cesar caught him in the cargo area. "Captain."

"What's up?"

Cesar seemed to have a hard time.

"Spit it out."

"I need to find someplace else to work. Not that this is a bad ship or your a bad captain or anything like that. I've been on the verge of having some relapses with all the combat and high stress. I don't want to go there again. I'm sorry."

"I understand and it's not a problem. I'll make sure I get funds transferred to your account in the next couple hours. I appreciate your help."

Rosalie stepped in beside him and looked at Roger sheepishly. "I need to go too, sir. I'm not cut out for this kind of thing."

"Neither of you need to feel bad about this. The work I seem to get stuck doing isn't always easy, and not just anyone can do it. I wish you both the best of luck in getting reestablished in something that suits you."

Roger shook the hands of both of them. They both left to pack their belongings and say their goodbyes to the rest of the crew. Roger left to take care of an errand while he still had the chance to do it.

When he returned to the ship a couple hours later he was greeted by John, Faith, and Sonja chatting about something in the cargo bay. They stopped when he walked in.

"What?" Roger asked.

Faith looked to Sonja, "Do it!" she whispered.

Sonja looked apprehensive. She eventually walked up close to Roger. "Faith and I have both become believers in I AM. John has been helping us. John laid a hand on Faith and she received the same gift that you passed on to him." She put a hand to the side of Roger's face. "John was going to do the same for me. I asked him to let you do it. Will you do this for me?"

Roger was struggling to hold the emotions back. "I did. The same day I laid a hand on John. I laid a hand on the pearl and nothing happened. I think I have to be able to touch your physical person for it to work. You'll die if we try to take you out of there."

She smiled at him and slightly shook her head. She whispered, "I wasn't a believer back then. I am now." She could see the pain in his eyes. "Please just try."

She had a point. He put a hand on her forehead and spoke. "Anyone that accepts I AM as their God, He will receive them back as His child." White light swirled around his forearm. "As proof of His Word, He gives His Spirit to you."

The light flowed into the eyes, ears, nose, and mouth of Sonja's droid form. After what seemed like several minutes, the light faded. Sonja's face looked vacant.

"Sonja?"

John and Faith both rushed over to look.

Her face was devoid of all emotion. "Returning to charging station." She said in a flat voice. Roger took off in a run. John and Faith followed.

"Where is everyone running to? Somethin about to blow up?" Randall called out as he entered the bay.

Roger climbed past the fold space generator to the stairs leading to the Pedlar's Omen. He could hear her coughing up fluid. He ran through what now felt like a dinky ship. Roger got to the room with the pearl and stood there staring.

Sonja was sitting up on the metal edge, breathing deep. She coughed again and spit the fluid back into the tank. She smiled at Roger. "Hi."

She looked just like the day she went in. She got up and climbed down the ladder. John and Faith reached the doorway and saw. Randall wasn't far behind.

Roger wrapped his arms tightly around her. She wrapped her arms around him. "You forgot my towel, mister."

Roger laughed. Sonja laughed with him as did the other three crew members.

He gave her just a little space. "I've been thinking you might need a name change soon."

"Can we talk about that later? I agree, but right now..." she put a hand to the side of his face.

Roger reached into his jacket pocket and pulled out a small box. "Would you consider changing your last name to Vance?" He dropped to one knee as he opened up the small box and presented it to her.

She started breathing really hard and started to cry. She cupped his face in her hands and kissed him, deeply.

When she finally let him up for air he asked, "I take that as a yes?"

"Yeah," she said. She seemed deliriously happy. "Now please get me a towel."

John looked up at Randall and smiled.

Randall was still having a hard time believing what he was seeing. He finally saw John looking at him. "Yeah, okay. I believe now."

"Good," John turned from the new couple, "Let's go talk someplace more appropriate."

Faith had gotten a large towel and tossed it at Roger. She just smiled and shook her head before leaving the two of them.